RYDER REVISITED

QUINN VALLEY RANCH
PAMELA KELLEY

SWEET FAMILY SAGA SERIES, 3 BOOK COLLECTION

PAMELA M. KELLEY

PIPING PLOVER PRESS

Chef Bethany Davis needs a job. Ryder Quinn needs a Chef. But she'd
never make his short list.

Bethany Davis has worked in some of the most exciting restaurants in
New York City. She's from Quinn Valley, a small Idaho town and she
hasn't been home for more than a few days in years. Her mother is sick
and it's a blessing in a way that her restaurant just closed and she's out of
a job, because now she can take as much time as she needs to be with her
mom. If she's going to stay though, she needs a job ASAP. But the only
option available is at Quinn's Pub, owned by her first love, Ryder, and his
sister Maggie.

Ryder tried to put Bethany out of his mind completely when she left him
so many years ago. He's desperate for a good chef, but she is the last
person he'd choose. He doesn't trust that Bethany is back for good and
he's wary of getting too close and getting burned again.

Everyone else thinks they belong together. Will the two of them ever
realize it?

We need to do something about Ryder. It's time he found someone and got married," Gertrude Quinn said as she set a platter of raspberry jam filled thumbprint cookies in the center of the table. It was Wednesday afternoon and as usual, her friends Maude, Nellie, Betty and Ruby were over for tea. They'd met every Wednesday at Gertrude's home, Quinn Valley Ranch for ages. Ryder was one of Gertrude's many grandchildren and the oldest of five children born to her son Richard and his wife, Marcia, who was a widow.

"Has he been dating anyone?" Nellie asked as she reached for a cookie.

"Not as far as I know. Not seriously anyway. Not since that girl he dated in high school, Bethany. She was a lovely girl."

"She moved away, didn't she?" Betty asked.

"Yes, she went off to cooking school somewhere in

New England. I hear she's a chef somewhere in New York City now," Gertrude said.

"Speaking of chefs, has Ryder hired a new one yet?" Ruby asked.

"No, and I think he's been under a lot of stress after what happened." Gertrude made a face as if she'd tasted something unpleasant.

"Yes, that really was shocking," Maude said.

They all nodded in agreement as it had been quite a scandal.

"Marcia's been doing the cooking again, right?" Ruby asked.

"Yes, but that's just temporary, until they find a new chef," Gertrude said.

"You know, it's funny you mention Bethany. I could have sworn I saw her a few days ago at the grocery store," Betty said.

"She may be home visiting her mother as I know she's been sick. I don't expect that she'll stay long, unfortunately," Ruby said.

Gertrude was silent for a moment and looked deep in thought. "I'll talk to Marcia. She's friends with Bethany's mother. She can find out for us. It's a long shot, but you never know. Maybe we'll get lucky and Bethany will decide to stay a while…."

CHAPTER 1

Y ou look tired. Is the new computer system still driving you crazy?" Ryder Quinn leaned back in his seat at the bar of Quinn's Pub. He was worried that his mother was working too hard. He and his sister Maggie had bought her out last year, and she was supposed to be retired. But, given their recent drama, he was grateful for her help. It was Friday night, almost midnight, and the restaurant was empty except for the three of them.

His mother sat up straight and gave him 'the look'.

"Ryder Quinn. You should never tell a woman she looks tired. Ever. I'm fine. And I am getting used to that silly computer of yours. Maggie, honey, I'll take a splash of that new chardonnay." Even though the pub was closed, Maggie was still behind the bar, wiping the counter down.

Maggie laughed. "Mom's right, Ryder. Don't ever say that." He watched as she poured two glasses of wine, put one in front of their mother and brought her own to the other side of the bar. She settled into a chair between them and smiled at her mother.

"I heard a lot of compliments on Mom's food tonight. The regulars don't want her to ever leave." His mother looked pleased to hear it.

But Ryder still felt guilty that he was going to be away for the whole weekend. "It's not fair for her to be in the kitchen all day every day though. I can cancel my trip. I'm sure Brad will understand."

"Don't be ridiculous. Your college roommate is getting married, and you haven't had a day off in weeks. I can cook in my sleep. You know that," his mother assured him.

He also knew by the tone of her voice that the discussion was over.

"No one misses Gary's cooking. He'd really been letting things slide," Maggie added. It was true. Gary did a fine job at first, but over the past six months, it seemed as though he wasn't trying as hard. His specials were lackluster and even standard items didn't seem as good as they used to be.

"Gary and Suzanne have to turn up, eventually. Have you heard any updates from the police?" his mother asked.

"Nothing yet."

Maggie sighed. "I still can't believe they were stealing from us and for so long. I considered Suzanne a friend."

The betrayal stung for all of them. "Gary and I used

to have beers together after work. I never suspected it," he admitted.

"No wonder they were so insistent that we didn't need to computerize," his mother added dryly.

"I still can't believe we missed it." Ryder lifted his glass and took a sip. The beer was a new one, a local IPA and was his current favorite.

"Suzanne used to always brag that she made more tips than anyone else," Maggie said. "I never thought much of it, but it makes sense now."

His mother chuckled. "And she always made those elaborate birthday cakes for everyone. Probably so no one would suspect she was up to anything."

Ryder sighed. "They were clever about it too, not taking enough that it would be noticed."

He'd only discovered their scheme by accident when he picked up a handwritten order off the kitchen floor. It was lucky for him that it had missed the trash can. It was a week after the new computer system had gone in and there shouldn't have been any more handwritten orders for the kitchen. He'd matched up credit card receipts at the end of the night for the order amount and there wasn't one, which meant the customers had paid in cash But, the amount of the order wasn't in the register. It was as if it had never happened.

That's when he realized that Suzanne had pocketed the cash and that Gary was in on it too as he threw the order slip away as if it had never existed. Ryder took a long hard look at his orders and profits for the past few months and realized the deception had been going on for a long time.

He'd questioned them and both vehemently denied any wrongdoing. But the next day, neither showed up to work, and no one had heard from them since. That was two weeks ago and while Suzanne was easily replaced, it was taking longer than he'd expected to find a new chef.

"Any promising resumes come in?" he asked hopefully. He'd called all the local schools and posted an ad for a chef and put it in the Quinn Valley newspaper and online as well. His mother had insisted on handling the hiring since she was the one that had designed their menu and was the only true cook in the family. Ryder managed the day to day running of the restaurant and Maggie handled everything related to the bar.

His mother nodded and for a moment he thought he saw a flash of a smile, but it was gone just as fast. "They have been trickling in. I have a few interviews scheduled for tomorrow morning. I'll keep you posted."

"Oh, that's great news." The job market was tight and there weren't many qualified people to choose from in Quinn Valley. It was a small town, like the neighboring one, Riston, and while there were a lot of tourists that came to stay at the inn and enjoy the hot springs, there weren't a lot of year round residents. He'd also posted ads in the Riston and Lewiston papers, hoping to cast a wider net of applicants.

"Have you closed out the month yet?" Maggie asked with a worried look. He nodded. He knew what she was really asking was if things were looking up. Unfortunately they were not.

"It was pretty dismal. Down another ten percent from the month before. I won't be taking a check again this week."

"Well, if you're not taking one, I won't either," Maggie said.

"I'm happy to help you out, if you need a short-term loan," his mother offered.

"No!" Both he and Maggie said at the same time and then laughed. "Thank you, but we want to do this ourselves. I know we can turn things around," Ryder said. It was important to him and to Maggie that they were able to run the business on their own.

His mother reached over and gave his hand a squeeze. "I know you can. I have complete faith in both of you. This is just a blip, a minor hiccup to get past."

That was one of the things he'd always loved about his mother. Marcia Quinn was one of the most positive people he knew. And she'd helped to instill that belief in all five of her children—that with hard work and the will to succeed, they could do anything.

He looked around Quinn's Pub, at the gleaming dark wood bar and beams, the soft leather chairs and cheerful watercolor paintings on the walls, and the big windows that let in plenty of daylight and even now, a bit of moonlight. Quinn's Pub was a family restaurant with a bar area that closed at eleven sharp every night. On the weekends, they had local live music and during the week, they ran specials and fun events like music bingo to bring people in.

When his mother ran the restaurant and was in the kitchen, they had a reputation for excellent comfort food and a strong base of regular customers. But since she'd retired and Gary took over the kitchen, business had slowed. It wasn't an immediate slow down, but rather a decline that almost wasn't noticeable at first. And it wasn't helped any by Gary and Suzanne skimming some of the profits.

Some of the customers were starting to come back though, now that word was getting around that Marcia Quinn was in the kitchen again. But Ryder knew that he needed to get someone good in there as soon as possible so they could start rebuilding and so his mother could enjoy her retirement. He smiled thinking about what being retired meant to her.

She still came by the restaurant every day, often bringing a batch of homemade ravioli that they could run as a special or a batch of her blueberry muffins that they ate together for breakfast before the day got underway. He knew that she still liked to keep her pulse on the business and to visit with her children.

"Ryder, I have one request I'd like you to agree on before you head out for the weekend?" His mother took a sip of chardonnay and smiled, waiting for him to respond.

"What's that?" He was ready to agree to anything.

"If I meet someone and want to hire them, I want your permission to do so."

"I don't get to meet them first?" As the general manager, he felt like he should be involved.

"If we have to wait around for you, we could lose a good candidate. Besides, I believe the last hire was yours?" Ouch! She had him there. Gary had been his pick.

He sighed. "Of course. I trust you. If you meet someone that knocks your socks off, by all means hire them."

"Thanks, honey. I've always been good at reading people. I'll find us someone."

Ryder relaxed and began to look forward to his weekend away. The restaurant would be in good hands, and maybe his mother would surprise him and find someone that could start right away. Anyone would be better than Gary.

CHAPTER 2

Bethany Davis peered in her rearview mirror, smoothed a few strands of flyaway blonde hair into place and added a swipe of sandy pink lipstick. The time on her cell phone showed that she was still five minutes early for her interview. She glanced at the blue front door of Quinn's Pub and felt butterflies in her stomach. She'd been back in Quinn Valley for almost two weeks and she needed a job, fast. The chef position at Quinn's was the only local opening she'd seen advertised, and she really didn't want to have to commute to Lewiston which was over an hour away.

The original plan had been to come home, spend a week with her mother and then head back to Manhattan. But, her mother had downplayed how serious her condition was. She needed her and truth be told, Bethany wanted to stay. She'd always planned to return to Quinn Valley someday. And now that she didn't have a job to return to in New York, she didn't need to rush back anytime soon. But her savings was dwindling, and she needed to get something, anything soon.

But, could she work at Quinn's Pub? Would they even want her? To say she had mixed feelings was an understatement. But, beggars couldn't be choosers. She took a deep breath, grabbed her purse and got out of the car.

Barely a minute after she knocked on the front door, it opened and Bethany felt as though she'd fallen back in time. Ryder's mother, Marcia Quinn, stood there, just a hair over five feet tall, with her chin length shiny brown bob, her warm blue eyes and the smile that made everyone feel right at home.

She looked exactly the same as Bethany remembered, except maybe there were a few tiny lines here and there and a slightly thicker middle, but she looked wonderful. And she immediately pulled Bethany into a bear hug.

"You look just as lovely as I remember! Come in, let's have a cup of tea and catch up, shall we? You're still a tea drinker?"

Bethany nodded and followed Marcia into the well-equipped kitchen that was a sea of spotless stainless steel. Marcia stopped at a coffee station and poured hot water for both of them and added tea bags.

"Milk, sugar or honey?" she asked as she slid the cup towards Bethany.

"Nothing, thanks."

Marcia added a splash of milk and a heaping spoonful of sugar to her cup and gave it a stir.

"Let's go get comfortable, shall we?" She led the way into the dining room and to a booth with soft padded seats. Once they were both settled and sipping their tea, Marcia began the interview.

"It's been a long time since you've been gone from Quinn Valley. How long are you planning to stick around?"

Bethany smiled. Marcia never was one to beat around the bush. And she could understand her concern. She didn't want to be replacing the position again in a few months.

"My intention is to stay in Quinn Valley."

Marcia looked pleased to hear it. But also a bit confused. "Your resume is impressive. You've worked at some fine restaurants in Manhattan. Why would you leave that?"

Bethany took a deep breath. She knew some would think her decision was crazy. She was at the prime of her career now and it wouldn't be difficult to find a new position in NYC. She'd had several offers already as soon as word got out that she'd left her last role.

"I never intended to stay long-term in Manhattan," she began softly. "I love Quinn Valley and it was always my intention to come back here when the time was right."

"And the time is right now?" Marcia leaned forward in her chair, listening intently.

"It's as right as it's ever going to be. I was going to stay in Manhattan another year or two," Bethany admitted. "I still have things to learn and when I came home, it was just going to be for a visit. But, I've changed my mind and have decided it's time to stay."

There was a long moment of silence as Bethany debated how much to share. But then Marcia asked, "How is your mother doing?" Her tone was so kind and caring that Bethany was surprised to feel her eyes watering as the emotion welled up.

It had been a stressful two weeks since she'd been home. Her mother was her rock, and it had been a shock to see her so weak and sick. She wasn't sure, by the way Marcia said it, if she knew what was going on with her mother.

"She hasn't been well. But she's on the mend. I'm not sure if you've heard, but she has breast cancer."

"I did hear, and I'm very sorry." Bethany wasn't sure, but for a moment, Marcia's eyes looked a bit damp.

"Thank you. It's very treatable, stage one and has an excellent prognosis," she assured her. "She didn't tell me right away because she didn't want me to worry. She's had radiation and just finished with chemotherapy. It seems to be working well, but she's been very tired and not up to doing much."

"I can imagine. Please give her a hug from me. I told her I'd stop by whenever she's up for company. We're actually in a book club together and I see her often."

Bethany smiled. "I'll do that." She looked around the room at the warm dark wood, polished brass trim and the light that poured through the large bay windows. It was a cozy place, and cheerful. She could imagine herself working there.

"I own a condo in Manhattan but will eventually put

it on the market and buy something here in Quinn Valley. For now I'm staying with my mother."

"I'm sure she is thrilled to have your company." Marcia picked up Bethany's resume, and they talked for a bit about the different restaurants she'd worked at and what the focus of each had been.

"I've heard of some of these places. Are you sure Quinn's Pub will be enough for you? We're not terribly fancy here." For the first time, Marcia looked worried.

"I'm not interested in fancy. I like to make good food. Meals that people crave. Comfort food."

Marcia looked delighted to hear that. "Really? What's your favorite comfort food meal?"

Bethany laughed. "That's easy. I make an insanely good turkey pot pie. Or rotisserie chicken. It's all good. My short ribs and mashed potatoes are pretty amazing too."

"Those are both favorites of mine," Marcia said.

"The short-ribs takes hours to braise, but if you have a leftover chicken or turkey on hand, I could whip up a pot pie pretty quickly," Bethany offered. "We could keep chatting while I do it."

"That's a fabulous idea. I usually ask candidates to make a dish, but given where you've worked, I know you can do the job. If you don't mind though, it would be lovely to see how you work and taste your pot pie."

"I'm happy to do it and I'd love to get the feel of your kitchen. It looks like it has just about everything I'd need."

Marcia beamed. "It does. I designed it myself. And we have a few roasted chickens in the refrigerator. I was going to make chicken salad, but we can use one for a pot pie."

When they stood to head into the kitchen, Marcia froze for a moment as she faced the big bay window that looked out over the sidewalk. She looked like she'd seen a ghost or was maybe about to faint.

"Is everything okay?" Bethany asked.

Marcia turned her way and smiled though she still seemed a bit shaken. "Oh, everything's fantastic. I just thought I saw someone I knew for a minute there. An old friend that I haven't seen in years. But I'm sure it was someone else. Follow me."

Marcia showed her where everything was in the kitchen and they continued chatting while Bethany worked. She quickly made a pie crust first and Marcia looked surprised when she asked for vodka.

"That's a first," Marcia said as she handed her a bottle of vodka.

Bethany added a generous splash of it to the dough. "I learned this trick a few years ago. A little vodka makes for a light and flaky crust."

"Well, isn't that something?"

Once the crust was done, Bethany moved on to a saute pan where she added a generous glob of butter and some sliced onions. Once they were browned, she added chicken broth and sliced cooked carrots and potatoes and shredded chicken that she'd tossed with a bit of flour, salt and pepper. She stirred it all together and a few minutes after the mixture thickened up, she poured it into a pie pan lined with the dough. She added the top crust, poked a few holes in it for ventilation and slid it into the heated oven.

While the pie cooked, she and Marcia continued talking, moving past her experience and onto people they knew in common in Quinn Valley. Marcia caught her up on just about everyone.

"Oh, and there's another amazing chef in town. Do you like tacos?"

Bethany laughed. "Of course. Who doesn't like tacos?"

"Right. Silly question. Anyway, you must stop by Ciran's Taco Truck. He spent time in Texas and studied taco making. He's also back with his high school sweetheart, Roxane."

"I remember Ciran. I thought he was going to be a lawyer? Or maybe I remembered that wrong?"

"No, he was. He did. But tacos are his true passion."

Bethany smiled. "Well, I'd much rather make tacos than be a lawyer too." She hesitated and then asked the question she'd been dying to ask since she walked through the door. "How's Ryder doing?" Marcia had mentioned everyone they had in common, except her oldest son.

A curious gleam came into Marcia's eyes. "I'm so glad you asked. Ryder is fantastic. Better than ever. He's away this weekend at his college roommate's wedding. Otherwise he'd be here."

"He still works in the pub?" Bethany had known it was possible, likely even, but she hadn't been sure. She'd known he'd gone to college and was going to study business. At one point, she'd known everything Ryder wanted to do, all his hopes and dreams. But those dreams had included her and when she broke his heart, he'd cut her out of his life.

"He and Maggie bought me out a little over a year ago. Maggie runs the bar and Ryder oversees all the overall operations." Bethany's heart sank. Ryder was in charge. And there was probably no way he'd approve hiring her.

"So, I'll have to meet with Ryder too?" She was already dreading it.

But Marcia cheerfully shook her head. "No, that won't be necessary."

"No?" Bethany wasn't sure if she'd heard right.

"Ryder gave me permission to hire whoever I like. I told him to trust me."

Bethany wondered if his mother knew what she was doing. She couldn't imagine that Ryder would be happy about this, if she was offered the job without his input.

"I can't wait to try your pie. It smells delicious." Marcia smiled as she changed the subject.

Bethany could tell by the smell that the pie was ready. Some chefs went by a timer and a recipe, but she went by feel and taste and smell. She pulled the pie out of the oven and it was perfectly golden brown. She found two small plates and a spatula and scooped some of the pie onto each plate. She looked around for forks and Marcia was holding two of them. She handed one to Bethany and took a bite.

Bethany watched and waited for Marcia's verdict.

Marcia took another bite, closed her eyes and made a happy sound.

"Mmmmm. Bethany, I make a good pot pie myself, but this is outstanding. Really exceptional."

Bethany was pleased to hear it. Nothing made her happier than hearing that people enjoyed her food. "I'm so glad you like it."

"I was going to offer you the job anyway," Marcia admitted. "How soon do you think you could start?"

"As soon as you want me."

"If you like, you could start tonight and work side by side with me. I could use the help as Saturdays can be busy."

Bethany grinned. "I'd love to."

CHAPTER 3

Ryder was unusually relaxed and refreshed as he walked into the dining room of Quinn's Pub Monday morning. Taking the weekend off and spending time with his old friends was exactly what he'd needed. He'd liked Jenna, Brad's new wife, the moment he met her. She and Brad fit together so well—it was as if they'd been together for years. He'd been skeptical at first when Brad said he'd proposed to a girl he'd only been dating for a few months, but when he met her, he understood.

When Jenna and Brad weren't teasing each other, the love in their eyes was evident. Ryder was happy for his friend even if it made him a little sad for himself. He'd thought he'd found that kind of love once too, but it hadn't lasted. He put all his energy into the restaurant and while he dated often, no one had captured his heart since.

"What smells so good?" he asked as he slid into the

booth where his mother and sister sat drinking coffee and eating some kind of muffin. His mother put one on a plate and slid it over to him.

"Zen muffins, try a bite."

He broke off a piece and popped it in his mouth. A rush of cinnamon, nutmeg, ginger and something unusually fragrant… lavender, maybe? collided with shredded carrots and raisins. The muffin was hot from the oven and it was delicious. As he continued to eat, a curious calmness came over him. The muffins were aptly named. Or maybe he'd just had a good night's sleep for the first time in a long time.

"New recipe? You've outdone yourself this time. These are really good."

His mother smiled mischievously, and he wondered what she was up to.

"Not me. Our new chef."

He raised his eyebrows. "You hired someone? You didn't mention anything when I checked in last night."

"I didn't want you thinking about work while you were off having fun. Just remember, you gave me permission to hire anyone I wanted."

"Yes, we talked about that." What was she going on about?

"Well, I just wanted to remind you, that this can't be undone."

"Who did you hire?" His mother was acting so strange.

"Oh, here she comes now." Ryder heard footsteps

coming up behind him. "I think you remember Bethany Davis?"

"Hi Ryder. It's good to see you." Bethany's voice was soft and a little nervous. Ryder looked her way and felt a rush of emotions, everything from anger to confusion to attraction. Bethany looked even more beautiful than he remembered. Her hair was glossy and still so blonde. Lemon pie blonde he used to call it. It fell into long curls that she tied back in a ponytail. A few stray pieces fell in tendrils to frame her face.

And her eyes were as big and blue-gray as he remembered. She had a small straight nose and full lips. He used to love watching them as she tasted a ripe strawberry or as they came his way. He could kiss those sweet lips for hours and he had.

She was still as trim as he remembered, which was impressive considering that he knew she'd been working as a chef for years. Most chefs he'd met were not thin. Bethany was slim and small. She was just a few inches taller than his mother who didn't quite hit five feet, no matter how tall she stood.

Ryder looked at Bethany and then back at his mother. He didn't quite know what to say. His whole world had changed, just like that.

"How long are you in town for?" he finally managed.

"I'm here for good now." For good. Why now? Why his restaurant?

There was a long, awkward moment of silence as both his sister and mother watched the two of them with fascination. It was too much for Ryder to take in.

"I'll be in my office." He stood and took the rest of his muffin with him. The last thing he saw as he walked away was the warmth and concern in Bethany's eyes. What was his mother thinking offering her a job? And what was she thinking by taking it?

BETHANY FELT LIKE ALL THE AIR HAD RUSHED OUT OF THE room when she laid eyes on Ryder that morning. She hadn't seen him in so long and he'd looked so good, with that thick, wavy hair that he always wore a little too long, the scruffy shadow along his jaw, that deep single dimple in his cheek when he smiled, and those eyes. Ryder's green eyes always seemed to look right through her. But this morning they'd held so much emotion. She could sense a mix of confusion, betrayal, anger, curiosity and attraction.

On some level it was reassuring to see that the attraction was still there. It had always been strong between them. It had been so hard to leave Ryder. And no matter how she'd tried to explain, she knew that he'd never understood why she had to go. She wondered if he could ever forgive her and she was curious if there was anyone in his life. She knew he wasn't married. She would have heard about that. Her best friend, Jill, still lived in Quinn Valley and she would have heard about that as it was a very small town. Too small it sometimes seemed as everyone knew everyone else's business.

She hoped that it wasn't going to be too awkward

working together. They were not off to a promising start. But she knew that Ryder had been blind-sided. She hadn't realized until that morning that his mother hadn't filled him in about his new chef. Maybe Marcia thought it would be easier somehow, she wasn't sure about that.

Or maybe Ryder just needed time to digest it. He'd never been one for sudden changes. She was glad she'd made her zen muffins for them that morning. The ginger and lavender had calming properties, and she'd had a feeling Ryder could use a little zen that morning of all days.

At a little past three, she felt his energy around her and glanced up. Ryder stood in front of the line, looking deep in thought. She guessed that he was ready for something to eat.

"What can I get for you?" she asked.

He looked wary. "I don't know. What's already made? I don't want you to go to any trouble." Or maybe he was so hungry that he didn't want to wait anymore.

She smiled. "It's no trouble. I have a tray of braised short ribs that are ready. I could plate that right up with some mashed potatoes and sautéed spinach."

"Sure. That sounds good."

She piled a plate high with food and added a generous drizzle of gravy over the short ribs and potatoes.

"Here you go. Hope you like it."

"Thanks. It smells great." He took the plate and walked off. Once he was gone, the air in the room suddenly felt flat.....the charged energy had deflated.

A half hour later, Ryder brought his empty plate back

to the kitchen and handed it to the dishwasher. He strolled back over to the line and looked at her curiously.

"Those were the best short ribs I've ever had, anywhere. And I've had my fair share." He seemed almost angry as he said the words.

"Thank you."

There was a long awkward moment of silence before he finally broke it by asking, "Why are you here? This restaurant, of all places?"

Bethany shrugged. "It was the only opening in the area. I didn't want to commute to Lewiston."

"I wouldn't want to do that either," he admitted. He turned to leave and then added, "I heard about your mother. I'm sorry. Please tell her I asked for her."

"I will."

He nodded and then left again and Bethany felt tears come to her eyes. It had been a long day and ever since she'd been home, she'd been feeling emotional. It was harder than she'd thought it would be to see Ryder again, and to be around him. Her mother had adored Ryder and at first hadn't understood why Bethany needed to go to New York when she could have just stayed in Quinn Valley and married him.

But at nineteen, she had wanted more. She needed to experience life outside Quinn Valley and to become the chef she wanted to be, she'd needed to work at the best restaurants. She'd wondered more than once if she'd made a mistake, but in her heart, she knew that she'd done the right thing, the only thing, that she could, for herself.

WHEN BETHANY WALKED IN THE FRONT DOOR, HER mother was curled up on the living room sofa, with a soft fleece blanket wrapped around her. Her mother's oversized orange cat, Simon, was sprawled across the back of the sofa and didn't even glance Bethany's way as she entered the room.

"Hi, honey, how was your day?"

Bethany knew that her mother was secretly hoping that Bethany and Ryder might get back together now that they'd be working together. But Ryder had made it clear when she left for New York that it was over for them. He'd immediately started dating Natalie Palmer, who graduated high school with them and had been a cheerleader and active on the beauty pageant circuit. Although she also knew that hadn't lasted long. She hadn't been home often after that, just for an occasional long weekend when she could get away, so she hadn't run into him before now.

She sighed. If her mother had seen Ryder's lack of enthusiasm when he saw her, she wouldn't be as hopeful. Bethany just hoped they'd be able to work together. She flopped onto the love seat facing the other sofa.

"It was pretty good. I like it there for the most part." If Ryder wasn't there, it would be ideal. She loved the kitchen, and it was the perfect place for the type of food she wanted to focus on. Marcia welcomed her ideas for new menu items and specials and while he'd been less than happy to see her there, Ryder at least seemed to like her food.

"Did you see Ryder?"

"I did. You should have seen the look on his face when he realized that his mother had hired me while he was gone. If they weren't so desperate for a chef, I think he might have told her to keep looking."

"Oh, that's too bad. I thought he might be happy to see you." The light went out of her eyes a little and Bethany knew she was disappointed. She was too. Though she didn't share her mother's hope that they'd reunite, she was hoping that since so many years had passed that he'd be glad to see her at least as a friend.

"I'm sure it will be fine, once he has a chance to digest it all. Ryder never did like surprises." Her stomach rumbled, and she realized she hadn't eaten since lunch.

"I'm going to make a green drink, would you like one?"

"That sounds nice, honey. The one you made this morning was delicious."

Bethany went to the kitchen and returned a few minutes later with a cold juice smoothie for both of them. She'd juiced green apples, beets, ginger, carrots and kale. The combination of fruits and veggies had a sweet fresh taste, and it was a way to get healthy, organic nutrients into her mother.

She was trying to build up her immune system to support the chemotherapy and help her mother heal faster. She'd just had her last treatment a few days ago and her doctor said if all went well, she could be cancer free soon. Bethany handed her mother her drink and settled back on the sofa with her own.

"Thanks. Are you working next Tuesday night?" her mother asked.

"I'll be working on Tuesday but my regular hours are going to be ten to seven or so during the week and later on Saturday nights. I'll get all their daily specials prepped and get them through lunch and dinner and Bryan, the sous chef will finish up. Is something going on Tuesday?"

Her mother smiled. "The girls asked if I might be up for music bingo. I haven't been for weeks and I think I might be ready to get out again. You could join us if you're not working."

Bethany was thrilled that her mother was feeling up to going out soon.

"I'd love that. I can just join you all when I finish up."

"Good. We need someone young on our team. There's always music we have no idea about."

Bethany laughed. "I'll try my best. But I wouldn't get your hopes up."

CHAPTER 4

Ryder leaned against the bar waiting for Maggie to finish up a phone call so they could go over the bar order. While he waited, he glanced over at his grandmother, Gertrude Quinn, and her cronies, Betty, Maude, Nellie and Ruby as they enjoyed their late lunch. It was half-past three, and the restaurant was almost empty except for their round table by the window. He'd noticed Grandma glance his way more than once in the past ten minutes, and he was pretty sure that he wasn't imagining that she looked quite pleased with herself.

Maggie was also smiling as she hung up the phone and turned his way.

"Do you think it's possible to fall in love with someone's voice? I look forward to calling my order in to Charlie Keane every week just to listen to him talk."

Ryder laughed. "Anything's possible. Have you ever met him?"

"No. And he probably looks nothing like I imagine. I picture a young Brad Pitt or Bradley Cooper. I don't even know if he's single. He's probably happily married with five kids."

Ryder thought for a moment. "It's been a long time since I've run into Charlie, but last I knew, I think he was single."

Maggie sighed. "I know I'm being silly. The last thing I'm looking for anyway is a new relationship."

"It has been a while, Mags. It might be time to get back out there," he said gently. Maggie had ended her last relationship almost a year ago and hadn't really dated anyone more than once or twice since.

"It's not time yet, Ryder. I'll know when it is." She said firmly as two new customers walked up to the bar.

Ryder noticed his grandmother and two of her friends looking his way again.

"What is Grandma up to? Do you have any idea?"

Maggie looked surprised. "I haven't the foggiest. Why don't you go ask her?"

"I think I will." He strolled over to the table of women and his grandmother beamed when she saw him coming their way.

"There's my favorite grandson! We were just talking about you." Ryder knew that she said that to all her grandsons, but it was still nice to hear.

"I thought my ears were ringing. All good things, I hope?" he teased.

"Of course. We were just saying how smart you were

to hire Bethany. She's a marvelous chef. I always did like her you know."

Ryder sighed. His grandmother loved to play matchmaker. But he needed to nip this in the bud fast. Once she had her mind set on something, she was known to be relentless.

"She is a very talented chef. I agree. But I'm sure this is a short-term thing for her and she'll be going back to Manhattan once her mother is better."

"Oh, I think you're wrong about that. We heard that she's here to stay."

"Why would she want to stay in Quinn Valley? She couldn't wait to leave years ago."

His grandmother gave his arm a squeeze and smiled as if she found him amusing and maybe a little dim. "Oh, I can think of lots of reasons why she might want to stick around. We'll just have to wait and see, I suppose. Please tell her how much we enjoyed everything today. I've never had such a delicious macaroni and cheese."

"I'll tell her. It was nice seeing you, Gram, ladies." He nodded at the rest of the women who all looked almost as excited about his love life as his grandmother did.

BETHANY DIDN'T SEE RYDER UNTIL LATER THAT afternoon, a little after four when she set out the evening staff meal and was writing up the evening specials.

"What are you serving us tonight?" he asked as he strolled into the kitchen. He almost sounded friendly, which was a nice surprise. She'd made one of her favorite meals for the staff and was pleased to see that so far it was a hit with just about everyone. They had the option to eat the provided meal before their shift or to order something off the menu and pay half price.

"It's a chicken stir-fry over wild mushroom risotto."

"Sounds good." He grabbed a plate and helped himself to a little of both. "My grandmother was in earlier. She said to tell you hello. She liked your mac and cheese. She insisted that I tell you that too." He smiled as he went to take a bite of risotto.

"Please tell her hello as well, next time you see her."

"I will." He stood quietly eating for a few minutes while she finished writing the specials on the whiteboard.

"Are you having any trouble with the computer system?" he asked. "We just started using it a few weeks ago."

"We actually used the same program at the last two places I worked. So that made it easy."

"Good. Our last chef wasn't a fan of it." He told her the story of how his chef and one of the waitresses had been pocketing money from customers that paid with cash.

"I'm sorry to hear that. Unfortunately, you're not alone. Something like that has happened at a few different places I've worked at."

"Oddly enough, that does make me feel a little better. I was feeling pretty foolish that I didn't figure out what they were up to sooner," he admitted.

The kitchen door swung open and Ryder's brother, David, walked in.

"There you are! Maggie told me you were in your office." He glanced Bethany's way. "She also told me that you're the new chef here. It's great to see you again. It's been a while."

Bethany smiled. "It has. Good to see you too David." She knew that she'd be ordering most of her food supplies from David as he ran a local restaurant food distribution service. And Ryder's other brother, Carter, was one of his suppliers. He raised organic livestock and produce.

"I was on my way back there. You hungry?"

David shook his head. "No, I had a big lunch. It smells good though."

"Alright, let's head to my office then."

"Bye, Bethany," David said as the two brothers walked off. She watched them go thinking how similar they looked. All the Quinn boys had that same, single dimple and were all tall with thick, dark hair. Yet their personalities were very different. David was friendly and outgoing while Ryder was more reserved and somewhat intense. She'd been so drawn to him in high school and even now, she had to admit, that for her, the attraction was still there.

A LITTLE PAST SEVEN, AFTER THE DINNER RUSH WAS winding down, Tom, her line cook and assistant, assured her he was fine handling things for the rest of the night.

Bethany took off her apron and grabbed her purse. She'd planned to go straight home, but Jill had texted that some friends who recently got married were in town and they were going to have a few drinks at Quinn's and she should join them. She ducked into the ladies room, quickly ran a brush through her hair after taking it out of the elastic ponytail holder and added a little lipstick.

As soon as she walked into the dining room, she saw Jill sitting at a table with a couple. Jill waved as soon as she saw her and Bethany slid into the empty chair.

"Bethany, this is Cameron and Ethan. I work with Cameron, she's a nurse at the hospital. She and Ethan are on their honeymoon!" Jill's practice was located in Quinn Valley, but as an ob/gyn doctor she was often at the Riston hospital delivering babies.

"Congratulations!" The two of them looked very much in love as Cameron told her how they'd known each other since elementary school, but it was actually Ethan's grandmother who played matchmaker after having Cameron for a nurse.

"I agreed to marry Ethan because it was only going to be for a month."

"But then, I won her over with my irresistible charm," Ethan said with a grin.

"You did, actually!" She leaned over and gave him a sweet peck on his cheek.

"Are you staying at the inn?" Bethany asked. The Quinn family ran the nicest hotel in the area, close to the natural hot springs.

"We are. It's a lovely getaway. We are here for the rest

of the week and it's nice to be so close to home."

"We'll do a longer vacation in the Caribbean later this year," Ethan added.

"This is perfect for now." Cameron leaned in. "The rooms at the inn are so luxurious. We have massages scheduled for tomorrow and in the afternoon we're going to the hot springs."

"Don't forget to stop by Ambrosia's crystal shop too. You'll enjoy that," Jill suggested.

"It's on my list. Jaclyn told us at trivia last week that she heard it's a must-see shop. She believes that crystals have magical healing properties."

"We play trivia almost every week at the River's End Ranch," Ethan explained. "Jaclyn is an older woman who plays with us and she seems to know everyone in this area."

"I heard about Ambrosia's shop too," Bethany said. "Maybe I'll stop in there soon too." She could pick up a healing crystal for her mother.

"If you like trivia, we could try our hand at music bingo," Jill suggested. "It's like trivia sort of, but all music related. You guess the name of the song after hearing a few notes. It's actually a lot of fun."

"Oh, I'd love to do that. What do you think, Ethan?" Cameron sounded excited.

"Sure. Sounds fun," he agreed.

"It will be starting in a few minutes. I saw Eddie handing out score sheets. I'll try to flag him down." She got his attention and a few minutes later, they joined a dozen or so teams as the game began.

Bethany ordered a glass of chardonnay when their waitress, Ivy, came by. She was Ryder's youngest sister and was humming along to the song they were supposed to guess the name of as she set her glass of wine down. It sounded so familiar, but they were all struggling to recall the name. Ivy looked as though she knew it. Suddenly it came to Bethany.

"Is it Landslide, by Stevie Nicks?" she asked her.

Ivy grinned. "That would be my guess."

Bethany conferred with the others and they agreed that it was their best guess. While they waited to hear the answer, she saw a familiar face at the bar. Ryder was just settling into an empty seat and Maggie was laughing as she slid a draft beer his way. He took a sip and slowly looked around the room, stopping when he saw her sitting at Jill's table.

He looked surprised to see her and lifted his glass. She nodded and smiled for a moment before turning her attention back to the others. Just a look from Ryder could still fluster her. And it didn't escape Jill's attention.

"Is that Ryder at the bar? Why don't you invite him to join us?"

"I don't want to bother him. He's chatting with Maggie."

"Who's Ryder?" Cameron asked.

"Ryder Quinn is one of the owner's of the restaurant. And he's Bethany's ex."

Cameron raised her eyebrows. "How interesting! And now you work here. How is that going?"

"It's fine. And it was a million years ago that we

dated. Another lifetime."

"So, you're friends then. You could still invite him over. He looks so alone at the bar," Cameron said.

Maybe she should reach out and ask Ryder to join them. She'd like it if they could be good friends again at least. She was about to get up when Ethan spoke, "It doesn't look like he's alone anymore."

Sure enough, a tall woman with gorgeous long blonde hair settled into the empty seat next to Ryder. Bethany couldn't see her face until she turned slightly and then her jaw dropped. It was Natalie Palmer. And her hand was on Ryder's arm as she leaned in to talk to him. A moment later, they were both laughing and Bethany was feeling a bit foolish to have assumed that he wasn't involved with anyone.

Jill raised her eyebrows. "Well, that didn't take her long."

"What do you mean?" Bethany took a sip of wine. The chardonnay was rich and creamy.

"Natalie's divorce was just finalized a week or so ago. She's always had a thing for Ryder."

"Oh, they're not a couple?"

Jill laughed. "They were for two seconds years ago But it looks like Natalie wants to try again."

Bethany glanced over to the bar where Ryder was leaning back in his chair and looked amused by whatever Natalie was going on about. She was still a beautiful girl, and he looked like he was enjoying her company.

"Maybe he does too," Bethany said. Though the idea of it bothered her more than she was willing to admit.

CHAPTER 5

The next morning, on her way to the restaurant, Bethany drove to the far end of Main Street to Ambrosia's crystal shop which was on the first floor of an old Victorian home. It was hard to miss because it was painted a pale purple and had scalloped gingerbread trim. A large bay window filled with crystals and jewelry twinkled as the sunlight fell upon it.

When Bethany opened the front door, soft chimes rang and Ambrosia looked up from the counter where she was sitting and thumbing through a book. A chipped teacup sat by her side. The faint smell of lavender incense danced across the room. Ambrosia smiled and her face lit up. She stood and stepped out from behind the counter, ready to help. She was a pretty woman, maybe around thirty-five or so, Bethany guessed. She was wearing a gorgeous long, flowing ivory sweater over a purple and blue print skirt that swirled around her ankles.

"Welcome. Are you looking for anything in particular?

Let me guess, you've lost a ring or something and you need some guidance to find it?"

Bethany guessed that she probably had a lost look about her as she knew very little about crystals. But, she had heard that they had healing properties and her mother could use all the help she could get.

She smiled. "No, I haven't lost anything. My mother just finished a round of chemotherapy and radiation. Can you suggest a stone or crystal that might help with her healing?" It sounded a bit crazy as she said it out loud, but Ambrosia nodded.

"I'm very sorry that your mother has been sick. I do have a few crystals that I would suggest." She led her over to an area filled with crystals of all sizes and colors. She carefully picked out three stones and handed them to Bethany one by one. The first was a pretty green color.

"Malachite. It helps with all forms of cancer and strengthens the immune system."

Bethany ran her hand over the stone, it felt cool and smooth.

"And this is Smoky Quartz. The darker the color the better. It is especially helpful with the after effects of chemotherapy." She dropped the coffee-colored crystal into Bethany's palm.

"Lastly, Yellow Kunzite helps with healing after radiation. It helps to strengthen the cells." This crystal almost seemed to glow from within. The color was like pale yellow light.

"Do you know how to use the crystals?" Ambrosia asked.

"No. I'm really not sure." Bethany had no idea what to do next.

Ambrosia smiled. "There's no one correct way, but you want to cleanse your crystals before using them and recharge them for at least four hours by setting them in either sunlight or moonlight. Whichever you prefer. Then you gather your stones close to you and you think about what you want them to do. It's really that simple."

"How do I cleanse them?"

"Wave them through a cleansing incense. This one is good." Ambrosia plucked a box of incense off a shelf and handed it to Bethany. "And once the stone is cleansed, some believe that the fairy inside will speak to you if you are deemed worthy." Ambrosia seemed to be waiting for some kind of a reaction from Bethany, but the comment left her speechless. *Fairies?*

"Let me get you a little pouch for your stones." Ambrosia led the way to the register and pulled a pale silvery blue velvet pouch with a silk drawstring from a drawer and held it open so Bethany could drop the crystals into it.

"Is there anything else I can get for you?" she asked

"No, I think that's all I need."

"Hmmmm. Hold please." She wandered off to the far corner of the room and came back a moment later with a pretty pink stone. "This one is with my compliments. Rose Quartz. You need it."

"I do? What is it for?"

Ambrosia smiled. "It's for giving the heart the love it

deserves. It will bring positive energy into your life. Trust me."

It sounded silly to Bethany, but it was sweet of Ambrosia to give her the stone. "Thank you. That's very kind of you."

"Make sure you do the same process with this stone that I told you to do with your mother's. Once it's recharged, hold it close and keep it near you. By your bedside is a good spot."

"I'll do that. Thanks, Ambrosia."

———

When Bethany got home from work that evening, her mother and cat were in their usual spots. Her mother was reading a novel for her book club and Simon was kneading a blanket and purring so loudly that Bethany could hear him from across the room. They both looked up when she walked in.

"You're home early." Her mother closed the book and set it on the coffee table.

"It was slow tonight."

Her mother frowned. "I've heard that Quinn's isn't as busy as it used to be. I hope for their sake and for yours that they are doing ok?"

Bethany had the same concern. The pub had been busy the night before for music bingo but it had been very slow the next day for lunch and dinner. So slow that as much as she hated to do it, she was planning to talk to Ryder about it when she went in. She knew about the issues they'd had with the old chef but thought it was just about him stealing. It seemed as though business itself was down and she wondered what Ryder's plans were to turn things around.

"I'm going to talk to Ryder tomorrow and see what they have planned for marketing. People seem to love the new food."

"It might just take a while until word gets out that there's a new chef," her mother said.

"I agree. So, are you up for a smoothie?"

"Yes, I'd love one. I had your shepherd's pie for dinner, honey and it was excellent. You do comfort food well."

Bethany smiled. "Thank you. I'm glad you liked it. I'll be right back."

She returned a few minutes later with their green smoothies, handed one to her mother and settled onto the love seat.

"I stopped at Ambrosia's shop today. Have you ever been there?"

"With the crystals? No, I haven't. But I've always been curious about that place. Did you get anything?"

Bethany pulled the little pouch out of the bag Ambrosia had given her. She handed it to her mother.

"What's this?" She looked intrigued as she took the little pouch and peeked inside.

"Three crystals, for you. They're to help with your healing."

Her mother looked touched and curious. "Really? Thank you. How does it work?" She poured the crystals into her hand and held them up to the light. "They're so pretty."

Bethany explained what Ambrosia had shared about how to start using the crystals.

"We can start the process tonight. I bought the incense too. And I have a stone of my own."

"You do? What is yours for?"

Bethany hesitated for a moment. "For bringing positive energy into my life."

"Oh, that sounds lovely."

After they finished their smoothies, Bethany lit a stick of incense and waved it around the room and around their crystals. They took the crystals outside and set them on the front steps where the moonlight shone down upon them.

"They have to stay in the light for at least four hours. So we can just collect them in the morning."

"Perfect. We can gather them close and think happy thoughts while we have our morning coffee."

Bethany smiled. "That sounds like a good plan"

CHAPTER 6

Bethany arrived earlier than usual the next day. She was hoping to catch Ryder alone before the rest of the staff arrived so she could have a serious conversation with him about the financial health of the restaurant. She was admittedly a bit nervous to ask such sensitive questions, so she'd baked another batch of zen muffins, going even heavier on the lavender and ginger to help put Ryder in a more receptive mood. She'd noticed that he'd eaten every last crumb of the last batch she'd brought in, as had the rest of the family.

His door was ajar as she approached it and lightly knocked.

"Come in."

She stepped inside and was dismayed to see his mother and sister already there too, sipping coffee and all looking quite serious.

"I'm sorry, I didn't mean to interrupt anything," Bethany said and took a step backwards while Ryder and

Maggie exchanged glances. Finally, his mother broke the ice by reaching for a muffin.

"So thoughtful of you dear to bring more of these delicious treats in for us. Why don't you have a seat and join us?"

"Are you sure that's a good idea?" Maggie said.

"Yes, I'm sure. Bethany is the chef here, she should know more about what's going on."

Ryder sighed. "You're right. Bethany, please pull up a chair and thank you for bringing muffins. Are these the same ones you made before?"

She smiled. "Yes, these are my zen muffins. I tweaked the recipe a little."

Both Ryder and Maggie eagerly reached for a muffin. Bethany had already had one, so she just sat sipping her coffee and wondering what they'd been discussing.

"You haven't really missed anything yet," his mother said. "Ryder was just going over the monthly numbers and projected forecasts for the coming weeks. We're a little below where we'd like to be."

"That's an understatement," Maggie said.

Ryder looked up from his spreadsheets and met her gaze straight on. "Our sales are down, way down from where they used to be. Gary, our old chef, had let things slide and we've lost some of our customers to other restaurants in the area."

"But now that Bethany's here, they'll come back," his mother said. She didn't seem overly concerned. But both Ryder and Maggie looked worried and Bethany didn't blame them. She'd seen more than one place have to close during a slowdown when they couldn't keep up with the daily expenses of running a restaurant.

"Bethany has only been here for a week. It may take a while before word gets out that the food here is really good again," Ryder said. He ran a hand through his hair and kept tapping a finger against his papers. It was a nervous habit she remembered from when they used to date. He got fidgety when he was stressed out.

"Are you open to suggestions?" she asked quietly.

"Why, have you run a restaurant before?" Ryder snapped.

"Ryder...." His mother cautioned.

He sighed. "I'm sorry. Yes, of course we're open to any suggestions."

"Well, I haven't run a restaurant before, but I was always involved in these kinds of meetings and I have seen a few things that worked to get the word out and turn things around. Do you do any advertising?"

"We have a radio ad that runs every weekend and a display ad in the weekly paper."

"Okay, and I'm guessing your budget is fully allocated?"

He laughed. "There's no extra money, if that's what you mean."

"That's what I figured. I'd suggest making a few changes, if you are open to them. I'd stop the radio ads and I'd put that money into printing coupons that you can give to area hotels for money off their meal, maybe $5 off or something like that. And I'd change your newspaper ads to highlight daily deal specials, like burger

Wednesday and Prime Rib Thursday. That kind of thing."

"You want us to switch from radio ads to coupons?" Ryder looked skeptical.

"Radio is expensive and you might see a better ROI from the coupons. People that stay at the inn will be looking for places to dine and that discount will get them in the door."

"I like the idea of the daily deals. Comfort food classics that are family friendly cheap eats," his mother said.

"Exactly. Both of these things have worked really well for some of the places I've worked at."

"It's worth a shot, maybe. And it won't cost us any more than we're already spending," Maggie said.

"Okay, we can try it out. Thank you." Ryder reached for a second muffin and Bethany was happy to see that he seemed to be in a better mood already. "Oh, what was it you were coming to see me about?"

Bethany smiled. "This actually. I just wanted to learn more about how the restaurant was doing."

His mother reached for another muffin and smiled. "We're doing much better now that you're here, dear."

Maggie turned at the sound of the front door opening. "I think that's my liquor delivery. I'll catch up with you all later."

His mother stood and stretched. "I should be on my way as well."

"Where are you off to?" Ryder asked.

"I'm going to visit with Bethany's mother for a bit. She invited me over for tea."

Ryder looked as surprised as Bethany felt.

"I didn't realize that you two were friendly," he said. Bethany didn't either but kept quiet, curious to hear what his mother would say.

"We've been friends for a number of years now. We're also in the same book club. Bonnie hasn't been up to going lately, so we're going to chat about the book and anything else we feel like gossiping about."

Ryder smiled. "Well, have fun then, and please give her my regards."

"I'll do that. And Ryder, get on that advertising stuff today. I never did like that radio commercial much."

He grinned. "I never did either."

AFTER THE LUNCH RUSH DIED DOWN, RYDER VISITED WITH Maggie at the bar while she restocked and got the bar ready for the evening shift. She had the night off and was going out with friends to the other pub in town, O'Shea's, where Ivy was going to be singing with a friend's band. It was her first time playing there, and she was a little nervous. Maggie wanted to go and support her and tried to recruit Ryder too.

"So, you'll come by, at least for the last set? They'll probably go on again around nine."

"I should be able to manage that. Mom called earlier too, to remind me." Ryder stayed until closing most nights, but he really didn't have to. His assistant manager, Paul, was more than capable of closing things down.

Ryder just usually liked to do it himself, especially after what happened with Gary and Suzanne.

He was pouring himself a glass of water when he noticed an older man about his mother's age walking toward them.

"You must be Ryder? And Maggie?" He glanced at his sister and Ryder tried to place him, but he had no idea who the man was.

"Yes, and you are?"

"Harry. Harry Peterman. I'm actually here to see your mother. Is she in?"

Maggie raised her eyebrows. It was clear that she had no idea who the guy was either.

"No. She's not. I can tell her you came by though."

"Oh dear. I was hoping she'd be in. Yes, of course. Let me give you a card. He fished in his pocket and drew out a thick ivory business card. It had his name and his business, Peterman Productions. Whatever that was.

"Please ask her to call me. It's been many years since I've seen her, but at one time we had a strong friendship. I've just recently moved back to the area."

"I'll let her know as soon as I see her," Ryder said.

As soon as the door closed behind him, Maggie spoke. "What was that about? Did mom have some kind of mystery life that we never knew about? What do you suppose Peterman Productions is?"

Ryder shook his head. "I have no idea. Funny that he knew our names though."

Maggie looked thoughtful. "Right. He must be an old friend or something." A mischievous look crossed her face. "Speaking of old friends. I noticed you and Natalie Palmer were chatting up a storm last night. Anything brewing there?"

"With Natalie? No."

"Well, she's single now, and available. She looked as though she wouldn't mind."

"Natalie is just lonely and recently divorced. She's a sweet girl." He'd always been fond of her.

"She's gorgeous too."

"I suppose." As pretty as Natalie was, she wasn't his type. Natalie was glamorous and turned heads wherever she went. Ryder preferred a softer, quieter beauty.

"You should take her on a date. See if there are any sparks there."

Maggie didn't usually push this hard. "Why do you care if I date Natalie?"

"Oh, I just thought she might be good for you. You were giving me a hard time, but truth is you haven't dated anyone seriously in a long time either."

Since Bethany.

"Natalie's not my type."

"Who is then? Bethany?" and there it was. Maggie was worried that he might try to get back together with Bethany.

"I take it you wouldn't approve?"

Maggie glared at him for a moment, her lips pressed in a thin line. Finally, she sighed. "No. I wouldn't. I saw what it did to you the last time she went away. I don't want to see that happen again. Do you really think she's not going to run back to New York as soon as her mother is healthy again?"

"She says she's not, but I don't really know. There's not much here for her."

"No, there's not," Maggie agreed. "I'd hate to see you hurt again, that's all."

He and Maggie were super close, and he appreciated her concern.

"You don't have to worry about me. I'm keeping my distance."

"Good." She poured herself a glass of diet soda and took a big sip. "So, we'll see you sometime between eight and nine?"

"I'll be there."

CHAPTER 7

"Good night, Ryder," Bethany said as she walked past his office on her way home. It was a quarter to eight, and she was tired. It had been a long day.

"Bethany, hold on a minute." Ryder closed his office door behind him and had his jacket on. "I'll walk out with you."

As they stepped outside he turned to her and asked, "Do you have plans or were you just heading home?"

"No plans. Why?"

"Ivy's playing at O'Shea's for the first time, I told her I'd go to support her. Maggie's already there with some friends. Do you want to come along?"

Ivy had mentioned to them the night before that she was going to be playing tonight and was excited about it.

"Sure. I can go for one drink. I don't want to be out too late though."

"It won't be a late night for me either. I just want to catch one of her sets. "

"Perfect, I'll meet you there then."

Bethany was still smiling as she got into her car and drove the short distance across town to O'Shea's. Ryder seemed to be warming up to having her around and she was hopeful that they could maybe be friends again. She could use a friend here in Quinn Valley. Aside from Jill, she'd lost touch with her old friends. Many had moved away or married young and were busy with their families.

She found a spot right in front of O'Shea's and walked inside. Ryder was waiting for her and led the way through the bar to where Maggie and her friends had a big table near the stage. Maggie waved when she saw them and looked surprised to see Bethany with Ryder. Bethany hoped she didn't mind that Ryder had asked her to come along.

She used to really like Maggie, but since she'd started at the restaurant, Ryder's sister hadn't been all that friendly towards her. She knew that Ryder and Maggie weren't just co-owners of Quinn's Pub, they'd always been close and she guessed that Maggie was being protective of Ryder. But still, it didn't make her feel great.

Though when they reached the table, Maggie smiled and made room for them to slide in and take the two empty seats. She seemed to be in an unusually good mood.

"Thanks for coming. Ivy's more nervous than usual about this gig. She usually plays at smaller places."

Bethany looked around the room. O'Shea's had a

much bigger bar area than Quinn's. The room was packed, and the crowd was all ages. The environment was a bit more casual. There were lots of young people in their twenties playing darts or pool while what looked like a group of regulars in their fifties were laughing and eating burgers at the bar. O'Shea's was an Irish bar. The Irish flag was proudly displayed along with the American one and there were paintings of Guinness beer on the wall and Irish music played in the background.

"Sally, I'll have another draft beer and these two probably want something," Maggie said to their very Irish-looking waitress. Sally had black hair, blue eyes and a spattering of freckles. She was also one of Maggie's best friends.

"I'll take a Guinness draft too, what do you want Bethany?" Ryder asked.

"Chardonnay please."

Sally went off to the bar and returned a few minutes later with their drinks.

It looked like Ivy would be on soon. There were two other guys in the small band and they were checking their equipment.

Bethany took a sip of her wine and noticed that Maggie was deep in conversation with her friends. There were four of them and she'd been introduced, but the names had gone in one ear and out the other. Maggie was two years younger than her and all of her friends were from high school. They'd all stayed in Quinn Valley after going to college. The town was growing, and she was glad to see everyone doing well. Ryder looked deep in thought as he lifted his beer.

"I'm looking forward to hearing Ivy sing," she said.

"Oh, she's great. Really talented. She'd probably do well to leave Quinn Valley to be honest. Like you did." He didn't look happy at the idea.

"I didn't want to leave, you know. But, I felt like I had to," she said softly. She still felt a little guilty for leaving even though she knew she'd make the same choice again.

"I know. I was angry with you for a long time," he admitted. "It took me a long time to get over you."

"It took me a long time too."

They were both quiet for a moment and then Ryder said, "I was so surprised to see you that morning. I had no idea that you were back in town. You didn't come back often."

"No, I didn't. I came when I could, but you know how it is in the restaurant business. It's hard to take more than a few days at a time."

He grinned. "Yeah, I know. What was it like, working in Manhattan?"

"It was an adventure. Magical, wonderful and sometimes maddening." She paused to take a sip of her wine before continuing. "Culinary school in Vermont was such a special time and several summer co-ops on Nantucket and in Manhattan led to my first full-time position after graduating. I've worked at some incredible restaurants, cutting edge places as well as established icons. I learned a lot."

"It must seem so slow and ordinary here compared to that."

"It's nothing like Manhattan, but that's what I love about it. This is home. I always knew I'd come back, when the time was right."

"You weren't planning to come back this soon though?"

He was right about that. "Well, no. Not just yet. I thought probably in another year or so. But, I think things happen for a reason sometimes. I lost my job two weeks before I found out my mother was sick. I would have come immediately anyway, but it meant I could stay as long as I liked and the more I thought about it, I started to realize that I didn't need or want to go back."

"What would you have done if we didn't hire you?"

"I would have found something. There are lots of restaurants in Lewiston. I wouldn't like the commute, but I could do it if I had to. Or I might have tried to start up my own catering business. That's something I'd thought about too."

"Oh? What would that look like? Would you want to do weddings? That's a big undertaking."

"I know. And not really what I had in mind. I was thinking more personal chef type of thing. Dinner parties and to-go meals. I could imagine a small shop full of prepared meals that people could pick up and heat and eat when they got home."

"That's a really good idea, actually." Ryder looked thoughtful and Bethany thought he was about to say something but stopped when the music started and Ivy stepped up to the microphone. It was too loud to talk, so they sat back and listened. It was the first time that Bethany had heard Ivy sing and she was impressed.

They played a popular mix of covers, country as well as pop rock and some classics. Ivy had a way of singing that drew people's attention. The whole room seemed to focus on her. The last song she sang was an original song, and it was hauntingly beautiful. When she finished, the room was silent and then erupted in applause and cheers.

"She's really good," Bethany said.

"Yeah, she keeps getting better. I hadn't heard that last one before."

Maggie leaned their way. "She's amazing, huh? I keep telling her she should go to Nashville."

"Yeah, she probably should," Ryder agreed, but he didn't look thrilled at the idea. Bethany knew he wanted what was best for his sister and just hated the thought of her moving. He was a homebody and always had been. But now that she was older, Bethany could see both sides better. She knew it must have been hard for her mother for her to be so far away. They'd always been close and talked every few days. But since she'd been home, they'd grown even closer and Bethany couldn't even think about the possibility of her not overcoming her cancer.

"I should probably get going," Bethany said as she took the last sip of her wine and pulled out some money to put toward the bill. But, Ryder handed it back to her.

"I've got this." He handed some cash to Maggie and stood up. "I'll walk you to your car. I'm going to head home too."

"Thank you."

They said their goodbyes to Maggie and her friends and congratulated Ivy on the way out.

"You were amazing," Bethany said.

"Oh my gosh, thanks so much for coming."

"That last song was your best yet," Ryder told her and she looked thrilled by the compliment.

"Thank you. See you both tomorrow!"

When they reached Bethany's car, she took him by surprise by pulling him in for a hug. "Thank you for inviting me out. It was good to talk and just have fun."

"Yeah, it was good catching up with you. And fun. We might have to do it again sometime." He grinned.

"See you tomorrow, Ryder."

———

BETHANY WAS STILL SMILING AS SHE PULLED INTO THE driveway. She was relieved that she and Ryder seemed to be in a better, friendlier place. And it wasn't too late, just a little after nine. Her mother should still be up so they could hang out a little before she went to bed.

When she walked in, her mother was in her usual spot, but her eyes were closed and she was holding the pouch of crystals against her chest while one of Simon's paws rested on her shoulder. She looked sound asleep but even though Bethany closed the door softly behind her, her mother's eyes fluttered open at the sound.

"Bethany, is that you?" she sat up a little and looked around the room.

"Hi, Mom. Sorry that I woke you."

"Oh, don't be silly. I was just resting my eyes for a minute."

"Can I get you anything? I'm going to make a cup of herbal tea."

"If it's not too much trouble, I'll have one of your green drinks. I think I'm addicted to them now."

Bethany laughed. "That's a good addiction!"

While her water was heating, she juiced a smoothie for her mother and brought the drinks back to the living room.

"Thanks, honey. Did you have fun at O'Shea's?"

"How did you know that's where I went?"

"Oh, I just assumed. Marcia mentioned this morning when she came over that Ivy was playing tonight. She was going to suggest that Ryder invite you. She knew Maggie was going too. David and Carter would have gone, but they were at some industry event." Hmmm, so it wasn't necessarily all Ryder's idea to invite her. Still, he didn't have to agree, and they'd had a good time.

"I didn't realize you and Marcia had become good friends."

"She's been wonderful since I've been sick. All my friends have really. Marcia is easy to spend time with and now that she's retired, she has more time to visit. She likes to come a few mornings a week for tea after she stops by the restaurant.

"I see you're trying out the crystals."

"Oh, yes. I did just what you said earlier. I held them in both hands and focused on thinking about healing.

And then I felt so relaxed that I must have drifted off to sleep. Hopefully that's a good sign that they're working?"

She was so enthusiastic. Bethany had always loved that about her. Her mother was the most positive person she knew. And she had a good feeling about those crystals and her mother's cancer. She'd been eating well since Bethany came home and was due for a followup visit the next week. Her color looked better, and they were both hopeful that her numbers would show improvement too.

"I think it's a very good sign," Bethany agreed.

———————

LATER, WHEN SHE WENT TO BED, BETHANY PICKED UP THE pretty pink rose quartz crystal and held it in both of her hands. She closed her eyes and let her mind drift. The stone felt warm as she focused on wishing for positive energy for herself, her mother and for Ryder and the restaurant. She wanted it to do better for all of their sakes. After a few minutes, she set the crystal on her nightstand and slid into bed. She felt relaxed and content as she drifted off to sleep.

CHAPTER 8

Ryder was in a good mood the next morning as he sat drinking coffee at the bar with his brothers. Both David and Carter had stopped in for a quick visit as they knew their mother would be there too. Maggie, Ivy and Bethany would be arriving any minute.

"So, Ivy was good last night, huh? I was sorry to have missed it," David said.

"She was great. We all thought so."

"Who went?" Carter asked.

"Me, Maggie, a bunch of her friends and Bethany." His brothers exchanged glances while his mother just smiled and sipped her tea. He knew if their mother wasn't sitting there that one or both of them would have asked more questions. He was grateful that she was there because he wasn't ready to answer them. He just knew that he'd had a better time than he'd imagined with Bethany.

It had been good to talk, really talk to her and it felt comfortable, almost like it used to feel. She'd always been easy to talk to. And when she surprised him with that hug at the end of the night, he'd been blown away by how right it had felt and how familiar.

He'd inhaled her sweet scent and wanted to hold on longer. Bethany had always felt like home to him, which is why it was so devastating when she left. He understood why she went. He hadn't understood at first though.

"Don't forget about the tasting event Friday afternoon," David reminded him as Bethany walked in.

"Come have coffee with us, dear," his mother called her over.

Bethany slid into the chair next to her and took a sip from the coffee she'd brought with her, from Fresh Brew, the takeout coffee shop down the street.

"You should bring Bethany with you," David suggested.

"Oh, that's a marvelous idea!" his mother agreed.

"She can taste our new meats," Carter added.

"What are you talking about?" Bethany looked confused.

"We are having our annual tasting. It's when we invite all of our clients in to sample products from our vendors. It's a great way to try what's new."

"Oh, those are always fun. But what time is it? I might not be able to go."

"It's Friday afternoon from two to five."

"That's during the slow time," his mother said. "Tom

can cover for you if necessary. And I can always pop in too. I'm just a phone call away."

Ryder chuckled. "It sounds like it's settled then. Bethany will join me Friday afternoon." He found himself looking forward to the event more than he usually did.

"I'm looking forward to it," Bethany said.

Ryder realized he'd forgotten to do something. He pulled out his wallet and found the thick business card he'd put there the day before and handed it to his mother.

"I almost forgot to tell you this. A Harry Peterman stopped by to see you yesterday. He was disappointed that you weren't here. He wants you to give him a call."

He watched as his mother's fingers shook as she took the card and looked at it. She gazed out the window for a moment and then back at them.

"I thought I saw him the other day. He was just walking along the street and stopped for a minute by the bay window. I was sure that I imagined it. He's been gone for so long."

"Who is he?" Ryder asked.

"He's a very old, dear friend. I knew him before I met your father. We were high-school sweethearts. But his family moved away during our senior year. We kept in touch for a while, but he had big dreams. I knew he wasn't coming back to Quinn Valley any time soon."

"What is Peterman Productions?" Ryder was curious about what he'd read on the card.

"I'm not really sure. Harry had always loved theater and movies. His dream was to do something with film."

"Are you going to call him?" David asked.

"Of course I am. It would be rude not to!"

THE REST OF THE WEEK FLEW BY AND BEFORE BETHANY knew it, Friday afternoon had arrived and it was time to go to the tasting event with Ryder. They'd had a very busy lunch which was both wonderful and concerning as she didn't want to leave if it was still really busy. But by one thirty, the rush was over and only a few customers were still there. She'd be coming back for the dinner service but it would be nice to get out for a few hours.

"Are you ready to go?" Ryder walked into the kitchen, wearing his jacket.

"Just about." Bethany slipped off her white chef coat and hung it on a hook by the door and pulled on her own jacket. "I'm ready."

She followed Ryder to his navy blue Honda CRV and climbed in the passenger side. She noticed a few boxes on the back seat as she buckled in.

"I picked those up from the printer this morning. I need to drop them off with Rachel at the Inn. She loved the idea of discount coupons. Said it was another great perk they could offer their guests." Rachel was the assistant manager there. It was a big job but according to Marcia, who had just mentioned her a few days ago, Rachel was doing a fabulous job.

"That's great. Do we have time to drop them off on

our way? Then maybe they could start giving them out this weekend."

Ryder checked his watch. "We go right by there, so we can make a quick stop."

Five minutes later, he pulled up to the valet station in front of the main entrance. A young man came rushing over and smiled when he saw Ryder.

"Hey, Dylan. Can we just leave the car here for a minute while we drop a few boxes off?"

"Of course. I'll keep an eye on her for you."

There were two boxes in the back seat. Ryder grabbed the bigger one and Bethany picked up the smaller one. It wasn't heavy, just a little bulky. When they walked in the front door, Rachel was coming their way and looked surprised to see them.

"Hey, Ryder. I didn't think I'd see you until tomorrow."

"We were coming this way anyway, so I thought we'd go ahead and drop the coupons off."

"Well, that's great. Follow me." She led them into her office and told them to set the boxes on the floor. She reached in and pulled out a stack of coupons and smiled.

"I'll bring these up to the front desk now. We'll put some in our tourist attractions room, where guests can browse brochures of all the local sights. And I'll make sure that every guest that checks in from now on gets two coupons."

"Thanks, Rachel. I really appreciate it," Ryder said.

"It's a fantastic idea, and it's something we can give to our guests. I really think they're going to love it."

"I wish I could say it was my idea, but it was all Bethany's."

Rachel looked at her with interest. "Really? I heard you've been working in Manhattan. Did they use coupons like this there?"

"Yes. And in Nantucket too when I spent a summer there. Tourists love a good deal."

"Keep me posted how it goes," Rachel said

"I will. We're off to David's annual tasting event now."

"That's today? I think I was supposed to go to that too. Maybe I can sneak out a little later."

"It goes until five I think," Ryder told her. They said their goodbyes and ten minutes later pulled up to David's giant warehouse.

"Wow," Bethany said. It looked like quite an operation.

"David has done well for himself."

"It looks like he has enough food to serve most of Idaho in there."

Ryder laughed. "Every year he expands. He has trucks that go to Riston, Lewiston, and beyond."

He parked, and they made their way inside. As soon as David saw them he came over and gave Bethany a tour. He seemed to carry just about everything a restaurant could need. When they came back to the main room where the tasting was being held, he gave them both a printout that listed all the attending vendors and what they were going to be sampling.

"I hope you're both hungry?"

Bethany nodded. She was actually starving. Normally she would have eaten something once the lunch rush started to slow, but she hadn't had anything since breakfast.

"Good. I'd start with Bella Cheese, their baby fresh mozzarella balls dipped in oil and balsamic glaze are a hit."

Bethany headed straight there and happily popped one in her mouth. They were as delicious as David had said. Ryder agreed, and they spent the next hour strolling around the room, chatting with the various vendors who were all friendly and interested in learning about Quinn's Pub and how their products could fit in there. There were quite a few things they tasted that impressed them both and Bethany's mind whirled as she imagined different ways to serve the various foods she'd tasted.

They spent quite a bit of time with Carter as he explained to Bethany all about what he did and the various humanely raised and organic meats he sold. She tasted everything and the quality and freshness rivaled the best meats she'd had in Manhattan and she told him so.

"I believe in our quality, but I have to say it made my day to hear that. Thank you." He told them about some new products he hoped to have in the coming year before they made their way to the final table which was desserts. Although every restaurant Bethany had worked at made some of their own desserts, almost every one bought some too. And desserts was one area that she thought they could improve on at Quinn's.

They tried small bites of at least a dozen different

desserts—everything from cheesecakes to rich chocolate layer cakes to fancy pies and even a few frozen desserts. There were two that stood out to Bethany. A deceptively simple apple crisp that had toasted walnuts, oats, lots of brown sugar and butter and perfectly cooked apples. They served it with vanilla bean ice cream on top, which was how she would serve it too.

The other standout was the chocolate cake. It was six layers of rich decadence and she knew it was the kind of dessert that people would talk about. It was oversized and outrageous. And who didn't like chocolate cake?

It reminded her of one she'd had in Boston at Abe and Louie's. She'd gone there for lunch with a fellow student and before she even decided what she wanted to order, she'd seen three chocolate cakes go by and knew that was what she was having for dessert. It was magnificent. Almost as good as this one.

"You're in love," Ryder said with an amused smile.

"I am. And you will be too as soon as you take a bite. We're ordering this today. The apple crisp too. This is exactly the kind of comfort food dessert that people are going to go crazy for. And it doesn't make sense for me to make it when they do it so well."

Ryder took a bite of the chocolate cake and while he was still swallowing gave it the thumbs up.

"I was thinking the cannoli until I tasted this. But you're right. This makes much more sense."

Bethany smiled. "Cannoli are delicious too but they are messy and get soggy too fast."

"It's hard to top the cannoli from the bakery down the street, anyway."

"That's true and we can always get them occasionally for a special. But this cake is going to be our signature dessert." Bethany was so enthusiastic that Ryder looked amused and just nodded in agreement.

"Whatever you want works for me. You're the expert."

David came over as they finished up.

"So, what do you think? See anything you want to add to the menu?"

Bethany and Ryder both laughed.

"Bethany wants to add a lot of things, I think. But we'll start with the chocolate cake and apple crisp," Ryder said.

"Great, I'll include some of both in your next order. Bethany can let me know when she wants to add some other items."

"Perfect," Ryder said.

As they drove back to the restaurant, Bethany looked forward to getting the desserts on the menu and had a few new ideas for some of the other things she'd tasted. She was excited to see how their customers would respond

When they parked and walked toward Quinn's, Ryder asked, "So, are you glad you went?" He was smiling and she knew he was teasing her.

"So glad. Ryder, I really think we can turn things around for Quinn's."

She saw something warm and appreciative in his eyes. "I sure hope so."

CHAPTER 9

Quinn's was busier than usual Friday and Saturday night. David arranged for a delivery of the desserts they'd ordered for Saturday morning, so Bethany ran them as specials until they could get them added onto the new menus. They were still working on what the final changes to the menu would be. She wanted to test out a few things and see how customers responded before finalizing anything.

She was pleased to hear that some discount coupons were already being redeemed. They had a few trickle in on Friday and a steady flow of them Saturday night. She was also glad she'd suggested that Ryder accept them on weekends too, instead of just during the week as many restaurants did.

Feedback on both desserts was as she'd hoped. Customers loved both and particularly raved about the chocolate cake. Bethany had added her own touch to the decadent cakes-a sprinkling of crushed lavender. It was one of her favorite herbs and she thought it might help promote romantic feelings. The slices were so tall that most people ended up taking half of it home with them and the overall consensus was that they more than got their money's worth.

Bethany worked late both nights and let her assistant go home early, to give him a break. By the time she left each night, she was ready to fall into bed, but it was the good kind of tired, when she felt like she was making a difference. The energy in Quinn's was already different.

She sensed that slowly but surely, people were coming back, and were curious if they'd been away, to see if the new chef had made improvements. She heard from the servers that they loved the new dishes that she'd introduced. The chicken pot pie she ran as a special was so popular she'd added it to the regular menu, along with the short ribs and meatloaf.

Sunday and Monday were her days off and she wasn't used to having two full days off. Everywhere else she'd worked the chefs and sous chefs worked six and often seven days a week and usually from open to close. It was a punishing schedule and part of what had attracted her to the possibility of starting up her own catering business. She would work long hours no doubt, but she'd also have a flexible schedule. She was glad though that she didn't have to do that yet. The position at Quinn's seemed tailor made to her and the expected hours were more than reasonable.

She and her mother had a relaxing Sunday. Her mother wanted to get out of the house and go to an early church service, which wouldn't be as crowded. They both enjoyed the peacefulness of the small, quiet service. And her mother was happy to see some of her friends afterward at coffee hour.

They went for a walk when they got home as the weather was cool and clear. Her mother rested after that, curled up on the living room sofa with a book while Bethany puttered in the kitchen making a roasted chicken and vegetables. The house quickly smelled amazing, and she planned on making a chicken soup from the bones the next day. Bone broth was supposed to be extra nutritious and so far her mother's diet seemed to be helping.

They enjoyed a lazy afternoon together. Bethany also read for a while, a Melinda Leigh mystery that had her on the edge of her seat. And they both snacked on a frozen treat that she made. As an experiment, she froze one of her green smoothies as popsicles and they turned out better than expected.

She got a good night's sleep and met up with Jill the next day for lunch. It was a last minute invitation as Jill had a cancellation and was just going to walk next door and grab a salad. Bethany met her at Smith's and also ordered a salad. Jill always made her laugh with some of her funny stories about her patients. She never shared any identifying details of course, and Bethany wouldn't know them anyway, but it was still fun to hear them.

"I had a young couple that had their first baby delivered yesterday. The husband was in the delivery room. I told him that the baby's head was starting to crown and that it was time to push. He put on gloves and then stepped back and squatted as if he was preparing to catch a football! Everyone in the room laughed while I explained to him that babies don't get tossed out of the womb."

Bethany laughed. "He must have been so out of his element."

"He was. I heard he was a star quarterback in high school. It was probably instinctual for him."

As they finished eating, Bethany asked if Jill had plans the next night. "I'm meeting my mother and her friends after work at Quinn's for music bingo. It's my mother's first official night out since she finished her treatments."

"Oh, that's wonderful. I'd love to join you."

When they stepped outside, Bethany noticed a new shop a few doors down. At least it was new to her. "Have you been to there yet? It looks cute."

"Scentiments? Yes, I've been in there a few times. Their stuff smells amazing. They have all kinds of things made with essential oils. You should stop in. They haven't been open long, but Lindy, the woman that runs the shop is great and they're doing a good business."

"I will stop in there. I bet my mom would love a sweet smelling candle." She grinned. "Who am I kidding? I'd love one too."

Jill headed back to her office while Bethany walked down the street to the new shop. When she stepped inside a tangle of wonderful smells teased her nose. She was curious to learn more about essential oils as she thought she remembered hearing something about them being useful for healing too. A woman about her age looked up from behind the counter and smiled.

"Hi there, I'm Lindy. Can I help you find anything?"

Bethany hesitated. She wasn't really sure what she was looking for. "I was just curious to look around. I don't know much about essential oils, but my mother has breast cancer. Is there anything you might suggest?"

"Many people believe that there are a few essential oils that have some healing benefits for cancer. Frankincense, Myrrh, Lavender, Peppermint and especially, curcumin. You might know it as Turmeric."

"The yellow spice?" Bethany often used it to add a golden glow and subtle flavor to rice pilafs.

"That's the one. I have a collection of all five in small purse size vials. There's a pamphlet that explains each one. If she just dabs a little oil behind her ear or on her pulse points that's all she needs to do."

"Thank you." Bethany continued to wander around and selected a few candles as well as a lip balm for each of them.

"How long have you been here?" she asked as Lindy took her credit card and put everything in a pink shopping bag.

"I haven't been here long. Just about a week or so. It's actually my aunt's shop, but she hurt her back so I'm helping her out for a while." She handed Bethany her credit card slip and added with a smile, "I've always enjoyed helping her in the store. The essential oils are fascinating and seem to be helping so many people. I hope they help your mother."

"Thank you."

Ryder was in an unusually good mood when he walked into the kitchen Tuesday afternoon. It was a little after two and Bethany was experimenting with a new green smoothie recipe.

"What are you making?" he asked as she flipped the blender switch on.

"I'm trying a new smoothie recipe. I've been making these green drinks for my mother. She's coming in tonight for music bingo with her friends and I wanted to have this for her. All her friends will be drinking alcohol. But this is much better for her."

"Can I try a taste?"

"Sure." She poured the smoothie into two plastic cups and handed one to him. He took a sip and looked surprised.

"This isn't bad at all. I thought it might be awful."

Bethany laughed. "I don't do awful. But it's missing

one key ingredient. I couldn't find lemongrass anywhere in Quinn Valley."

"Lemongrass, Hmmm. Let me think about that. It still tastes good without it."

"It does. But the lemongrass is a known cancer fighter and immune booster."

"I'll keep an eye out for some for you."

"Thank you."

"So, on another note, I just wanted to share that our receipts were up by over thirty percent this weekend. The coupons were a hit and the chocolate cake gives us a huge profit margin. That was a good call."

Bethany smiled. "Thanks. I'm glad to hear it."

"Well, I'm off to the bank and to run some errands. I'll be back before the dinner rush."

Bethany watched him go and was glad to see him in such a good mood. He seemed a little more relaxed than usual and she guessed that he'd been carrying around a lot of stress, worrying about the restaurant's financial situation.

"That's the first time I've seen Ryder smile like that in ages," Tom said. He was busy prepping pot pies and had overheard their conversation. "It was busier than it's been in a long time last night. I have to say, I much prefer working with you over Gary any day."

"Thanks, that's nice to hear." She liked Tom. He was young, but he was a talented cook and had some fun suggestions for their menu too.

"Your food is much better than his and you're a lot nicer too. Gary was never interested in any of my ideas."

An order came into the kitchen which got his attention and he wandered off to the computer to see what it was. Bethany finished her smoothie and started thinking about the night's specials.

A little past four, Ryder came back into the kitchen holding a small plastic bag and wearing a smile. He handed the bag to Bethany. She peeked inside and her jaw dropped. It was filled with fresh lemongrass.

"Where did you find this?"

"Carter has an extensive herb garden as well as produce. I totally forgot to mention it to you, but he has everything you could imagine and said he could keep you well stocked with lemongrass if you want it."

Bethany felt her eyes water, she was overcome with gratitude and emotion. It was such a sweet, thoughtful gesture.

She nodded. "I'd love that. Thank you."

"Maybe you should try adding that smoothie as a special. People are really into nutrition these days, it might be a decent seller."

"It might. That's a great idea. Oh, and Ryder I'm joining my mother and her friends for music bingo when I finish up here. Jill is coming too. Would you like to join us?"

He looked surprised and pleased by the invitation. "I just might. Thanks."

———

At a quarter past seven, Bethany hung up her chef

coat, fluffed her hair, and carried her mother's lemongrass kissed smoothie out to her table. They were sitting at a big round table. Bethany sat next to her mother and Jill was on the other side of her. Her mother's friends Glenda and Janie were also there, and they were all sharing a piece of the chocolate cake. Bethany smiled when she saw it.

"Hi honey," her mother said as she dug her fork into the cake. Bethany set her smoothie down and waved to Ryder who was looking around the room. When he reached their table, he sat in the empty seat beside her.

"Are you playing with us? We'll be unstoppable!" her mother exclaimed. She looked excited to be out and happy to see Ryder.

"Ryder found the lemongrass for your smoothie, mom," Bethany told her.

"Did you? Well, isn't that impressive? Thank you." She took a sip and pushed it toward Bethany. "Have you tried it? This is your best yet."

"I had some earlier. I'll take a bite of that cake though " She had a mouthful of chocolate cake when Ivy came over to get her drink order.

"I'll have that new draft IPA and I'm guessing Bethany wants a chardonnay?" Ryder said.

Bethany nodded, her mouth still full of cake. A moment later she thanked him.

They spent the next few hours laughing and trying to win at music bingo. It wasn't as easy as it seemed. Too often they all knew the song but none of them could remember the name of it. But somehow they managed to come in second. Her mother was just as thrilled as if they'd won first place.

Bethany suspected she was just happy to be out with her friends and glad to be feeling better. Her blonde hair was like peach fuzz, just starting to grow back. She left her head bare around the house, but when they went out, she usually wore a pretty scarf or a hat, or sometimes both. Tonight she had on a pink baseball cap and it made her look younger than her fifty-five years.

"That was so fun," she said as they paid their bill and got ready to leave. Glenda, Janie and Jill said their good-byes and left. Bethany's mom wanted to use the ladies room first, so they waited for her to return and then Ryder walked them out. When they reached her mother's car, she suddenly slumped against it and grabbed Bethany's arm in a panic.

"Honey, I feel really funny all of a sudden." She went limp as Bethany grabbed hold of her to prevent her from falling.

"Did she faint?" Ryder asked.

"Yes, I'm not sure what's going on."

"Hold tight. I'll drive my car over and we can bring her to the ER."

Her mother was already starting to stir when Ryder pulled up. He jumped out and helped Bethany to get her into the back seat. They laid her down, so she wouldn't fall over if she fainted again.

Bethany got into the passenger seat and Ryder drove off toward the Riston hospital. It was on the outskirts of town, near the Quinn Valley line and there was no traffic so it took them less than twenty minutes to get there.

"Has she ever done this before?" Ryder asked as he pulled up to the front door and helped Bethany to get her mother out and into a wheelchair. There were a row of them, waiting outside for those who were too weak to walk.

"Yes, once, right after she started chemo. It knocked her socks off and she ended up in the ER. Her red blood cell count was low as a side effect of the treatment."

Bethany told the triage nurse about her mother's history and that she'd fainted before. They brought her right in and started running tests. Bethany and Ryder stayed with her in her area that had curtains for walls. Her mother was awake now, but weak and sleepy. She drifted off to sleep while they waited for the doctor to come.

When he walked over, both Bethany and Ryder recognized him. They'd graduated high school with Kevin Murphy. He'd been the class valedictorian and Bethany relaxed a little, knowing that her mother was in good hands.

"Hey, I know you two!" Kevin smiled and tried to put them both at ease. "Sorry to be running into you under this kind of circumstance though. What brings you all in?"

Since her mother was asleep, Bethany explained what had happened and her mother's history. "She's all done with treatments, both radiation and chemotherapy and we're hopeful that it's worked. But, this doesn't seem like a good sign, does it?" Bethany bit her lip. She'd been worried sick the whole way there.

"Not necessarily. I see this often. It could just be a delayed reaction to the chemo. Your mom might be a little anemic again. We will get to the bottom of it though. We're going to run a bunch of tests and then figure out our next step. Sound good?"

"Thank you." Bethany stretched and glanced at her mother who was still sound asleep. Ryder reached out and massaged the back of her neck, kneading the tight muscles. It felt absolutely wonderful. She knew she'd been carrying a lot of tension there.

"Don't worry. Your mother's going to be fine. I know it."

Bethany forced a smile. "I feel better now that we're here. And she has Kevin for a doctor! Did you know he was a doctor?"

"I think I heard that years ago. It makes sense. He was always the smartest guy I knew."

"He was." She yawned and looked at the clock. It was already nine-thirty. "You don't have to wait with us, Ryder. We can get a cab home. It's probably going to be awhile."

"I'm not going anywhere. Except down to the cafeteria to get a coffee. Do you want one?"

"I'd love a hot chocolate, actually."

"You got it."

While he was gone, nurses and other medical people were in and out of the room, checking her mother's vital signs, drawing blood, and putting an IV in. Her mother woke up again briefly and fell fast asleep again once they were done poking and prodding her. By the time Ryder returned with her hot chocolate, the room was quiet again.

"Do you remember that time I broke my leg?" he asked as he settled back into his chair.

"Of course I remember." He broke it playing football during his senior year.

"You stayed with me the entire time in the hospital. I never forgot that." He looked around the room. "It's scary being here when something happens. Your mom could use the extra support."

"Thank you." Bethany took the top off her hot chocolate and blew on it to cool it a little. She took a tentative sip. It was still too hot to drink. She thought back to that day when she'd come to this hospital with Ryder. It had been terrifying for both of them. It had happened so fast, a normal play that had dangerous consequences.

He'd been rushed to the hospital and no one knew how bad it was at first as he'd passed out too, knocked unconscious. Bethany's mind had imagined the worst, brain damage, paralysis. When the doctor told them the verdict, a broken leg, they were all so relieved. His mother had cried happy tears. And Ryder had been so cranky. All he knew was that he was in a lot of pain and his football year was over.

It had brought them closer together though as they spent even more time together once he wasn't going to football practice or games every week. She'd helped him to carry his books and they spent every afternoon together. It was nice to feel needed and useful. And loved. It was soon after the accident when Ryder first told her that he loved her and couldn't imagine not having her in his life.

He'd gotten so serious quickly after that and wanted to get engaged as soon as they both graduated from high school. Her mother was hesitant but supportive if that's what Bethany wanted to do. She knew then that she loved Ryder more than she'd imagined she could love anyone, but she also knew just as strongly that at nineteen she was too young to get married.

She'd told him then that she might be open to getting engaged but that it would be years before she'd be ready to get married. He was heading off to college and she still had culinary school to go to, and she knew she needed to work her way up in good restaurants where she'd have opportunities to learn from the best in the business. Waiting to get married seemed perfectly sensible to her.

But Ryder had felt very differently. He thought she was being selfish and that she obviously just didn't love him enough. She tried to explain over and over again but it fell on deaf ears. They were both upset and heart-broken at the time, but she knew now that he just wasn't mature enough to understand why she had to go and that it had nothing to do with not loving him.

"What are you thinking about?" Ryder asked softly.

She smiled. "Just remembering our senior year, your accident. It was awful but I think it brought us together more too."

"It did. You helped me get through a hard time.

That's when I knew I was falling in love with you. And it's why it was so hard when you left," he added.

"I know. It was really hard leaving you too. You bounced back quickly enough though," she said.

His eyes narrowed. "What do you mean by that?"

"Well, I heard you started dating Natalie a week after I left for school."

He sighed. "We didn't date long. Natalie is a great girl, but she wasn't you. After I took her out a few times, I didn't date anyone for months."

"I saw her chatting with you at the bar last week. And I heard she's divorced now. You could have your second chance," she teased.

He stared at her intently for a moment and then shook his head. "I'm still not interested in Natalie."

Bethany wasn't sure what to say to that so she just sipped her hot chocolate.

"What about you? Is there anyone waiting for you in Manhattan?" Ryder asked casually.

The question made her laugh. "No. Hardly. I've had a few relationships over the years, but never anything long-term or serious. It's hard in our business, with the hours we work. I mostly dated other chefs or bartenders."

Kevin walked back over to them, carrying his clipboard and test results.

"So, we've run our tests and as I suspected, it looks like your mother is a little anemic. We're going to give her a blood transfusion which takes a few hours and then you'll be able to take her home soon after that. There's a waiting room if you want to relax and watch some TV while we give her the treatment.

Bethany watched as they wheeled her mother to the treatment room and then followed Ryder to the waiting room. There was a comedy playing, and they settled on the sofa to watch and wait. They chatted for a bit then got lost in the movie. Bethany felt her eyes grow heavy about half-way through and woke up a while later feeling disoriented. She was leaning against Ryder and his arm was around her. She sat up and looked at the time. Several hours had passed. Ryder was asleep too and stirred when she moved. She settled back against him and closed her eyes.

An hour or so later, Ryder was gently shaking her awake. "Bethany, your mother is all done. It's time to take her home."

Her mother was more awake than both of them when they returned to her area of the ER. Kevin was there going over her discharge orders.

"You should feel a lot better after this and have more energy. All of your other data was very good." He looked at Bethany. "Her white blood cell counts were actually improved by a lot. Whatever you're doing, keep it up."

An aide brought the wheelchair for her mother and she sniffed at it. "I don't need that thing. I'm perfectly capable of walking."

Kevin smiled at her. "Of course you are. But consider it part of the service. Save your strength for getting well."

"All right then." She eased herself into the wheelchair and Ryder wheeled her out to his car. They got her settled in the backseat and headed home. When they reached the house, Bethany and Ryder walked her mother inside.

"Ryder, thank you so much," her mother said and then surprised him with a hug. "I always did like you." She wandered off to her bedroom with Simon trailing behind her. Ryder looked exhausted. Bethany walked him to the door.

"Thanks a million. I'll see you in the morning."

Ryder smiled and his dimples stood out. "Good night, Bethany."

R yder was half-asleep when he walked into Fresh Brew to get a to-go coffee to bring into the restaurant. He stopped short when he saw a sight that he'd never seen before—his mother with a man that wasn't his father. It had been nearly ten years since they'd lost his father to a massive heart attack and his mother hadn't dated anyone or shown any interest in dating at all since. And now she was sitting and having coffee with Harry Peterman. They were laughing and so lost in their conversation that they didn't even notice him. He watched them curiously as he paid for his coffee and then had to walk right by them again on his way out.

This time his mother saw him and he hadn't seen her so happy in a long, long time.

"Ryder, come meet Harry!"

He stopped by their table and nodded. "Nice to see you again, Harry."

"Oh, that's right. I forgot that the two of you already

met. Harry's moved back to Quinn Valley. Isn't that marvelous?"

"Sure, that's great. Where did you move from?"

"Hollywood. I worked in the movie business for many years. Still do actually, but now that everything is digital, I can do a lot of my work remotely."

"Harry is a film editor. He has a fancy studio at his house."

"You've seen it?" Ryder wasn't sure how he felt about his mother going to a strange man's house. Though he realized that Harry wasn't a stranger to her.

"No, not yet. But I will tonight. Harry's having me over for dinner. We have so much to catch up on."

"I'm not much of a cook, but I can order a mean pizza," Harry said.

"I love pizza." His mother was a little too enthusiastic for his liking.

"I have to get going. Have fun you two."

———

WHEN HE REACHED QUINN'S HE SAW THAT BETHANY'S CAR was already there. And when he walked in the kitchen to say hello, she was behind the line, making pie crust. She looked as exhausted as he felt.

"How's your mother doing?" he asked.

"Much better. I think she slept better than I did. I made her a smoothie and a spinach omelet before I left."

"For the iron?"

"Yes. I know it's silly as the transfusion took care of

the anemia, but I figure it can't hurt to have her eat iron-rich foods too. Speaking of mothers, I haven't seen yours yet. She's usually here soon after I get in."

"I ran into her at the coffee shop. With a man." He told her about Harry Peterman and how he'd stopped by the restaurant a few days ago hoping to see his mother."

"And they were high school sweethearts before she met your father? How romantic that they'd find their way back to each other after all this time."

"I suppose. I just want her to be happy." He frowned. "I thought she was done with all that."

Bethany gave him a look. "With all what?"

"You know, romance."

She laughed. "Your mother is still young. I think it would be great if she could find love again."

His mother in love again. Ryder couldn't picture it.

"I'll be in my office, holler if you need anything."

BETHANY HAD SEVERAL CUPS OF COFFEE THROUGHOUT THE day, hoping a second wind would kick in. She'd gotten to bed so late the night before and slept badly. Fortunately the restaurant was too busy for her to think about how tired she was. And just before the dinner service, the caffeine finally kicked in and the next few hours flew by. She finished up at about a quarter to eight and when she left the kitchen and was going to head out the front door, Ryder waved her over. He was sitting at the bar chatting with Maggie.

"Have a quick drink with me?" He had a freshly poured beer in front of him and it suddenly looked good. Or maybe he looked good, who was she fooling?

"Okay, just one though." Maggie started pouring the chardonnay that she liked and set it down on the bar as Bethany settled into her seat.

"You always get the same thing, so I figured I was safe with this." Maggie smiled and Bethany sensed that her iciness was beginning to thaw. She liked friendly Maggie much more.

"Thank you."

"I was just telling Maggie about Mom and Harry."

"She hasn't been in at all today. That's a first," Maggie said.

"I'm happy for her." Bethany was curious to see how Maggie felt.

"Hmmmm. He didn't look like he belonged around here. How do we know he'll stick around?"

"We don't. But if he breaks our mother's heart, I'll just have to kill him." Ryder spoke with such seriousness that Bethany and Maggie stared at him until he started laughing and they joined in.

"It would be great for her if she found someone. She's still young," Maggie said.

"That's what I said earlier too," Bethany agreed.

"I have to run to the ladies room for a minute. Ryder can you keep an eye on the bar for me?"

"Sure thing."

As Bethany took a sip of wine a well-dressed couple

walked in and took seats at the bar. She couldn't place him, but the man looked vaguely familiar. She noticed Ryder stiffen before he stood and went behind the bar to take their drink order. When he came back her way to pour a draft beer, his eyes were cold and his jaw was clenched. She glanced at the couple. The man was dark-haired and in a suit and the woman with him was in a stylish suit too. She was petite and blonde, with long, feathery hair and a huge diamond engagement ring. It sparkled when the overhead light hit it.

"That's Jason. The one that broke Maggie's heart. And he's already engaged to someone else," he said softly when he came back to Bethany's end of the bar.

"Oh no!" Her heart went out to Maggie.

A moment later, Maggie returned to the bar, with a smile on her face, until Ryder pulled her aside and warned her. Her face turned ashen. He said something else, and she nodded. But first she walked over to Jason and his fiancé.

"Hello Jason. It's nice to see you. My shift is just ending, but I wanted to say hi first. I see congratulations are in order."

Jason at least looked somewhat uncomfortable. "Hi Maggie, I didn't even think that you might be on the bar. We're meeting some friends and got here a little early. This is Tiffany. She works with me at the bank."

"It's nice to meet you." Tiffany's voice was high pitched and annoying.

"Well, enjoy your evening." Maggie turned and left and when she glanced over at Ryder and Bethany, she looked on the verge of tears. She nodded at both of them and grabbed her purse from under the bar.

"Thanks, Ryder. I owe you."

She disappeared into the kitchen which led out to the back parking lot as Ryder let out a heavy sigh. "I told her to just go, that I'd cover the rest of her shift tonight. Poor kid."

"Is she still hung up on him?" Bethany asked.

"No, I really don't think she is. But I knew the shock of seeing him here with his new fiancee would be too much for her. She doesn't need to wait on them. Not while I'm here."

She smiled. He was a great big brother.

"She's lucky to have you."

He shook his head and reached for his beer. "I'd do the same for anyone in these circumstances." He turned as a crowd of guys came in and lined up at the bar. Bethany took her last sip of wine and put it in the bar dishwasher.

"I'm going to head out. I'll see you tomorrow."

CHAPTER 12

Y ou're flying out to New York tomorrow morning and coming back the next day? Are you sure you want to do that?" Bethany's mother looked at her as though she'd lost her marbles.

"I'm sure. I've had all week to think about it and I think it's a sign. It's time to put the condo on the market. And I need to get it ready to be shown and meet with the realtor." Gina Corcoran had texted her earlier in the week and asked if she might be ready to list her unit as they had several buyers interested in her building.

The market was hot, and she didn't expect that it would take long to sell if it was priced right. It was Bethany's last connection to Manhattan, but it was silly to keep paying the mortgage every month if she wasn't living there and if she had no intention of moving back.

"It's a good time to sell." She got all the ingredients

for her mother's favorite lemongrass smoothie and made one for both of them. She brought the smoothies and a cup of black coffee to the kitchen table where her mother was reading the paper.

"Thanks, honey." Her mother stuck a straw in the smoothie and took a sip. Bethany noticed that her hair was growing in nicely now and was a little curly. That was new though they said it often happened to people who had chemotherapy. Overall, her mother looked and felt really good. And her doctor was encouraged by her progress.

"How are you feeling?" she asked.

"I'm great. Marcia's going to stop by later this morning and we're going walking and then out to lunch with Glenda and Janie."

"That sounds fun."

After she finished her smoothie and cleaned up the kitchen, Bethany took her last sip of coffee and headed to the restaurant.

All the Quinn's were there when she arrived and it looked like they were having some kind of family meeting. Ryder looked up when Bethany walked in. She didn't want to interrupt and was going to keep walking to the kitchen but Ryder called her over.

"Let's ask Bethany's opinion."

She smiled. "My opinion for what?"

"Once a month, the whole family gets together for dinner. Just the family. It's this Sunday night, and she wants to invite Harry Peterman. It just doesn't seem appropriate. What do you think?"

"Oh, um. Well. Who is hosting?" she finally managed.

"My mother always hosts," Maggie said. Her eyes were stormy and it was clear how she felt about the matter.

"Well, if your mother is hosting, then I think it's her decision who to invite."

"Thanks, Bethany. I quite agree." His mother looked pleased.

Ryder sighed. "You're no help at all."

She laughed. "Sorry about that."

A mischievous gleam came into his mother's eyes. "Would it make you feel better if I told you to invite Bethany? I'm sure she'd enjoy having dinner with us."

Family dinner with the Quinn's. Bethany didn't know what to think.

"What do you say, Bethany? Want to join this crazy bunch for dinner?" Ryder asked.

She did actually. In the past two weeks, she and Ryder had been spending a lot of time together. Just about every night they had a drink or two after work. They hadn't gone on an actual date yet, but Bethany was comfortable with how things were progressing and she imagined that Ryder was being cautious since she worked for him too. But, she definitely sensed the interest. She could see it in his eyes. She was happy just spending time with him. And she felt bad that she had to decline their invitation.

"I'd love to, but I can't this Sunday night. I'm flying to New York in the morning and meeting with a realtor. I'm putting my condo on the market."

"Oh. Okay. Well, that's good then. When do you come back?"

"Monday, late afternoon."

"That's a fast trip," Maggie commented.

"I know. It's not ideal, but I didn't want to miss work."

"You can't do it over the phone?" his mother asked.

"No, not really. I need to declutter my condo a little and get it ready to show well."

She didn't mention that she was also going to meet with her former boss, Mark Newton. He said he wanted to show her the new restaurant he was going to be opening. He also said he wanted her to come with him as his executive chef and the salary he mentioned was dizzying.

But it was an easy decision to say no. It wasn't what she wanted to do or where she wanted to be anymore. And she told him as much, but he still insisted that she come see the restaurant and have a drink with him 'for old times sake.' She knew Mark well enough to know that he was going to try to put the pressure on to change her mind, but she didn't mind meeting him for one drink. She owed him a lot, and she was curious to see what his new venture was going to be like.

She had one drink at the bar with Ryder and Maggie at the end of the night. They were both in great moods as it had been a busy night and in the past two weeks, sales had gone up significantly and word was getting around about the new menu. They had a steady stream of tourists coming in too using the discount coupons. And Bethany was thrilled to see that they were now rated the top restaurant in Quinn Valley on TripAdvisor.

She smiled as she saw two couples at the bar drinking coffee and sharing a piece of chocolate cake. As she'd hoped, it had become a popular favorite and was mentioned in most of their rave reviews. One of the reviews even said that after eating the chocolate cake, a woman's boyfriend went out the very next day and bought an engagement ring. Stories like that warmed Bethany's heart.

"So, I'm finally going to meet my mystery man with the great voice," Maggie said.

"Charlie Keane?" Ryder asked.

She nodded. "He told me yesterday that Sean, the regular salesman, is going on vacation in April. And he'll be covering then and making the deliveries."

Bethany laughed. "In April? That's like six months or so from now. That's funny"

"I know, right? It's all just teasing fun. I do look forward to talking to him though. I have to admit I'm curious to see what he looks like."

"You need to go on a date before then," Ryder said.

Maggie surprised them both by agreeing. "I know. And I have one lined up for next Thursday night. A friend of Sally's new boyfriend. We're going to see a concert in Lewiston."

"That sounds fun." Bethany was glad that Maggie

was going to put herself out there. A new customer came to the bar, and she went to take his order.

Ryder looked thoughtful as he took a sip of his beer. He set the glass down and turned to her. "What do you say we go on a real date when you get back? Like out to dinner. Wherever you want to go?"

"Oh. I'd love that. It would be nice to see some of the other local restaurants. I really haven't been anywhere since I got home, except for here and O'Shea's."

"There's a few good places in town and in Riston there's an Italian restaurant that I love. They have good cannoli."

"That sounds perfect." Bethany yawned as she checked the time on her cell phone. It was getting late, and she had to be up really early. She pushed her half full glass of wine away and fished in her purse for some cash.

"You didn't even finish your wine. Your half-glass is on me. Have a safe trip, Bethany."

CHAPTER 13

Bethany drove to the Lewiston airport at the obscene hour of three am to get there an hour ahead of her five am flight. There were no good options for flying to New York City from Lewiston. There were no direct flights and even leaving this early didn't get her there until after three in the afternoon because of the time difference. But it would work out because she was meeting Mark later that evening, and the realtor was coming first thing in the morning.

She took an Uber from the airport to her tiny condo. It had one small bedroom that barely fit her bed, a galley kitchen and a small sitting area. It was in an up-and-coming area of the city though and had a small balcony where she used to love to sit and have her morning coffee when it was nice out. She looked around the small space which felt even smaller after coming from her mother's house, which wasn't big but was a lot more spacious than this. Bethany remembered when she'd first moved in and was so excited about buying her first home.

But with what she'd get for it, she could buy a house three times the size or more in Quinn Valley. She didn't have any plans to buy anything anytime soon, but it would be nice to not have to worry about making the monthly payments anymore and to have a nest egg in the bank.

She spent the rest of the afternoon straightening up and throwing things out that were just taking up space. By the time she finished, she had about an hour to get ready and meet Mark at the address he'd given her. A hot shower felt great and a half hour later, she was dressed and in an Uber on her way to Mark's new restaurant.

The address was a trendy brownstone in mid-town Manhattan and Mark was sitting on the front step checking something on his phone when she stepped out of the car. He looked up when he heard her footsteps and pulled her in for a hug.

"Thanks for coming. You look amazing as always." Mark always was a flatterer. But Bethany did feel good. She hadn't had a reason to get dressed up since she'd been back in Quinn Valley and the black dress she wore was one of her favorites. It was modestly cut and flattering.

"You look great too. Your hair looks different. Did you color it?" His hair was thick and choppy and she was pretty sure it was also blonder than she'd last seen it.

He laughed. "Ssssh, don't tell anyone. I'm going for the hot, surfer look. What do you think?"

She just shook her head. "I think you haven't changed at all!"

"Ha! Come on inside. I want to show you what I'm planning."

She followed him inside and gasped when he turned the lights on. The space was absolutely gorgeous. Huge bay windows looked out over a courtyard that was draped in tiny white lights. All the tables were covered in a shimmery blue gray fabric and accented with creamy white napkins. Black vases filled with white flowers sat in the middle of every table. The overall look was both elegant and warm.

"It's beautiful. What's the menu like?"

"That's the best part. It's right up your alley. I'm thinking upscale comfort food. That's why I thought of you first."

The space and overall concept would have been her dream situation if she wanted to stay in the city.

"It's tempting. I can't say it's not. But I'm selling my condo and staying in Idaho. It's time."

Mark looked at her as if she had two heads. "How can you say no to this? To living here? There's no greater city on earth."

Bethany laughed. "I agree. But I don't want to live in any city anymore."

Mark sighed. "Okay, I'll give up, for now. Let's have a glass of wine and then grab a bite to eat. There's a new place that opened up in Soho that I've been meaning to check out. You okay with red?" He began rummaging through a wine closet until he found what he was looking for.

"Red is fine."

"Good. Because this one is going to knock your socks off."

Bethany had a bit of a headache the next morning when the realtor knocked at the door. She was glad that she'd taken the time the day before to straighten up so the place looked neat and ready to show. Gina bounced through the door and was so perky and chipper that Bethany wanted to groan.

"Would you like some coffee?" she offered.

"Oh no, I'm fine. I already had mine at the office."

Bethany topped off her mug and walked around the condo with Gina while she asked questions and took notes.

"This is such a great neighborhood. Will you be looking to buy something else in the city?"

"No. I don't think so. I've loved living here though." It was going to be bittersweet to leave.

"So, I think I can get this sold for you quickly, if you're ready to get started?"

"I'm as ready as I'll ever be." They discussed a starting price, and Bethany signed the necessary paperwork. She gave Gina a spare set of keys and told her she could show the condo anytime as she wouldn't be there.

"Okay, stay tuned. I'll be in touch!" When Gina left

all the energy went out of the room and Bethany sank into a chair at her small kitchen table. She sipped her coffee and slowly felt her headache ebb away. She and Mark had stayed up late, drinking wine and eating so many wonderful things. He insisted on getting the tasting menu and knew the chef, so there was much discussion about the different dishes and cooking in general.

It was the kind of night that Bethany loved. She could talk about food until the wee hours. And they did. It was after one by the time Mark dropped her at her building. Several times throughout the night he'd asked her again if she'd reconsider but she told him no every time.

"You're a tough nut to crack," he said when he stopped outside her building. "If you change your mind, call me. I'm looking to nail down my chef in the next few weeks."

"Thank you for a wonderful night, Mark. It was great to see you again. And I wish you all the best with the new restaurant."

"Safe travels, Bethany."

CHAPTER 14

Ryder was earlier than usual Tuesday morning. He'd been antsy since Sunday when Bethany left for New York. He knew she was going there to list her condo, which he thoroughly approved of but a small part of him still worried that she might change her mind and decide to move back there. What if she realized how much she missed the city?

He wanted to believe her though when she said she was back in Quinn Valley for good. Until he'd walked in that morning and his mother announced that she was his new chef, he'd pretty much given up on the possibility. And he'd tried to move on. He really had. But there was only one Bethany.

And unless he imagined it, she was feeling some of the same things he was. He loved everything about her, her laugh, her shy smile, her amazing cooking, her sense of humor, the way she laughed at his lame attempts at a joke and the way she looked. She took his breath away, she always had. There was no one else he'd rather spend time with and he'd been surprised by how much he'd missed not seeing her for the past few days.

He'd quickly grown so used to seeing her every day, and looked forward to sharing a drink after work and chatting about all the crazy things that had happened that day. Yes, it was definitely time for he and Bethany to officially start dating.

"Morning." The familiar voice made him feel warm inside. He turned and saw Bethany standing in a pool of light that streamed through the open window. She was wearing faded jeans, her hair was in a ponytail and she was carrying a hot coffee. And she'd never looked so beautiful. He fought the urge to go and kiss her senseless. He knew that wouldn't be appropriate. Instead he smiled and asked how her trip was.

"It was fine and fast. I'm tired today as you can imagine, but I got the condo listed and my realtor thinks it should go quickly. There's not much available in my price range."

"So, you're back to stay awhile," he teased.

She hesitated for a second and then smiled. "Of course I'm here to stay. How was your family dinner? Did Mr. Peterman go?"

"He did. He seems to go everywhere with my mother now. She keeps insisting though that they are just good friends."

Bethany laughed. "Well, it sounds like they are really good friends."

"Right. Oh, I had a message that my grandmother

and her friends are coming today for a late lunch. And she has a special request."

"Oh? What's that?"

"Apparently they all want that lemongrass smoothie that you made for your mother. Word has gotten around that it's some kind of cure all. My grandmother also wants you to set aside three pieces of chocolate cake for the table to share."

"Is that all they want? Smoothies and chocolate cake?" Bethany was amused.

"I don't ask questions. I just do what she says," Ryder said.

Later that afternoon, Ryder came into the kitchen and looked a bit uncomfortable.

"My grandmother wants to talk to you. If it's not too much trouble. Her words."

She laughed. "I'd be happy to talk to her. Where is she?"

"Round table by the window, white hair, purple sweater and pearls."

Bethany ducked into the bathroom to smooth her hair, added a bit of lipstick to freshen her look and made her way into the dining room. She immediately recognized Ryder's grandmother. She was sitting in the middle of the table, and the surrounding ladies were hanging on her every word. She finished her story just as Bethany reached the table and the ladies broke into peals of laughter.

"Well, hello there. It's been a long time since I've seen you Bethany. It's very kind of you to come see us."

"I hope that you enjoyed your lunch? Ryder said that you wanted to talk to me?"

"Yes. Tell me dear, how is your mother? Is she doing better? I heard that she's been ill."

Bethany smiled. "She's doing very well. Her doctor says her tests are all showing significant improvement."

"Oh, that is wonderful news." All the ladies nodded in agreement.

"That smoothie we had, with the lemongrass, is that what your mother drank?"

"Yes, she still has one every day."

"You don't say. And will these be available here regularly now?"

"The smoothies? I think so yes."

"Good, because we're all hoping that they might help us too. None of us are as sick as your poor mother of course, but we figure it might be good to keep ahead of things. Build up our immune system."

Bethany was impressed. "I really do think it helps."

"And what about the chocolate cake?" His grandmother winked. "Do you suppose that helps too?"

Bethany grinned "I know that it helps. It feeds the soul."

"That it does. So, my grandson. Are the two of you dating yet?"

"Gertrude!" Her friend Nellie nudged her.

"It's an honest question. Inquiring minds would like to know." The ladies all leaned forward in their chairs, listening hard.

"Ryder and I are very good friends," Bethany said.

"Hmmmm. Well, I suppose that will have to do for now. Thanks for coming to see us." Bethany fought back the urge to giggle. She was being dismissed.

"Enjoy the rest of your day, ladies."

SHE STOPPED BY THE BAR TO GET A GLASS OF WATER ON her way back to the kitchen. Maggie was unloading the dishwasher and looked up when she saw her.

"Was my grandmother giving you the third-degree? She prides herself on her matchmaking abilities."

Bethany chuckled. "Not too bad. She was equally interested in making sure the lemongrass smoothie stays on the menu."

"Now she's into smoothies? She's too much."

"I hope I have half her energy when I get to be her age."

"She does pretty well. She doesn't miss much that's for sure. Grandma seems to know about everything that goes on around here."

"I heard Mr. Peterman came to dinner. How was it?" Bethany asked.

"Not as bad as I thought it might be. He's actually a pretty nice guy. And he's obviously crazy about my mother, so I have to like that about him."

"Ryder says that she says they are just friends."

"That's right. Very good friends. I don't think she's looking to rush anything, which is smart of her. Oh, gotta go. New people needing drinks."

Bethany made her way back to the kitchen and got ready for the dinner rush. When it quieted down, a few hours later, she joined her mother and her friends. Jill was delivering a baby so she couldn't make it. But Ryder joined them too.

"I hear you put your Manhattan condo on the market?" Glenda asked as Ivy set down Bethany's wine and Ryder's beer.

"I did, yes." Bethany's phone beeped alerting her that she had a text message. It was from Gina. She read the message and smiled.

"That was just my realtor, letting me know that she has two showings scheduled for this week."

"That was fast," her mother said.

"She said the market is hot. We'll see what happens."

"Well, cheers to a quick sale." Ryder lifted his beer glass and the others all did the same.

"So, I had an interesting phone call a few minutes ago too. Gary and Suzanne were arrested in Las Vegas for running a similar scam on the restaurant they were working at."

"Wow, they caught them pretty quickly," Bethany said.

"In Vegas they have cameras everywhere because of the casinos. It wasn't very smart of them." He explained to her mother's friends what they'd done at Quinn's.

"How awful," Janie said. "Will they go to jail now?"

"It looks like they will. They won't be able to rip anyone else off for a long time now."

"Are you all playing music bingo tonight?" Eddie, the game's host was handing out score sheets and pads of paper for their answers.

"We're in," Ryder said.

Two hours later, they officially came in last place after blowing the final question.

"Oh well, you win some, you lose some," her mother said.

"That's right, but it's always fun," Glenda agreed.

They settled their bill and everyone left together. Ryder and Bethany walked her mother to her car and then as soon as she drove off, Ryder pulled Bethany to him and brought his lips to hers. He took her by surprise but his kiss was welcome and just as sweet as she remembered.

"I've been waiting a long time to do that. I've missed kissing you." he said.

"I've missed it too."

"Are you ready for that real date we talked about? We could go Sunday night if you're interested?"

"I'm interested."

He took her hand and walked her to her car and kissed her again. This time the kiss went on forever, but it was still too short for Bethany's liking. Ryder gave a final hug before she got into her car.

"Sleep tight, Bethany."

CHAPTER 15

The rest of the week flew by in a happy blur. Every night after work, she sat with Ryder and Maggie and then Ryder walked her to her car and they kissed, for a long time. On Sunday they were going to his favorite Italian restaurant in Riston, the next town over and she was looking forward to it. Though she didn't really care where they went as long as they were together.

And when Sunday morning came, she and her mother went to the spa at the Quinn hotel for massages and then a long hot soak in the hot springs. They'd both been before of course, because how could you live in Quinn Valley and never visit the hot springs? But it had been many years since either of them had been. She knew it was supposed to have healing properties too.

"How does it feel?" she asked her mother as they relaxed in the warm water.

"Heavenly. It's like nature's hot tub."

Bethany smiled. "We really should do this more often."

Once they were done soaking and got dressed, they took a drive downtown and had a nice lunch at Phil's diner. She'd been going there with her mother for as long as she could remember. And they almost always got the same thing. Chocolate shakes, cheeseburgers and onion rings.

"I love all that healthy food you've had me eating, but sometimes a little grease is good." Her mother winked as she took a big bite of her burger. A minute later she asked, "So, Ryder's taking you out to dinner tonight. Will this be your first real date?"

"It will. In a way though, because I see him every day and night, it almost feels like we've been together longer."

"Well, you do have some history."

"That's true. Though it feels like it was a million years ago."

"You're still the same people. Just older, and hopefully wiser." Her mother reached for an onion ring and dunked in ketchup before taking a bite.

"I hope we're wiser. We'll find out I guess."

Her mother frowned. "Well that doesn't sound very optimistic. I think the two of you belong together. I always have. Don't worry so much. Just enjoy every day as it comes. That's something I've learned recently."

"You're right." Bethany took a sip of her chocolate shake. It was rich and creamy and probably not at all what she should be having since she was going out to dinner later. "Your pet scan is tomorrow right? I can go with you if you like?" She knew her mother was nervous about what the results of the full body scan would be.

"I'd like that. I've been falling asleep with my crystals every night....I'm feeling hopeful."

"I am too."

BETHANY TRIED ON AT LEAST A DOZEN OUTFITS BEFORE finally settling on her favorite faded jeans, a white top with a long, flowing caramel cashmere sweater over it and black leather cowboy boots. She ran a curling iron through her hair to add some soft, tousled waves and finished the look with a deep rose lipstick. She almost felt like she was back in high school as she waited for her date to come and pick her up. When she heard the knock at the door, the butterflies in her stomach went crazy. She told herself it was silly. It was just Ryder after all and she'd known him forever.

But when she came downstairs and saw him chatting with her mother, she just stared for a minute. She hadn't seen Ryder all dressed up in a long time. He was looking sharp in a button-down shirt and tie and a navy blazer over jeans. His hair was lightly gelled and when he turned her way and smiled, his cute dimple and his eyes fought for her attention. The eyes won as they always did.

"Hi, Ryder."

"Bethany. You look beautiful."

"She does, doesn't she?" her mother said proudly.

"Thank you. See you in a while, mom."

"You two have fun."

Bethany stepped outside and saw Ryder's car at the curb. They drove off and spent the whole ride laughing about silly things they'd seen that week at the restaurant. There was no shortage of stories to share. The ride to Riston went by in no time and they soon arrived at Mamma Mia's, the Italian restaurant Ryder liked so much.

She was glad to see that they were busy, but not too busy. There were a few empty tables, and they were led to a nice one by a cozy fireplace.

Their server appeared a minute or so later to take their drink order and they ordered a bottle of chianti.

Once the wine was poured, and they put their orders in, Ryder picked up his glass and tapped it against hers.

"To our first real date. First of many I hope."

Bethany looked around the room, at the cheerful glow of the fire, the hum of conversation around them and the smell of garlic and tomatoes. Their server returned to their table and set down a basket of hot crusty bread and a dish of olive oil and spices.

"I can see why you like it here," she said as she took a piece of bread and dunked it in the fragrant oil. And then she shared her big news.

"So, I got a call from my realtor today. She had two showings this week on my condo. And both people made an offer."

"Wow! That's good news. The market must really be hot there."

"That's what she said, but I didn't realize it would happen that quickly."

Ryder frowned. "Are you sure you want to sell?"

"Oh, I'm sure. I accepted one of the offers. We close in a month."

"That's great! Congratulations." He was quiet for a moment and then said, "Did I tell you I'm thinking about building a house?"

"No. What kind of house? Where?"

"I bought a lot of land a few years ago as an investment. It's on a lake and is a good size, over two acres. I thought at one point that I might want to subdivide and sell it, but it's a really pretty spot and I think I want to keep it as is."

"I've always thought it would be fun to build my own dream house. To get everything exactly the way I want it."

"What would that look like to you?" Ryder broke off a piece of bread and dipped it in the oil.

Bethany thought about that for a minute. "Maybe a rustic contemporary style with lots of big windows that would overlook the water, and a big deck to sit outside and have coffee."

"That sounds good. What else?"

"Three or maybe four bedrooms in case I have children at some point. A comfortable living room or family room and of course an amazing kitchen."

"Of course."

"What would you want?" she asked.

"Not too different. Most of what you said, plus a basement for a man cave and a three-car garage."

"But you only have one car."

"For now. I might want more and maybe I might live with someone someday and that person probably would have a car."

"True. Where do you live now?" The last time they dated, Ryder lived at home with his family.

"I'm renting for now, a condo not far from the restaurant. It's convenient but kind of vanilla. I'm looking forward to having a little more space. And the lake lot isn't far, maybe a ten minute drive to Quinn's."

THEIR MEALS WERE DELIVERED A FEW MINUTES LATER, chicken parmesan for Ryder and gnocchi with meatballs for Bethany. The potato based pasta was homemade and cooked to perfection, light and pillowy and the sauce was delicious. Ryder looked happy with his dinner too. As they ate and chatted, Bethany noticed the way Ryder's dimple and the laugh lines around his mouth and eyes made his face so attractive.

He seemed more relaxed now than when she first started at the restaurant too. There was a nervous tension around him then that she knew was partly due to her sudden appearance but also his worries about the restaurant's financial situation. She was relieved that sales were still trending upwards and that feedback so far on the food had been overwhelmingly positive.

"I had an interesting phone call before I left to pick you up," Ryder began.

"Oh?"

"A buddy of mine works at the newspaper and told me to be sure to check the review page tomorrow. Evidently their lifestyles editor that also does the occasional restaurant review was in last week sometime for dinner."

Bethany felt a pit in her stomach. She'd seen the damage a bad review could do to a restaurant before.

"Was he warning you? Or do you think it might be positive?"

"He didn't say, probably couldn't say until the review is live. But, he was in a good mood. And I can't imagine anyone would give your food a bad review."

"Well, I hope he liked whatever he had. A good review could be helpful."

"Don't be all worried now. I really do think this is probably good news. Let's toast to the possibility of it." He raised his glass and Bethany laughed and tapped hers against his and took a sip.

"Now, let's just hope you didn't jinx us!"

He chuckled. "I don't believe in jinxing. But I do believe in you. I wouldn't say this in front of my mother, but you're a better chef than she is."

"Thank you. And no, that can never be said to her! Besides, I had the advantage of formal training."

Ryder took his last bite of chicken and set his fork down. He'd cleaned his plate while Bethany still had more than half of her dinner left. She'd be taking the rest home with her.

"Did you save any room for dessert?" he asked.

"I'm pretty stuffed. But if you want something, I could probably take a bite or two to help."

He grinned. "Let's share a cannoli. "

Their server cleared their plates and set a single cannoli between them along with two forks. It was one of Bethany's favorite desserts and this one looked just like the ones she used to get in New York's Little Italy restaurants. The ricotta filling was rich and creamy with a hint of sweetness and the edges were dipped in tiny chocolate chips. The shell was crisp and the perfect vehicle for the filling. She had two small bites and let Ryder finish the rest.

"Good, huh?" he said as he polished off the last bite..

"So good."

Ryder reached for the bill when it was delivered and handed it back to the server with his credit card.

"Where should we go from here? Figs on Main Street usually has live music if you want to check that out. It's not too far of a walk from here."

"Sure. I could use a good walk."

After Ryder signed the credit card slip, Bethany put her bag with her leftovers in the car and they walked over to Figs. The air was brisk and cool with a slight wind as they walked. Bethany snuggled into her coat to ward off the wind and was glad when they reached Figs a few minutes later. The restaurant bar was warm and lively as they stepped inside. It looked like a small band was getting ready to play a set.

There were no open cocktail tables or seats at the bar, but there was a spot against the wall where they could be out of the way and also have a good view of the music.

"What can I get you? I'm going to go up to the bar."

"I'd love a coffee, with a little Frangelico in it."

Ryder smiled. "And whipped cream?"

"Of course!"

While he was getting their drinks at the bar, Bethany watched the band get ready. There were two guys on guitar and a pretty woman with long caramel colored wavy hair. She looked vaguely familiar and Bethany wondered if she might have seen her somewhere before.

She noticed Ryder chatting with a guy at the bar. It looked like they knew each other. He returned with their drinks a few minutes later and handed Bethany her coffee. She took a sip. The hot coffee and nutty flavor of the hazelnut liqueur warmed her right up.

"What are you drinking?" Ryder was sipping something clear with a lemon floating in it.

"Just soda water. I'm too full for anything else and still have to drive us back."

"True. Who was that you were talking to at the bar?"

"That's Wade. Wade Weston. He's the general manager of the River's End Ranch resort here in Riston. I know him from college. He's a great guy. He said that Lily, the singer in the band tonight, also works for him handling events."

"Oh, I thought she looked familiar! I think my mother

mentioned something about her a while back. There was an article about her in the local paper. She's a songwriter too, right?"

"I think so. Oh, and I talked to Wade briefly about our discount coupons. He thought that was a great idea and said he might want to have some to give out at the ranch too."

"Don't they have a restaurant at the ranch too?"

"Yes, but he knows the guests won't want to go there every night. And the hot springs in Quinn Valley is a perfect day trip for people staying at River's End. And if they come to our town, we're happy to feed them."

When the band began to play, Ryder put his arms around her and she leaned into him, listening and enjoying the music. So far, it had been a perfect night and being in Ryder's arms was exactly where she wanted to be. She sighed with happiness.

"Having fun?" he whispered in her ear.

"Yes. So much fun."

They left after the band finished their set. The temperature had dropped even more and the walk back to the car was a cold one. Ryder turned on the heat as soon as they drove out of town and it didn't take long to warm up. Bethany wasn't eager for the evening to end, but it wasn't long before Ryder pulled onto her mother's street and stopped in front of her house. He jumped out of the car and came around to open her door, which made her smile. He was such a gentleman.

"Don't forget tomorrow's lunch." He handed her the small bag that was on the floor of the car.

"Thank you. And thank you for a wonderful night."

"It's not over just yet. I still need to kiss you." He pulled her close and brought his lips to hers. She inhaled his scent, the fresh wonderful smell that was uniquely his. It was addicting, and she leaned into him and deepened the kiss. If it wasn't so cold, she could have kissed him much longer, but when she shivered, he pulled back.

"I think that's our sign to call it a night."

"I suppose you're right."

"And you have a big day tomorrow. Big for your mom that is." She'd told him about the scan her mother was going for and how they were hoping for good news.

"Yes. We're all praying hard."

"Well, let her know she's in my thoughts and my mother's too. And Maggie's."

"I will. Goodnight, Ryder."

CHAPTER 16

When Bethany came downstairs the next morning, her mother was already in the kitchen making herself a smoothie.

"Morning. Do you want me to do that?" Her mother had all the ingredients lined up on the counter and was staring at the juicer.

"If you could just show me how to work this thing, I'm happy to do it. That way I can make these anytime."

Bethany showed her how to feed the fruit and vegetables into the juicing machine and the best way to clean it immediately afterward so it didn't get all sticky

She poured herself a coffee while her mother sipped her smoothie. They had to leave for the hospital shortly.

"So, did you have fun last night? I went to bed early and never heard you come in."

"We did have fun. We went to Figs after dinner to hear some music."

"Figs. I think I went there a few years ago, right on Main Street?"

"That's the place. We didn't eat there, but the menu looked good. The food at Mamma Mia's was excellent."

Her mother nodded. "It's been a long time since I've been there, but I remember it always being very good."

Her mother looked serious and hopeful as she leaned forward and said, "So, what do you think about Ryder? Are the two of you an item now?"

"Yes. I think so. I know that's what I want."

Her mother smiled. "Good."

They spent the rest of the day at the hospital and Bethany spent most of her time waiting, while her mother got ready to have her Pet Scan, which involved injecting a dye that would allow the machines to scan her whole body and determine if there was any cancer left and where it was. The procedure itself took awhile and then the recovery period. Once she was done, they went straight home and Bethany served her mother a big bowl of chicken soup and some hot bread. She was starving because she wasn't able to eat solid foods before the test. The test results would take two business days her doctor told them, so they spent the next two days worrying and waiting. And on Thursday morning, a few minutes before Bethany left to go to work, her mother's doctor called.

She was silent on the phone, just listening as he told her the results of the scan. And she looked to be in a bit of a daze as she thanked him for calling and hung up the phone. She burst into tears which alarmed Bethany until she saw her smile emerge.

"He said that there was nothing on the scans. No signs of any cancer at all."

And suddenly Bethany was crying too and hugging her mother.

"I'm so happy for you, Mom."

"And I'm so grateful, honey. Everything you've done, the smoothies, crystals, oils, and the hot springs. I think it all helped so much."

"I don't know what worked, I'm just glad we tried everything, and that something did the trick."

"Marcia is coming by for tea today. I think we may need to go out to lunch and celebrate instead."

"Why don't you come into Quinn's? Maggie and Ryder are going to be so excited for you too."

"Maybe we will!"

RYDER WAS IN A BETTER THAN USUAL MOOD WHEN HE arrived at Quinn's Thursday morning. His night with Bethany had gone even better than he'd hoped and they'd spent the next few evenings together too. He could finally see himself building a future with her. It also made him feel more secure that she'd already sold her Manhattan condo, so in a month, when she closed on the sale, she wouldn't have any more ties there.

Maggie was already there, sitting at the bar going over her weekly order. She was on her phone and finished her call as he brought his coffee over to the bar and sat next to her. He noticed that she was blushing slightly and seemed a bit flustered, which was unlike her.

He smiled. "Have you been talking to Charlie again?"

Her flush deepened and she nodded. "I'm almost afraid to meet him. We have such a perfect relationship over the phone. He flirts with me and makes me laugh. And that voice."

"You have it bad."

She sighed. "I think it's a fantasy, really. It's not real."

"You never know. Stranger things have happened. You should meet him."

"I will. But not until April."

He laughed. "Whatever makes you happy."

Bethany came through the door and rushed over to them. She looked happier than he'd ever seen her.

"You look like you won the lottery!" Maggie said.

"Better. My mother got her scan results this morning and there's no trace left of her cancer."

Maggie came out from behind the bar, her eyes suddenly wet and pulled Bethany in for a hug. "That's the best news ever."

And Bethany's eyes were shiny too as she smiled up at him. There was so much love there, and he was happy for both of them.

He pulled her in for a hug too and kissed her forehead gently. "Please tell your mother we're both thrilled for her."

She grinned. "You can tell her yourself! I think your mother and my mother are coming in for lunch today to celebrate."

"Oh great. I'll reserve our best table by the window for them."

"Thanks. She'd love that."

Maggie went back to her ordering and Ryder walked with Bethany into the kitchen. They chatted about her next order from David. She wanted to try some of the products they'd tasted.

"Go ahead, I trust you completely on the menu. You haven't steered us wrong yet."

"Thank you. Oh, and I know I said it last night, but I had a really good time with you. It was the perfect date."

He smiled. He couldn't seem to stop smiling around Bethany lately. She had that effect on him.

"Let's do it again this Sunday. I'm not much of a cook, but I can grill a steak and I want to show you my lot by the lake. We can take a drive out there if you like?"

"I'd love to see it, and I'm always up for a good steak."

"Great, it's a date then."

————

BETHANY WAS HAVING A GREAT DAY. SHE COULDN'T remember when she'd last felt so happy. Her mother was healthy and she was looking forward to spending her day off with Ryder. She stayed busy in the kitchen through the lunch rush and then took a break to visit with her mother and Marcia. They'd come in for a late lunch when they knew it wouldn't be too busy so everyone could stop by their table and celebrate the good news.

After they left, Bethany was on her way back into the kitchen when a familiar face walked into the bar. Mark Newton. He looked around as if he was searching for someone and broke into a huge grin when he saw her.

"I was hoping I'd come to the right place!"

She walked over to him. He went to give her a hug, and she took a step back. Ryder and Maggie were watching with interest at the bar and she didn't want there to be any misunderstandings. Mark had no business being in Quinn Valley and at her restaurant as far as she knew. Which meant he'd come for one reason, to see her.

"What are you doing here?"

"Can we meet for a drink after you finish up?"

She knew that wouldn't go over well with Ryder and she couldn't blame him. Plus she had no interest in meeting Mark for another drink. "No, I'm working late tonight. What is it?"

He glanced around the bar and his gaze stopped for a minute on Ryder and Maggie.

"Is that your boss? The glaring man at the end of the bar?"

"Yes, he and his sister own Quinn's."

"Okay. Well maybe we should step outside for a minute. This won't take long."

"I've got about two minutes to spare."

"I'll make it fast."

She followed him outside and crossed her arms over her chest waiting for him to say what he came to say.

"Why did you fly all the way here? You could have just called me or texted."

"I did both, but I didn't hear back from you."

Hmmmm Maybe he did, she hadn't checked her text messages in a few days and she had ignored his last voice message.

"Here's the thing. I really want you to be my executive chef."

Bethany sighed. "We already had this conversation."

"No, I know. Hear me out. So, I've been thinking and I have the perfect solution. I'll cut you in, make you a partner. You'll get a share of all the profits. So you'll have a little skin in the game. What do you say? It's an opportunity you can't pass up right?"

She looked at him. A few months ago he would have been right. It was the kind of opportunity she'd dreamed of. But her dreams had changed. And Mark wasn't in them.

"I'm hugely flattered, but no thank you. This is where I want to be. Where I need to be."

Mark didn't look happy. He tried one last time. "But this isn't Manhattan."

She smiled. "No, it's not. It's home. Goodbye, Mark."

BETHANY WENT BACK INSIDE AND WALKED OVER TO RYDER and Maggie.

"Who was that?" Maggie asked. Ryder said nothing, just waited for her to explain.

"That's Mark Newton. I used to work for him."

"And he just happened to drop by Quinn Valley?"

Ryder raised his eyebrows. The wariness she'd seen in his eyes when she first saw him, was back.

"I saw him in Manhattan too when I went home to put the condo on the market. He wanted to meet me for a drink and to show me his new restaurant."

"He offered you a job." Ryder's tone was flat and cold.

She nodded. "He did. But I turned him down."

"Why did you even meet with him if you weren't considering it?" he asked

"I knew I didn't want it. But I felt I owed it to him to take the meeting, and I was curious to see what he was doing," she admitted.

"If you said no, why did he come here?" Maggie looked confused.

"Mark never was good at taking no for an answer. He raised the stakes and offered me shares in the restaurant."

"So you'd be an owner. I'd imagine that's hard to say no to," Maggie said.

"A few months ago it would have been." She looked at Ryder and smiled. "But today it was easy."

"You told him to beat it?" He sounded surprised, and unsure if he believed her.

"I did. I told you last night that I sold my condo."

"You don't close for a month. You could still get out of it," he said.

"I probably could. But I don't want to. I'm happy here. I don't want to go back to Manhattan. Except maybe for a vacation."

Ryder smiled tightly. "I can think of a long list of other places I'd rather go on vacation."

Maggie laughed and went off to help a new customer.

"So, are we good? Still on for Sunday?" Bethany asked. Ryder still seemed a little distant and closed off.

"Sure. We're still on for Sunday."

***

RYDER WATCHED HER GO BACK TO THE KITCHEN AND stewed for a minute longer before heading into his office. He'd been looking forward to Sunday and was eager to show Bethany his land and to cook for her. He needed to digest everything that he'd just heard though and make sure that they were both on the same page. Maybe Bethany wasn't as far along as he was with where he thought their relationship was going.

CHAPTER 17

R yder was quiet the rest of the day on Thursday which concerned Bethany a bit, but he still wanted her to stay after work that night and they kept Maggie company at the bar for about an hour or so before calling it a night. And he still walked her to her car and gave her a kiss goodnight. It wasn't as long or as passionate as the one she'd had the night before, but it was still a pretty good kiss as far as kisses went.

By Saturday, things seemed back to normal with them and Bethany relaxed fully. Her heart had sank when she saw Mark walk into Quinn's and then saw the look on Ryder's face. She never wanted to see that look again. She knew that he needed to process what he'd seen and heard and she was glad that he seemed to realize that Mark was unimportant to her and that what they had was real and solid.

Ryder was in an unusually good mood Saturday night as they shared a drink after a very busy and long night. It was their best night of the year so far and Bethany was still feeling the warm fuzzies from the review on Quinn's that was published that morning. Marcia had brought it into the restaurant and plunked it down on the table where they were sitting and drinking their coffee.

"We should frame this and hang it on the wall. We've never had a review like this one before," she said proudly.

Ryder picked up the paper and read the review out loud. It was full of accolades about the food and the service. What made Bethany happiest of all was the final line,

"If you're looking for the kind of comfort food that you wish your mother was able to make, come to Quinn's. You won't be disappointed. This is Manhattan quality fare in Quinn Valley. A true gem."

"A true gem," Ryder repeated holding her gaze until she felt herself beginning to blush and looked away.

"That's really great news," she'd said.

The mood all day had felt celebratory and when Ryder walked her to her car at the end of the night, the kiss they shared made her toes tingle.

"I'll be by late tomorrow afternoon, around three," he said.

———

AT THREE O'CLOCK SHARP, THERE WAS A KNOCK AT THE front door. Bethany heard it open and her mother's voice mixed with Ryder's. She took one last look in the mirror before heading downstairs. It was chilly out and since they were going outside to see his lake property, she'd dressed for warmth in a thick fisherman's knit sweater, turtle neck, jeans, heavy socks and her favorite old brown boots that were soft and warm.

When she came downstairs, Ryder and her mother were speaking softly. Her mother looked up and stopped talking. There was a gleam in her eye that Bethany hadn't seen in a long time. Her spirits had been great ever since she got the good news from her doctor.

"Have fun you two," she called out as they stepped outside.

"Do you have a hat?" Ryder asked before they got to his car.

"I do. I forgot to put it on." Bethany fished a knit hat out of her tote bag and pulled it on. She knew it wasn't the most flattering look, but it kept her warm. Ryder was wearing a thick knit hat as well and a down jacket. She had a thin down jacket over her sweater and even though it was cold out, she was warm enough.

"I made us a thermos of hot chocolate we can have when we get to the lake," Ryder said.

They reached his street fifteen minutes later, and he slowed as he reached a large empty lot that overlooked a large lake. There were boat ramps along the shore and the view from his land was beautiful.

"Come on, I'll give you the grand tour." He grabbed the thermos and a blanket and led the way around his lot and down to the shore. There was plenty of room for him to add a dock if he wanted to and he would have a large sunny view almost anywhere on the lot that he decided to build.

"What do you think?"

"It's awesome. I can see why you want to keep it for yourself."

He spread out the blanket and sat Indian-style with the thermos in front of him. He had two plastic mugs with him as well and poured out some hot chocolate for both of them. Bethany joined him on the blanket and gratefully accepted a mug of the steaming beverage. It smelled wonderful and had tiny marshmallows bobbing over the top.

They talked again about the kind of house he wanted to build and she told him all about what she envisioned her dream kitchen looking like. It was fun to dream even if it was for someone else's house.

"So, could you ever see yourself living here?" he surprised her by asking. His tone was serious, and she turned and the love that was reflected in his eyes took her breath away. She nodded. "Yes, of course."

He smiled, then stood up, which confused her, until he bent down on one knee and fished something out of his pocketed. A small, black velvet box. She hadn't expected this at all, not today.

His smile was shaky but about as big as she'd ever seen it.

"Bethany, there's no one else I want to be with. No one else I'd rather live in my dream house with. Our dream house. I want to build it the way we want it. I don't think I ever stopped loving you. You're my best friend and the person I want to spend every day with for the rest of my life. Will you marry me?" He held the ring up, and the diamond sparkled in the sunlight.

"Yes, yes of course I'll marry you! I love you too, Ryder. So much."

He stood and pulled her in for a kiss that went on and on. They sat down again and had more hot chocolate and she stared at the ring. It was beautiful, a cushion cut diamond surrounded by a ring of delicate, smaller diamonds in a platinum setting.

"How long have you had this ring?" She wondered when he'd gone shopping for it.

"My mother gave it to me years ago, before you went to Manhattan. She knew I wanted to ask you then. It was her mother's ring."

"And you've had it all this time." Bethany stared at the ring in wonder.

"Well, it's not like I had anyone else I wanted to give it to." He grinned and pulled her in for another kiss.

"Do you mind if I wait until after the house is built? I want to give my mother some time to get used to the idea."

"I don't mind waiting. She already knows though."

"She does?"

"That's what we were talking about before you came downstairs. I was asking her permission. She thoroughly approves."

"Oh, well we could do it sooner then."

"How about in a few months? I know my mother is going to have certain ideas about what she wants for a wedding and yours probably will too. That will give them both time to plot and plan. And there's plenty of room in my condo for both of us. We can live there until the house is done."

"I love that plan." She smiled and touched her finger lightly to his lips. "And I love you."

"I love you, too." Ryder kissed her again, and she sighed with happiness. Everything finally was exactly as it should be.

EPILOGUE

ONE MONTH LATER

R yder, do twins run in your family by any chance?" Bethany's mother asked as she set three perfect green smoothies on the kitchen table. It was Sunday morning, a little after ten and Ryder had stopped by to show them the house plans. Bethany picked one of the glasses up and took a sip. It was perfect.

"Mom, you've mastered smoothies. This is great!"

"Thank you, dear. Ryder?" She looked eager for his answer.

"I'm thinking, sorry. I don't think there are any twins in the family, actually. Why do you ask?"

"Hmmm. Well, I had the strangest dream last night. It was right after I'd drifted off to sleep and I was holding my crystals in my right hand, snuggled close to my chest. When I woke, it was all so vivid, and so real."

"What was it?" Bethany asked. It was the first time

she could remember her mother mentioning any of her dreams.

"It was lovely. I felt sad when it ended. I was in a beautiful garden, just relaxing, when three tiny fairies appeared. They were laughing and dancing and they kept saying the word 'twins' and then both of your names. Isn't that just the strangest thing?"

"That is strange. Did they say anything else?" Bethany asked.

"No. They faded away, and I woke up."

Ryder wrapped his arms around Bethany from behind and kissed her cheek. "Twins would be awesome," he said.

Bethany laughed. "We're getting way ahead of ourselves. We need to get married first."

"About that. How does four months from now sound? Bryan Baker, the builder says he can get it done by then. And that should give you time to plan whatever kind of wedding you want." Ryder grinned as he opened the cardboard tube and laid out the building blueprints.

"Finished in four months? That seems so fast," Bethany said.

"Oh, honey it will go by in a flash," her mother agreed. "But it still gives us plenty of time to plan a lovely wedding."

Ryder showed them the plans, and they were all impressed. It was one thing to talk about what you wanted your dream house to look like. It was something different to see it all laid out in black and white. The house looked amazing.

"Want to take a drive out there?" Ryder asked.

They said goodbye to her mother and drove out to the lot. The air was cool, but the sun was shining as they strolled to the shore of the lake. Ryder rolled out the blueprints on a large, flat rock and they went over them again. It was easier to visualize the house as they stood on the lot where it would be. Bethany smiled up at Ryder.

"This doesn't seem real."

He pulled her into his arms and gently touched his lips to hers.

"It is perfect. We're going to live the rest of our lives right here on this spot and who knows, maybe a year from now, we'll be a family of four."

"Twins. My mother's never dreamed anything like that before."

He grinned. "Fairies and twins. It would be pretty amazing. But a baby or two is just a bonus whenever they decide to come. I love you, and I just can't wait to live here with you, and start our lives together."

"Me too," Bethany said softly, and then she kissed him.

THANK YOU SO MUCH FOR READING! I HOPE YOU ENJOYED Bethany and Ryder's story. My next book in this series is Maggie's story, Calling Charlie. Fun bit of trivia, Calling Charlie was inspired years ago when I worked in recruiting and was on the phone with a candidate. His voice was so charismatic and charming and I was curious to meet him and see if he matched his voice--I was envisioning Brad Pitt and well, I was way off. But he was a great guy and I placed him in an awesome job. I never forgot that though and it inspired Charlie and Maggie's story.

CHICKEN POT PIE RECIPE

Chicken (or Turkey) Pot Pie recipe

This recipe first came about years ago when my twin nieces informed me on Thanksgiving that they really didn't like turkey anymore and we ended up with lots of leftovers. I also had an extra box of frozen puff pastry and felt like experimenting. And it was pretty amazing—and so easy!

Ingredients

Two cups chopped leftover turkey or chicken, pulled or chopped into bite-size pieces

3 carrots, chopped

One onion, sliced thin

One large potato, diced

1/3 cup peas (optional)

1 1/2 cups chicken broth

Two tablespoons flour

Two tablespoons butter
One sheet puff pastry, thawed
1/2 tsp thyme
Pinch salt and pepper

Preheat oven to 375. In a large saute pan, over medium heat, melt the butter and add the sliced onion. Cook about five minutes, until soft. Toss the chicken with the flour until well coated, then add to the pan and cook for one minute. Add the chicken broth and bring to a simmer. Add the potato, peas, and carrot and cook for another five to ten minutes or until the liquid thickens a bit. Add the thyme, salt and pepper. Pour into a 9 x 9 casserole dish and top with the sheet of puff pastry. Bake for 30-40 minutes until pastry is golden and filling is bubbling. Enjoy!

CALLING CHARLIE

Maggie Quinn loves her role as bartender and co-owner of Quinn's. Calling Charlie Keane to place her weekly order is something she looks forward to. It's no secret to her friends and family that Maggie has a crush on Charlie's voice. She's eager to meet him in-person—but Charlie keeps rescheduling their business lunch. He enjoys their weekly calls too, but is afraid that when they meet, Maggie will be disappointed. But he may have waited too long—Maggie has started dating someone new. Is it too late for Charlie?

CHAPTER 1

Maggie Quinn finished cutting the fruit she needed for the lunch shift and piled the oranges, lemons and limes into their containers. Mondays weren't generally all that busy, but she liked to be prepared, just in case. As one of the co-owner's of Quinn's, she ran the bar, while her brother Ryder oversaw general operations for the restaurant.

She glanced at the big, old wood clock on the wall. It was nearly eleven. They opened at eleven thirty and it was almost time for the call she looked forward to each week. She poured herself a fresh cup of coffee and grabbed her notebook with the information she'd need for the call. She slid into one of the bar chairs, took a sip of her hot, black coffee, and dialed his number.

"Keane's Liquors, this is Charlie."

As she always did, Maggie felt goosebumps at the first sound of his voice. It was mesmerizing and she could listen to him talk for hours if she had the chance.

"Hi Charlie, it's Maggie Quinn."

"Hey, Maggie. Did you have a good weekend?"

She smiled at the warmth in his voice.

"Yes, my weekend was good, busy and relaxing. How about you?" She'd had a date, first one in a long time, on Saturday night. But she wasn't going to tell him about that. Not that the date hadn't gone well. It was fine. It just wasn't with Charlie.

She hadn't actually met Charlie in person, yet. But she'd invited him to come into Quinn's for a lunch meeting. She claimed it was so he could see the bar and better advise her on ordering. He'd sounded enthusiastic, but had rescheduled their meeting twice already and put it off until April. But April was only a week away now, and there was no way he could cancel again.

"I'm sure my weekend wasn't as exciting as yours. But my twin nephews were in town. It was great to see Tommy and Tony and to visit with my sister." Maggie knew that Charlie was close to his sister Caitlyn and that her husband Billy was an optometrist. They lived in Riston, the next town over, and he saw them often and loved spoiling his ten-year-old nephews.

"That sounds nice. They're lucky to have you," she said warmly.

"They're great kids," he said. They chatted for a few more minutes about nothing in particular. Ryder walked out at one point and headed her way with a dark look on his face. He clearly wanted to talk to her about something, but once he saw her on the phone, he stopped short, watched her for a moment and his expression softened. "Tell Charlie I said hello," he said, before turning around and heading back into the kitchen.

"Tell Ryder I said hello, too. I hope he's not good at cards?"

"Ryder? He is, actually. Why?"

Charlie chuckled. He's coming here with a few other guys Thursday night. My buddy Josh knows him from the gym. One of our usual players can't come for a while. He and his wife just had their first baby. You know how it is."

Maggie laughed. "Well, not really. But I can imagine."

"So, the weekend was good?"

Maggie hesitated, feeling oddly guilty about her date, which was ridiculous as she'd never actually even met Charlie in person. And they really just had a business relationship.

"The restaurant was busy?" Charlie asked, and she realized he hadn't been asking about her weekend, but rather the reason for her call.

"Yes, very busy. I need to place a bigger order than usual."

"Well, that's a good thing. I'm ready when you are."

Maggie opened her notebook and told him what she needed, all the alcohol that needed to be replaced. When she finished, he made a suggestion, as he usually did for something new that she might want to try. This week it was a chardonnay from Washington State and a winery that she wasn't familiar with.

"They are a small, family-owned winery in Wood-inville. I think you'll like it." Charlie knew she had a weakness for chardonnay. She'd once mentioned that it was her drink of choice on the nights she went out instead of working.

"Sure, we'll take a few bottles. I'll run it as a weekly special."

"Is there anything else you need? It's always great to talk with you, as usual."

Maggie wanted so badly to tell him what she wanted. An actual date. A chance to meet in person. But she'd be meeting him in a week for their official lunch visit. It wasn't a date, but it was probably as close as she could get. She got the sense that Charlie didn't get out much. He seemed almost hermit-like.

She knew that he ran his very successful liquor distributor company mostly from his home office. She knew this because she'd stopped by once, months ago, on the pretext of needing to pick up a case of vodka. The older woman at his front desk had been lovely and explained that Charlie mostly worked from home, but she could have one of the guys bring a case of vodka right out to her car.

The next time he'd talked to her, he'd apologized for not being there when she came by. "Eloise told me and I'm sorry that I missed seeing you. I go in very early every morning, check the warehouse and outgoing deliveries, and then head home at lunch time and work from my home office the rest of the day."

"I think that's everything I need, for now," Maggie said. She was reluctant to end the call and go another week until she'd hear his voice again.

"All right, we'll get that right out to you this afternoon. Have a great day, Maggie."

"You too, Charlie."

Maggie set the phone down, looked up, and saw her
grandmother and her posse of four friends looking at her
with interest. She'd been so engrossed in her call and
looking down at her notes that she hadn't even heard
them come in.

She jumped up and gave her grandmother a big hug
and a kiss on the cheek. "Hi, Grams." She went and
hugged all her friends in turn--Maude, Nellie, Betty,
and Ruby. They came in at least once a week, usually
later in the afternoon, though.

"What brings you in so early today?" she asked as she
led them to their favorite round table by the bay window
that overlooked Main Street. They all loved to people-
watch. Her grandmother didn't miss much and she
looked particularly pleased as she slid into her chair and
took a menu from Maggie's outstretched hand.

"We signed up for a knitting class that starts this afternoon. It's shocking that none of us know how to knit at
our advanced age. Was that your young man you were
talking to?"

Maggie smiled. "I don't have a young man, Grams."

"Didn't you tell me you had a date this weekend?
With that lawyer, the one that owns the biggest law firm
in town? I thought that sounded so promising."

Maggie laughed. "Yes, I did. And he was very nice.
We might go out again sometime."

"That wasn't him you were talking to?" Her grand-mother looked puzzled.

"No, that was just Charlie. I was putting in my weekly order for the bar."

"Charlie Keane? I haven't seen him since he was a child. His father was a good man. Are you dating him?"

It was Maggie's turn to be surprised. "Dating Charlie? No. I've actually never even met him."

Her grandmother raised her eyebrows. "You don't say? My eyes must be failing me. You looked as though you knew him quite well."

Maggie smiled. "Well, I feel like I do. I've talked to him almost every week for several years now."

"How interesting. And yet you've never met him?"

"No, not yet."

"Fascinating." She looked around the table at her friends who were hanging on every word. They all nodded in agreement.

"It's really not that interesting," Maggie assured them. "So, let me tell you all the specials and get your drink order."

CHAPTER 2

Charlie hung up the phone and smiled. Talking to Maggie Quinn was one of the highlights of an otherwise ordinary week. He followed her on Instagram, through his business account. Keane Liquors was active on social media, but there wasn't a trace of Charlie Keane visible anywhere.

He didn't have a personal profile on Facebook or any social media. His office assistant, Emma, ran the social media accounts for the business. She did a great job generating buzz for them by posting pictures of all their newest wines and fun drinks.

Charlie only went on social media to see if Maggie had posted something new. She'd told him that Bethany, Ryder's wife, had suggested that Ryder film Maggie behind the bar, mixing one of her fancy drinks. She'd thought it was a silly idea, but it turned out that customers loved it and always ordered whatever she made in the videos.

Charlie liked watching her work. She had a smile that lit up her whole face, huge friendly eyes, and long, chocolate brown hair that fell in a cascade of waves to the middle of her back. She was always laughing in the videos. He knew that she wasn't entirely comfortable being filmed. She'd admitted it to him once, but she did it because it was good for the restaurant. He saw that she had a new video up and clicked on it.

"This one is called a S'mores Martini. It will take you back to your childhood and satisfy your sweet tooth." Maggie spread marshmallow fluff around the rim of a martini glass, dipped it in a dish of crushed graham crackers and then held a small baker's blow torch to the marshmallow until it was lightly browned all over.

"Then you mix ice with Twix flavored Vodka. We make that ourselves by soaking Twix candy bars in vodka, and adding Godiva white and chocolate liqueurs. Give it a good shake and pour into your martini glass, or enjoy your S'mores Martini on the rocks. If you don't want to make it yourself, come on in to Quinn's and I'll be glad to make one for you."

Charlie turned off the computer and stood up. It was time to go meet Josh at Brennan's dress shop in Lewiston, which was an hour away. It wasn't where Charlie usually went, but Josh had insisted it was the best place for what he needed, which was a tuxedo suitable for a black-tie event. Charlie had one, but it was old and hung off him now that he'd lost nearly twenty pounds. Ever since Maggie had invited him in for their lunch meeting, he'd taken the initiative to try to lose a few pounds and get into shape.

He'd started using the home gym that he had in a spare room. It had a full set of weights and a treadmill. And he was eating better and walking more. His doctor had also read him the riot act at his last physical and warned him that if he didn't change his habits soon, he'd be on the same track as his father, dead of a heart attack in his early fifties. His father had lived large, enjoying rich foods, strong martinis and his only exercise had been an occasional game of golf.

Sometimes Charlie imagined that he sensed interest from Maggie. Their conversations always went a little longer than necessary when she called in her weekly order. When he looked in the mirror, though, he was pretty sure that once they met, any interest would fade. His nickname in school had been Charlie Brown, because he had a round, bland face that most people didn't look twice at. So, he'd canceled their meeting more than once, each time rescheduling to put off the disappointment that he was sure he'd see on her face.

But still, he'd managed to find love. The kind of true love that people dream about. Meredith had been his high school sweetheart and soul-mate. They'd gone to college together and neither of them had ever dated anyone else. They'd married right after college and they'd had a wonderful life, although Meredith couldn't get pregnant. That had disappointed both of them and they were beginning to look into adoption when the accident happened.

He still felt guilt and confusion over it, though he knew deep down that there was nothing he could have done to save her. They'd been waiting to make a turn when a truck ran a red light and plowed right into Meredith's side of the car. They said she died on impact. The car was totaled, yet Charlie escaped with only a stiff neck and a few scratches. Everyone said he'd been lucky. He hadn't felt lucky at the time, though.

That was three years ago and while it was true that it got a little easier each year, he still missed her. And he knew that it wasn't likely that he'd find that kind of love again. Especially with someone as vibrant and beautiful as Maggie. Meredith had been beautiful, too, but hers had been a quiet, gentle beauty. Like Charlie, Meredith didn't stand out in the crowd. But she'd been beautiful to him.

Maggie's beauty on the other hand, scared him. She had the kind of looks and energy that made people stop and stare. He was surprised that she was still single, because he imagined that she could have her pick of men. He pictured her with someone more like his best friend. Josh looked like a walking, talking Ken doll, with his perfect blonde hair, blue eyes and dimples. He was also 6' 4" and his abs were insane. Charlie hadn't seen evidence of his own abs in years. Though his belly was getting smaller now that he was more active.

Charlie arrived at Brennan's before Josh and started browsing the racks. He caught a glimpse of himself in one of the full-length mirrors and groaned. Maybe he should have dressed a bit better. He was wearing a pair of

old jeans that had a paint splotch on one knee, but they
were the only jeans that fit him now. Everything else was
too loose.

He still had on his Keane Liquors navy blue sweatshirt which was a bit dusty from helping the guys in the
warehouse get the orders loaded onto the trucks that
morning. They'd been short a guy, so Charlie had pitched
in, like he usually did. Because he was in better shape
now, the work had gone quickly.

Josh texted that he was running a few minutes late so
Charlie continued to roam around, looking at the various
suits. He was surprised that no one had come over to
greet him or offer to help. The shop wasn't busy. There
was only one other customer and they were paying at the
register. He assumed when they finished, someone would
come his way.

But the customer paid and left, and when Charlie
glanced over at the two salespeople in their expensive
suits, he saw that they were both looking his way and
muttering. The expression on their faces was of distaste,
almost as if Charlie didn't belong in their shop. He was
sure he must be mistaken, though, and he was getting
tired of doing nothing and just waiting for Josh, so he
ambled over to them and smiled. He received two stony
glares in return.

"I'm waiting for a friend, but maybe we could get
started looking at some suits?" he suggested.

The two men exchanged glances, and one of them
looked Charlie up and down and clearly seemed to find
him not worthy.

"Are you sure this is the shop you're supposed to be meeting him at? The men's budget warehouse is a few doors down," he said with a sniff.

"Yes, they might have better options for you there," the other agreed and then added. "This is a premium store, we don't discount."

Charlie was equally amused and offended. "What makes you think I'm looking for a discount?" he snapped. He used his full business voice, the one he rarely used except for important negotiations. The two men looked at each other in confusion. And a moment later Josh came gliding in.

"Perry and James, how are you? I hope you've been taking good care of my friend Charlie. He's the business executive I told you I'd be bringing by today."

Charlie watched as their faces both lost color and they stammered to try to recover.

"Of course. How wonderful to meet you. Josh is one of our favorite clients. Let's get a room for you and we'll show you our very best suits."

"No, thanks. We won't be staying." Charlie turned to Josh who quickly sensed that something was off. "Didn't you mention that a new high end men's shop opened a few blocks away?"

"Yes, Jones Menswear. I haven't checked it out because I've always had such great service here."

"Well, I'm finding the service a bit…lacking. I'd like to go see if Jones is more my style. It's too bad, because I need to buy quite a few things, and I'm assuming you'd get a commission?" Perry and James nodded miserably.

"Sure thing." Josh glanced at the two salespeople, "Sorry, guys. Catch you later."

When they walked outside, Josh stopped and looked at Charlie's jeans and sweatshirt. "You could have made some effort. Those guys probably thought you were a bum off the streets."

"Well, that was a big mistake." Charlie laughed as he pictured the looks on the two salespeople's faces as they watched their fat commission disappear.

Josh grinned. "All right, then. Let's go shopping."

AN HOUR LATER, CHARLIE CARRIED THREE HUGE BAGS OF new clothes to his car. He'd gone a bit crazy, as it had been a long time since he'd bought anything new for himself. And unlike Brennan's, which only carried suits and tuxes, Jones Menswear had everything, including jeans and casual wear. He found a tux that fit him like a glove except for the length, and they measured him and pinned the minor alteration that needed to be made for it to fit him perfectly. He'd go back in a week for a final fitting.

Josh looked at him thoughtfully. "So, you're looking good these days. Are you ready to get back out there? I might know of a few people I could set you up with," he said as Charlie stashed his bags in his trunk.

Charlie dreaded the thought of a blind setup with one of Josh's friends. He couldn't imagine ever agreeing to that. But, he knew Josh meant well.

"Thanks. Can I get back to you on that? I don't think

I'm ready for a fix-up just yet. How are things with you and Liz? Have you gone ring shopping yet?"

Josh had been dating a great girl, Liz Cunningham, and Charlie thought they would have been engaged by now. He didn't know what Josh was waiting for. They'd been dating for three years now and it was obvious that they were perfect for each other. A pained look crossed Josh's face.

"She gave me an ultimatum, actually. Our three-year anniversary was two weeks ago, and I guess she expected a proposal. When I saw her mid-week, she sat me down and told me I had to make a decision and that if I wasn't ready to commit to marriage, she was out of the relationship."

Charlie shook his head. He couldn't believe his best friend was so stupid.

"And you told her no?"

"I told her that I wasn't going to be forced into a proposal!"

"I can't imagine that went over very well." As much as he liked Josh, he also felt that Liz deserved better than that. She was a great girl. Hopefully, Josh would figure it out before it was too late.

"So, are you missing her yet?"

"Of course. But, I'm getting right back out there. I had a date Saturday night with an incredible girl! We're going out again next weekend."

Charlie's jaw dropped. "Already?"

Josh nodded as his phone rang. He glanced at it, then waved at Charlie. "I gotta take this. Talk to you later."

. . .

CHARLIE WAS BACK IN QUINN VALLEY AN HOUR LATER. He was on his way to his home office when his phone rang and he saw it was Eloise, his office manager. He barely said hello when she started talking in a rush.

"Joe just called and his wife is being rushed to Riston. Her water broke early. He wants to know if anyone can finish his deliveries. He has two stops left."

"Of course. Tell him to bring the truck back to the warehouse. We'll get someone to finish up. Is anyone back yet?"

"No, I don't expect anyone back for a few more hours." Mary sounded worried. Charlie knew she was anxious for Joe, as it was his first baby. The whole office had a pool going on when the baby would arrive, though no one expected it would be this soon.

"I'll do it, then. I'm on my way back from Lewiston and will be passing by anyway in a few minutes. Tell Joe I said congratulations."

FIVE MINUTES LATER, CHARLIE ARRIVED AT THE warehouse and saw Joe's truck waiting for him. The keys were on the driver's seat, under the two stapled delivery sheets. He picked them up to see where he was going. His first stop was at Nick's Pizza and his second was at Quinn's Pub. And Maggie was working. He took a deep breath. This wasn't how he'd planned to first meet her. He hadn't been in Quinn's for years. He hadn't needed to. They'd been clients forever and Joe had been delivering to them for almost ten years.

He made his first delivery and then, with a pit in his stomach, he headed toward Quinn's. It was almost three and the restaurant was quiet. It was a good time for a delivery as he wouldn't be in anyone's way. They liked to avoid delivering during the busy times when possible.

He pulled into the loading spot near the front door, piled cases of beer, alcohol and wine onto a dolly and made his way in. He'd have to make a few trips as Quinn's always had a good-sized order. When he stepped inside, it was empty except for Ryder who was sitting at the bar, writing on a notepad and drinking coffee. To Charlie's relief and disappointment, there was no sign of Maggie.

Ryder jumped up when he saw him and started loading the cases onto the bar counter. "You guys must be short-handed today," he said.

Charlie nodded. "Joe's wife is having her baby early. They're on their way to the ER."

"Maggie's in the kitchen, she should be out in a few minutes. I'll help you get the rest of this in." Ryder followed Charlie out to the truck and helped him to load the rest of the order onto two dollies. They always had a spare in the trucks in case one broke or there was an extra pair of hands to help bring the order in.

Ryder led the way into the restaurant. Maggie was back behind the bar and smiled when she saw them. Charlie stopped short for a moment, dazzled by the power of her smile close up. He recovered quickly, though, and he and Ryder quickly loaded everything onto the bar. Maggie came to their end of the bar, held out her hand and smiled.

"Hi, I'm Maggie. I don't think we've met before? Joe must have the day off."

"His baby came early," Ryder said.

"I'm Charlie Keane. It's great to finally meet you, Maggie." He smiled and shook her hand, not surprised that her hands were soft, even though she worked them hard.

Surprise and something else, confusion maybe or disappointment more likely, flashed across her face.

"Oh, this is a nice surprise! It's great to meet you, too. Is..is everything okay with Joe's baby?" She looked worried suddenly. "It's very early, isn't it?"

"Just a few weeks. It should be fine, hopefully," he assured her.

"Oh, good."

Just as Charlie was searching for something to say, the front door opened again and a deliveryman came in holding a huge bouquet of red roses. He looked around and then walked toward the bar.

"I'm looking for a Maggie Quinn?"

"That's me."

"Well, then, these are for you!"

Maggie looked shocked and a bit uncomfortable as she opened the small card that was tucked inside the flowers.

"Wow, look at that. Who sent you those?" Ryder asked.

Maggie was quiet for a minute. "That guy I went out with the other night. I didn't expect this."

"Josh sent you those? You must have made quite an impression. Are you going out again soon?"

She nodded. "We're supposed to do something next weekend."

"Josh Winters?" Charlie felt a sense of dread as he asked the question. It couldn't be, could it?

Maggie looked startled. "Yes, do you know him?"

"I do. He's my best friend, actually. Josh is a great guy." He was, and now Maggie was completely and totally off-limits. Not that he ever really had a chance with her, anyway. Josh was definitely more her type. They'd make a very photogenic couple and Josh always liked having his picture taken.

"What a small world," Maggie said softly.

Charlie turned to leave. "I should probably get going. Great to finally meet you, Maggie. Ryder I'll see you Thursday night?"

"I'm looking forward to it."

"Bye, Charlie," Maggie said. The last thing he saw was her smile as he wheeled the dollies out to his truck.

CHAPTER 3

S o that was Charlie," Maggie said as Ryder sat back down at the bar and picked up his pen. He scribbled something on his notepad and then looked up.

"Yeah. He's a great guy. Not as much of a looker as Josh, though. Are you excited to go out with him again?"

Maggie thought about that. She wasn't nearly as excited as she should be. "Sure, I had a fun time with Josh. He's good company." He had made her laugh all through dinner with funny stories. But there had been a distance there, too, which made her all the more surprised when the roses arrived.

"Be careful not to fall too hard for him. He may be on the rebound," Ryder warned.

"Josh is?"

"He didn't mention that he just ended a relationship that everyone thought would turn into an engagement?"

"No! He didn't say a word." He hadn't revealed

anything personal, now that Maggie thought back to their conversation. It had been all light and fun, nothing personal other than that he'd grown up in Riston and his family still lived there. She realized that's where he probably knew Charlie from as he'd once mentioned that he'd lived there when he was younger until his family moved to Quinn Valley and his father started the liquor business that he eventually took over.

"Who was Josh dating?" Quinn Valley was a small town. If she was local, chances are that Maggie knew her or knew of her.

"Liz Cunningham."

Maggie nodded. She did know Liz, though not well. She was a few years younger than Maggie, the same age as her younger sister, Ivy, actually. Liz was a nurse, like Maggie's friend, Cameron. They both worked at the Riston hospital. Which explained why the few times she'd seen Josh in Quinn's, he'd been with friends. Liz was probably working the evening shift those nights. It explained why she sensed a distance during their date, even though Josh had been attentive.

She'd liked him, but as beautiful as he was, and Josh was one of the most handsome men she'd dated, she didn't feel that certain spark. She'd already agreed to go out with him again, though, and she was glad that she knew about Liz. Not that there was any danger of falling hard for Josh. He was fun, though, and it was a good way for her to ease back into dating.

She thought back to the look on Charlie's face when he'd introduced himself. He seemed uncomfortable and she guessed that it was because he hadn't planned on meeting her that way. She was glad, though, that she'd finally met him. He didn't look anything like how she'd pictured him, not at first. But once he'd smiled and said her name, she'd felt as drawn to him as she'd been to just his voice, especially when he took her hand. She actually got goosebumps for a moment and was rendered speechless. No wonder he looked at her funny.

And she wasn't at all happy to learn that he and Josh were best friends. She hoped that wouldn't scare Charlie off, though she was afraid that it might. It was possible her interest might be entirely one-sided, and Charlie could just be friendly with all his customers. She was still looking forward to their lunch meeting which was only a week away.

"Maggie? Did you hear a word that I just said?" Ryder asked.

She snapped back to attention. "Sorry, I was daydreaming. What did you say?"

"Remember I tried to talk to you earlier today when you were on the phone with Charlie? And then we got busy. I'm worried about Bethany."

"What's wrong?" Maggie was a huge fan of Bethany. She'd been Ryder's high school sweetheart, then moved away after graduation to go to cooking school and work in Manhattan. She eventually found her way back to Quinn Valley and to Ryder, and Maggie had never seen her brother so happy. Or the customers at Quinn's so satisfied. Bethany was a great chef.

"She hasn't been feeling right lately. She said her back

has been killing her and she's been exhausted. She looked ready to drop an hour ago. She was scheduled to work the evening shift, too, but I called Will in to cover for her." Will was one of their assistant chefs and he'd learned a lot from Bethany, enough to work several evening shifts a week on his own now.

"What do you think it is?"

"She says it's nothing other than her advanced age." He laughed at the ridiculousness of Bethany's joke as they were the same age. "Standing on her feet all day in the kitchen is catching up to her. But it's never bothered her before. She doesn't want to go, but I got her to agree to call her doctor just to make sure there's nothing serious going on."

"That's smart. Maybe she just needs some time off?" Bethany and Ryder really hadn't taken more than a few days off for months. "You guys should take a long weekend, head to Seattle or do a staycation and visit the spa at the hotel or at River's End Ranch. Pamper yourselves."

Ryder nodded. "I like your way of thinking. That's not a bad idea. And Will and Peter could hold down the fort for a weekend if Bethany prepared them for it." Peter was their broiler cook and about their mother's age. He'd been with Quinn's for years.

"Mom could always pitch in if needed, too," Maggie said. Their mother had run the kitchen at Quinn's until a few years ago when Ryder and Maggie bought her out and became co-owners. Their youngest sister, Ivy, worked in the restaurant, too, as a server. Their other brothers, David and Carter, ran their own food-related businesses.

"That's true. She might love it, actually."

Maggie nodded in agreement. Their mother still came by most mornings to have coffee with them and chat. Once she'd hired Bethany, she'd known Quinn's was in good hands and soon after, she reconnected with Harry Peterman and the two of them had been as thick as thieves since. She still insisted that they were just 'very good friends.' But her children knew better.

Maggie was thrilled for her, and Ryder too. Although they all still missed their father, he'd been gone for years now. They'd urged their mother to date, especially this past year, but she'd insisted that she had no interest, and she hadn't until Harry walked by the restaurant one day.

Bethany came out of the kitchen, untied her apron and slid onto the chair next to Ryder.

"Will's here. I'm going to take off in a few minutes." Her eyes looked heavy and tired, and she grimaced as she shifted position in the chair and touched her hand to her back.

"I'm sorry that you're not feeling well," Maggie said. "I have some Advil behind the bar if you need some? And I just made a pot of fresh coffee."

Bethany smiled, "I'd love an Advil. I forgot to put mine in my purse this morning. And a small cup of coffee sounds great, too. I need something to wake me up, especially if I'm going to make it through Dancing with the Stars tonight."

"Are you still coming to Gram's? I'm sure she'd understand if you skipped it." Most Monday nights, a bunch of women, mostly family and a few friends, gathered at their grandmother's house for a pot luck dinner and to watch Dancing with the Stars on her big screen TV. Maggie wasn't as much a fan of the show as she was just happy to spend the evening with her family. There were five sprawling branches of the Quinn family and she never knew who'd show up each week. It was nice to see some of her cousins that she didn't get to visit with as much as she'd like. She was feeling out of touch as she'd had to miss the last few Monday's due to work.

"I'm going to see how I feel. If I can lie down and rest for a bit, I might go. I like seeing everyone." She grimaced again and Maggie understood Ryder's concern.

"Have you made an appointment to see your doctor yet?" she asked.

Bethany nodded. "I checked my messages earlier and they confirmed an appointment for Wednesday morning."

"Good." That was just a few days away. Hopefully they'd have some answers soon. Bethany really did look exhausted. Maggie wondered if it was just being on her feet all day and working too much. Sometimes her own back ached if she worked a few doubles in a row, both lunch and dinner shifts. She tried not to do that unless it was absolutely necessary.

"All right, I'm off. Hopefully I'll see you tonight, Maggie." Bethany took a last sip of coffee, kissed Ryder goodbye and slid off her bar stool.

MAGGIE ADDED A BIT OF GRAND MARNIER, THE FINAL

touch to her contribution to the evening's pot luck—a pitcher of freshly mixed margaritas. Her grandmother wasn't much of a drinker, but she always liked to have one small glass of whatever Maggie made. Everyone else would be bringing an appetizer, or dessert. Their grandmother usually provided the main course, either lasagna or a roast of some sort.

When she arrived at the ranch, there was already a small crowd gathered. Her mother and a few of her aunts were sipping wine in the kitchen. Her sister, Ivy, was chatting with their cousin, Robyn. And two of her grandmother's close friends, Gertie and Ruby, were fussing over a platter of cheese and crackers, one cutting more cheese while the other arranged the crackers just so.

"Maggie!" her grandmother called out when she saw her. She pulled her in for a big hug and raised her eyebrow at the pitcher she was carrying. "What have you made for us tonight?"

Maggie smiled. "Margaritas." Her grandmother's favorite.

"Splendid!" She turned to her friends. "Could you girls get some nice glasses out for us?"

Once everyone who wanted a margarita had one, Maggie roamed around and chatted with everyone.

She looked up in surprise when Bethany walked in, holding a casserole dish covered in tin foil. Maggie went over to help and took the dish from her. "I can't believe you made something too. Are you feeling better I hope?"

Bethany smiled tightly. "A little. I did get a short nap

in, and cooking relaxes me. This is nothing impressive, though. Just my taco dip. I can make that in my sleep."

Maggie's stomach rumbled. Bethany's taco dip was legendary. And it was easy to make, Maggie could attest to that. It was just ground beef or turkey browned up with taco seasoning, a can of refried beans and a cup or so of shredded cheese. Bethany added more cheese on top, so that it got bubbly and delicious when she reheated it.

"Do I smell taco dip?" Maggie's mother gave Bethany a hug too. "Great minds think alike. I made a big batch of guacamole and Maggie brought margaritas."

"So, where is Josh taking you next?" Ivy asked a few hours later. They were all stuffed and gathered in the living room, around Gram's big screen TV. Bethany, Maggie and Ivy were sitting on a comfy, plush sofa and the show had just gone to half-time commercial break. Maggie smiled when she noticed that the room had grown quiet as everyone leaned in to hear her reply.

"It's almost two weeks from now. The Spinazolla Gala in Lewiston." Maggie saw a sea of impressed faces.

"What's the Spinazolla Gala?" Bethany asked.

"It's a big deal, creative black tie. A charity event that has food and wine tastings from the best restaurants in Lewiston and wineries from all over the country. It's named after a famous, retired food critic. I've never been, but I've heard it's amazing," Ivy said.

Maggie nodded. "It is a fun time. I went once a few years ago."

"When you were dating Eric?" Ivy asked.

"Yes. It was a memorable night." In more ways than one. She'd been head over heels for Eric and they'd dated for several years. But she'd sensed him growing distant and didn't know why. When he invited her to go, she'd been thrilled and told herself she'd been imagining things. And they'd had a wonderful, special night.

Until the end, when she'd gone off to find the ladies' room, went the wrong way, and walked into a closet where Eric and a skinny blonde girl were making out. She'd taken a cab home and never spoken to him again-- after telling him what she thought of him, of course. A year later, he'd moved away from Quinn Valley and she was glad to hear of it. But she hadn't dated anyone seriously since then.

"Bethany, are you and Ryder going, too?" Maggie's cousin Robyn asked.

"No, I don't think so. He hasn't mentioned it." She winced slightly and rubbed her back as she shifted position.

"Do you need more Advil? I have some in my purse," Maggie offered.

"Are you not feeling well? I'm sure I have some, too." Robyn sounded concerned. She worked as a midwife and Maggie often thought she knew as much as the doctors that she worked for.

"Thanks. I just took some a little while ago, it should kick in soon. I have a doctor's appointment this week. I'm sure it's nothing serious. Probably just standing for too long, and getting old," she joked.

Robyn studied her closely. "Is it just a back ache? Any other symptoms?"

"That's it, mostly. Oh, I have been really tired lately. Seems to hit me most afternoons out of nowhere."

"Is there any chance you might be pregnant?" Robyn asked quietly.

Bethany laughed. "Oh, I don't see how I could be. I'm on the pill."

Robyn nodded. "And you're probably not late either, then?"

Bethany thought about that for a moment. "Honestly, I've never been regular. It's not unusual for me to miss a month or be really late. I don't even track it that closely anymore."

"Maybe you just need a few days off," Robyn suggested.

"I think that's a great idea," Maggie agreed.

"Ryder does, too. I think we're going to try to take a long weekend soon and go away and just relax, maybe get massages."

"You should go see Maddie at River's End Ranch. She has a healing touch. I always feel better after I see her," Ivy said.

"That sounds wonderful."

"How've you been, Robyn?" Maggie asked. "I haven't seen you in ages."

"Good! Busy, with work and my newest addiction, Pinterest."

"Pinterest? Every time I get on there I fall down a rabbit hole and time seems to disappear. I redecorated my condo a few months ago and got so many great ideas from it. It was great for researching paint colors."

Robyn laughed. "I'm almost ready to buy a house, so I've been getting lots of ideas there, too."

"What are you looking for?" Bethany asked.

"I actually have my eye on one house. It's old and run down, but it has a lot of character and potential. It could be a really fun project!" She sounded so excited that Maggie was curious to see the house when she finished with it.

"That sounds great. Keep us posted how it goes."

"I will. Oh, I meant to ask. Do any of you know what's going on with Katie?" Maggie hadn't seen their other cousin Katie in even longer.

"No, why?"

"Well, she's usually here, but she hasn't been in a few weeks. It almost seems like she's avoiding the family. Oh, and did you notice she has a new car in her driveway? I wouldn't think she could afford a sports car like that making soap."

"Is she dating someone new maybe?" Maggie wondered.

Ivy leaned forward and lowered her voice, so that the rest of the room couldn't over hear. "I heard something yesterday and meant to mention it to you, but totally forgot. Two of Katie's friends were in for lunch and I overheard them talking as I brought their food to their table. One of them told the other that she heard that Katie has a man living there with her!"

"Our Katie?" Maggie didn't think that could possibly be true.

"Hmm," Robyn said. "Well, it would explain the sports car."

"I'm sure there's a good explanation for it," Bethany chimed in.

"That's true. Things aren't always what they appear to be," Ivy said.

CHAPTER 4

Ryder was fussing. Bethany knew he was just worried about her, so she let him fuss as he drove her to her doctor appointment Wednesday morning.

"So, we'll leave Friday morning and come home Sunday afternoon. Wade said he put us in the Copper Cottage. He thought you'd love it because it has a true chef's kitchen. We can go out to dinner, though, instead. If you don't feel like cooking."

Bethany reached over and squeezed his free hand. She loved that he was so worried about her.

"I'm sure I'll feel like cooking something, even if it's just breakfast. That was nice of Wade." Wade Weston was the general manager of River's End Ranch and he and Ryder had been friends for years.

"You look a little better today," Ryder said.

Bethany smiled. "My back seems to have eased up a

bit. I really do think it's nothing a long weekend away won't cure."

Ryder pulled into the parking lot of Finnegan's Family Care. Tom and Margery Finnegan were both doctors, and husband and wife. They were general practitioners and Ryder had been going to see them since he was a child. He saw Tom and Bethany had an appointment with Margery.

There was only one other person in the waiting room when they walked in. Bethany checked in at the front desk and then sat next to Ryder. She didn't have to wait long, as it was early in the day. A few minutes later, her name was called and she followed the doctor's assistant to an examining room where her blood pressure and temperature was checked and recorded. The assistant then told her that the doctor would be in shortly.

Almost immediately, there was a gentle knock on the door and Margery Finnegan entered the room and said hello. She quickly checked the assistant's notes and then smiled warmly at Bethany.

"It's nice to see you. Please tell your mother I said hello. She's not due to come in for a few more months. So, what brings you in today?" Bethany's mother had recently battled cancer and was now doing well. Bethany had seen Dr. Finnegan often while her mother was going through treatment. It was the reason she had come home to Quinn Valley and then decided to stay. She told the doctor how she'd been feeling.

"I'm actually feeling quite a bit better today and was

going to cancel the appointment. But, Ryder insisted that I keep it, just as a precaution."

"He's a smart man. It never hurts to get checked out. Your vital signs are all good. How long has it been since your last period?"

"I'm not sure, five or six weeks maybe? I'm on the pill, though, and I've never been regular."

"Hm." The doctor listened to Bethany's chest and lungs, had her cough and looked in her throat and ears.

"Everything looks good. I'd like to take a blood sample to check all your levels. Where you've been so tired, could be low vitamin D. That's common. We'll run a full panel and check everything. I should have the results by Friday afternoon and will give you a call as soon as I hear."

TWO DAYS LATER, BETHANY AND RYDER CHECKED INTO River's End Ranch for their long weekend away. The Copper Cottage was every bit as beautiful as Wade had said. Bethany was impressed with the six-burner stove in the sleek kitchen. After a relaxing lunch at Kelsey's Kafe, they made their way back to the cabin and had about an hour until it was time to go for their couples' massage at the spa. It was a new offering and Bethany was looking forward to sharing it with Ryder.

She and Ryder would share a room and each would have their own masseuse. Bethany was booked with Maddie, who Ivy had raved about. Later on, they had dinner reservations at the restaurant at the resort and planned to watch movies after that. It sounded like a perfect night, and Bethany was already feeling so much better. The stiffness in her back had eased quite a bit and she was sure the massage would help loosen her muscles even more.

As they made their way to the spa, Bethany's cell phone rang. It was the doctor's office.

"Hello, this is Bethany."

"This is Dr. Finnegan. I have your test results and all your levels look good."

"Oh, that's good. Thank you."

"Yes, that is good news. There is something else, though. Is there a chance that you've taken an antibiotic recently? I know I didn't prescribe one, but maybe someone else did?"

Bethany was surprised by the question. "Yes, I did, actually. I had a root canal a few weeks ago. I'd cracked a tooth and the dentist had me take an antibiotic before the treatment."

"That explains it, then. You'd said you were taking birth control, but an antibiotic can interfere with that and cancel its effectiveness."

"What are you saying?" Bethany asked quietly and stopped walking. Ryder looked at her in confusion.

"That congratulations are in order. You're pregnant."

"Really? Oh, my goodness. Are you sure?"

The doctor chuckled. "Blood tests don't lie. I'm positive."

"Okay. Thank you, then." She hung up the phone in a daze.

"What is it? Is everything okay? What did the blood test show?" Ryder's questions came out in a rush.

"I'm perfectly healthy, and quite pregnant."

Ryder grinned. "We're having a baby? Really? That's great news. But, I thought you wanted to wait. You were still on the pill, right?"

Bethany explained about the antibiotic. "I did want to wait. But it looks like our plans have changed. I guess we have something to celebrate over dinner."

"We certainly do. I can't wait to tell everyone."

Bethany laughed. "My mother is going to be thrilled."

"My mother will be, too. She's looking forward to being a grandmother." He pulled Bethany in for a hug and tenderly brushed a stray strand of hair out of her eyes. "This is such a gift. I love you so much, and now we're going to have a baby of our own. This is going to be incredible." He kissed her and she felt the same spark she always felt when Ryder's lips touched hers. The news had been a shock at first, but Bethany was excited now and nervous. Mostly excited, though, and looking forward to building her new family with the person who mattered most to her.

"You're going to be a wonderful father, Ryder. I love you so much." She patted her flat stomach lightly. "And I can't wait to meet our new baby."

MAGGIE ARRIVED EARLIER THAN USUAL MONDAY MORNING. It had been a quiet weekend with Bethany and Ryder gone. The restaurant was as busy as usual, but it felt different without two of her favorite people there. She and Bethany had grown close since Bethany started working at the restaurant and married Ryder. And of all her siblings, Maggie had always been closest to Ryder. He was the perfect co-owner because they shared the same approach to the business and got along so well. She looked forward to hearing all about their weekend and hoped that Bethany was feeling better.

Her mother was already there when Maggie walked into the kitchen to start the coffee.

"Are you looking for this?" Her mother handed her a fresh full pot of coffee.

"Thank you." Maggie filled her cup to the top, brought the pot out to the bar and set it on a burner to keep warm. Her mother followed her out and set a brown paper bakery bag on the bar.

"I couldn't help myself. They were just putting the pistachio muffins out when I walked in the door." She reached in and pulled out a giant muffin and handed it to Maggie then took one for herself.

They settled at the bar with their coffee and muffins. Maggie had just taken her first bite when Bethany and Ryder walked in together, holding hands and looking both excited and pleased with themselves. Bethany had a glow about her that Maggie hadn't seen before. To say she looked well-rested was an understatement.

"Well, don't you two look bright and shiny this morning," their mother said. "I take it the weekend was a success?"

Bethany and Ryder nodded and then Ryder spoke.

"We have some exciting news to share. Bethany is not sick."

"Well, that's a relief. The doctor said it was nothing, then?"

"The blood test did show something." He paused for dramatic effect and then grinned. "We're pregnant!"

"What?" Their mother screamed, jumped up and pulled the two of them in for a bear hug while Maggie sat there, shocked. None of them had even considered that possibility. But now it made sense.

Maggie got up and hugged her brother and sister-in-law, too. "That's the best possible news. I'm so happy for you both."

"Thank you. We found out on Friday and we've spent the long weekend dreaming and planning. We both agree that if it's okay with you, Maggie, we'd like you to be our baby's godmother."

Maggie felt tears well up immediately, she was so touched.

"Of course, I'd be honored."

"I HOPE I'M NOT INTERRUPTING ANYTHING."

They all turned at the sound of the familiar voice. Charlie was standing at the bar, looking much more polished than the last time Maggie had seen him. None of them had even heard him walk in, they'd been so distracted by the exciting baby news.

"I'm so sorry, Charlie. I'll be right with you."

Charlie was right on time for their long-awaited lunch meeting. She'd scheduled it for eleven, a half hour before the restaurant opened, so they'd have time to look over the bar thoroughly and then sit and eat before the lunch rush came at noon.

"Charlie, we have some good news to celebrate. I'm going to be a dad. Bethany and I just learned that we're expecting." Ryder was still grinning ear to ear and Maggie couldn't remember the last time she'd seen him so excited.

"That's fantastic," Charlie said warmly. "Congratulations to both of you."

"Well, I should probably get to work," Bethany said.

"I need to run, too. I have to go tell everyone I know that I'm going to be a grandmother. See you all later." Their mother grabbed her purse and headed for the door as Maggie went to meet with Charlie.

"Thank you for coming in. I'd love to show you how we have the bar set up and what we have stocked. We've been moving a lot of whiskey, lately, not as much gin. Wine and beer are always steady sellers and vodka is always on top."

Charlie came behind the bar and paid close attention as Maggie showed him around. He had some great suggestions for how to order more efficiently and also shared what was working for some of his other clients. He took her weekly order as they went along and she agreed to make a few changes based on his ideas and to try a few new beers and wines to see how they went over with their customers. When they finished, it was almost eleven thirty and Maggie's stomach rumbled. She was used to eating lunch early, before the rush got underway.

"Are you hungry?" she asked as she grabbed two menus. She set them down on the bar as they both settled onto bar stools.

"I'm always hungry. What do you recommend?"

"Well, everything's good, but Bethany does comfort food like no one else. The shepherd's pie with cheddar mashed potatoes is outstanding and the steak tips or grilled chicken on Caesar salad are always popular."

"What are you going to get?" he asked.

"I'm pretty hungry. I'm going to get a turkey club sandwich with chips."

"That sounds good to me. I'll have the same."

"I'll run this order into the kitchen. What can I get you to drink?"

"Water's fine."

Maggie quickly poured two glasses of water, set them on the bar, and brought the order into the kitchen and handed it to Bethany. It was the first lunch order of the day, so she knew it would be out quickly.

"Check back in five minutes," Bethany said.

Maggie made her way back to the bar and settled into her seat. Charlie was texting on his phone and finished up when he saw her.

"Sorry about that. My office had a question."

"No need to apologize." She noticed how much more

comfortable Charlie seemed. He looked sharp in his light blue, button-down shirt, gray tie and a navy blazer. And his black shoes were shiny and new looking. "I know yours is a family business, like Quinn's. Did you ever consider doing something else? Maybe selling the business when your father died?"

Charlie smiled. "I thought about it, but it was just a passing thought. I always expected that one day I'd take over the business. I just didn't expect it would happen so soon. I do enjoy it though. My father built a strong business, but we've tripled our sales in the past five years."

Maggie was impressed. "That's really something. Is the market booming?"

"The market hasn't changed all that much. We just got better at reaching new people and we broadened our service area. We go to Lewiston and beyond. And we put in a new computer system."

"Were you a business major in college?" she wondered.

He smiled. "I was. So it's been fun to put some of what I learned to good use."

Maggie enjoyed listening to Charlie talk about the family business that he took over. He was animated and passionate as he told her some challenges he'd faced initially and some more recent successes they'd had. He also shared his favorite Mojito recipe.

"The key is fresh mint, and lime. Muddle the two together, add a bit of coconut rum and the secret ingredient—a splash of Sprite."

"Sprite? That's different."

He grinned. "It's a shortcut, much easier than messing with club soda and simple syrup—which I never have at home. It adds the perfect amount of sweetness."

Maggie was intrigued. "Maybe I'll run that as a drink special today. I'm curious to try it."

"Two turkey club sandwiches," Ryder announced as he walked over and set their lunches down on the bar.

"Thanks! I could have gone to get them," Maggie said. She'd lost track of time while she and Charlie were talking.

"Bethany ordered me to bring them out, while the bread is still hot from the toaster. Enjoy."

Maggie picked up a wedge of sandwich, took a bite and wondered if Charlie was dating anyone. She knew that he was a widower and had lost his wife to a horrible car accident several years ago. She'd casually asked Ryder the day before as he was heading off to play cards at Charlie's house. He didn't have any idea, but hadn't heard that he was, for what that was worth.

"How did Ryder do playing cards with you guys the other night? I haven't had a chance to ask. He and Bethany were gone all weekend and the baby was all we've talked about so far."

"Well, it's exciting news. You're going to be an aunt." Charlie smiled warmly as he reached for a potato chip. "As it turns out, your brother is very good at poker. He surprised us."

Maggie laughed. "I wondered if anyone knew that about him. He's always been good at cards. I know better than to play with him."

They continued to chat easily as they ate, and Maggie learned that she and Charlie shared a lot of common interests. Besides working in the food industry, they both enjoyed playing trivia and listening to live country and blues music, both local bands and big acts, like Thomas Rhett, Luke Bryan and Kenny Chesney.

"Thomas Rhett is going to be in Lewiston in a few weeks. I tried to get tickets, but he sold out so fast," Maggie said.

"I saw him a few years ago. He was great. I missed out on getting tickets, too."

"We'll have to settle for local bands, then. My sister is actually really good. Have you ever heard Ivy sing? She once wanted to be a country music artist, but then had her dreams dashed. Which is too bad because she could have been really good. Now she just writes music as a hobby, and fills in when we have an opening or a local band needs a lead singer for a gig."

"I haven't yet. I'd like to, though. Where is she playing next?" Charlie asked.

"She's actually playing here Saturday night. You should come by." That was as close as she could get to asking him out. Besides, she was working Saturday night, anyway, but it would be fun to see him if he stopped in.

"Are you working that night?" he asked.

"I am."

Charlie grinned. "Well, I need to check my schedule." He pulled out his phone, glanced at it and laughed. "I'm wide open. I'll try to stop in."

"How are things going with Josh? Have you two gone out again?" Charlie wanted to go to Quinn's Saturday night, to have a beer at the bar, chat with Maggie and listen to her sister play. He wanted much more than that, but he didn't know if it would ever be possible. Not if Josh was who Maggie wanted to be with. And if they were to get serious, she'd be completely off-limits, anyway. Josh was too good of a friend. Even if he'd lost his mind recently when it came to dating. Charlie didn't want to see Maggie get hurt either if she were to fall for Josh. Josh wouldn't intentionally do anything to upset her, but he wasn't always known for thinking things through. And Charlie was pretty sure Josh's heart still belonged to Liz, even if he wasn't ready to admit it yet. The question seemed to take Maggie by surprise.

"Oh, um, fine I guess. We haven't gone out again yet. I think he said he's away this weekend, and I'm working. We have plans to go to the Spinazolla event next weekend, though. That should be fun. Are you going?"

Charlie was going with Josh, and he hadn't mentioned that he was bringing a date. Charlie hadn't really thought about it, though, and it wouldn't have surprised him if Liz was going and that would have been fine. He'd often gone out with the two of them before, to join others for trivia or dinner. But it did seem a bit odd that Josh had invited Maggie to join them. Charlie would have thought that he'd want her all to himself. If it had been Charlie inviting Maggie out somewhere, he certainly wouldn't have wanted Josh to join them.

So, he was inclined to tell Josh that he wouldn't go with them. He didn't want to be a third wheel on a date with the girl he'd kill to date himself. He could just go on his own, as he already had his ticket and a new tux on the way. Then it wouldn't be as awkward if he ran into them there. His phone buzzed just then with a text message, and he glanced at it and smiled.

"Can't wait to see you next weekend. Looking forward to a few days of relaxing and eating things I'm not supposed to have!" He'd almost forgotten his sister was coming home for a visit. Maybe he could get a ticket for her, too.

"I am going. A lot of the distributors I work with will be there, so it's sort of a work thing. But it's always a good time, too."

Maggie flashed a big smile, that made him momentarily dazed.

"Oh, good. I'm so glad you're going, too. It's going to be such a fun night."

A crowd of customers walked through the front door. Maggie glanced toward the bar, which was still empty, but Charlie knew the lunch rush was now underway.

"I should probably get going. I don't want to take too much of your time." He pulled out a credit card and put it on the table, intending to pay for their lunch. But Maggie had other ideas. She picked up the card and handed it back to him.

"Thank you, but I invited you here for lunch. And I

appreciate all of your suggestions for the bar. It's nice to finally chat in person, too."

"Very nice. I should do this more often. Get out of the office, I mean." He stood, reluctant to leave. Their time together had gone by too fast.

"I'll see you soon, hopefully on Saturday night?"

"I'll be here," he promised.

CHAPTER 5

Maggie arrived at Quinn's on Saturday a few minutes before four. She wouldn't actually go behind the bar until four thirty when the lunch shift ended and Paul, the day bartender would head home. But, she liked to come in early and relax a bit first. Quinn's always provided a staff meal for all employees to eat before their shift and Bethany always made something good.

When she went into the kitchen, the intoxicating smell of fried chicken tempted her. Ryder was loading up a plate for himself with chicken, mashed potatoes and gravy. Maggie debated doing the same, but she didn't want to eat too heavy a meal.

"I made a big Caesar salad, too. If you want some of that, I can slice up one of these chicken breasts and put it on top," Bethany suggested.

"That sounds perfect." She watched as Bethany made two plates of salad with sliced fried chicken on top.

"Who is the other one for?" she asked as Bethany set them both on the counter.

"Me! I'm going to join you and sit for a few minutes, too, before things get crazy in the kitchen."

They took their plates into the quiet back room, which was used for functions and served as a staff spot for meals or breaks. They joined Ryder and Maggie laughed when she saw that his plate was almost empty already. He laughed back.

"I was hungry. And I have to run a few errands. I'll be back before the dinner rush hits." He took his plate and headed to the kitchen.

"Ryder has been in an unusually good mood, lately," Maggie said once he was gone.

"He's pretty excited about this baby. It's funny, neither one of us was in a hurry to have kids, but now that we're expecting, we're both really looking forward to it."

"Have you thought about names at all?"

"We've talked about it a little, but we're all over the place. I thought he might want a Ryder, Jr., if it's a boy, but he said no. Possibly your father's name, at least as a middle name. If it's a girl, I haven't the slightest. There's so many choices."

"That's true and you have plenty of time to figure it out. I'm glad to see that you're feeling better. At least you look like you are?" Maggie asked. Bethany's color was good and she seemed to be moving around more easily.

"I am. I'm working more days now but shorter shifts, so that helps my back, and so far I haven't really had much morning sickness." She smiled and knocked her fist against the wood table for luck. "Hopefully that will continue."

"Have you had any cravings? Or food aversions?" Maggie was curious, especially as Bethany was such a foodie.

"Yes, to both. I've wanted mac and cheese almost every day and not my homemade recipe, I've been craving the orange Kraft stuff from the box. I can't get enough of it," she admitted.

Maggie laughed. "Well, it is pretty good. I haven't had that in years, but when I was a kid, I thought it was the best thing ever."

"Maybe that's it. I'm regressing to my childhood! And I have to have a small bowl of strawberry ice cream afterward, for dessert. The combo is a must. Isn't that strange?"

"It is a bit unusual," Maggie agreed.

"I know, right? I usually have chocolate swirl or coffee. Now, it's just strawberry. I might have to have some when I finish. Do you want a little?"

"No, thanks. Unlike you, I am not eating for two. I wouldn't mind dropping a few pounds. I always seem to gain and lose the same five pounds." It was frustrating. Maggie never had been as slim as Bethany, though. She had finally accepted that as long as she was healthy, she didn't have to deprive herself.

But, it would be nice to drop a few pounds before the Spinazolla event. Just so she'd feel more comfortable in the dress she was planning to wear. It was midnight blue, with halter straps and a nipped-in waist that created an hourglass effect.

"You look great, Maggie. You always do." Bethany smiled as she spread butter on a thick slice of sourdough bread. "How did Charlie like his turkey club the other day? I meant to ask you about your lunch with him earlier. I walked by to get a soda at the bar while you were eating, and it looked like the two of you were deep in conversation. You were both smiling and it almost looked like you were on a date."

Maggie set her fork down. "Really? It was just a business meeting. Charlie came in to see the bar and give me some pointers."

Bethany raised her eyebrows. "That's a first for him. And he is the one whose voice gave you goosebumps when you talked to him on the phone, right?"

Maggie nodded. "That's true. There is something about his voice. It's…mesmerizing."

"And he's nice in person, too?" Bethany looked intrigued.

"He is. He's easy to talk to and interesting. And smart. He took over his father's company and has done a great job growing it."

"He sounds impressive. So, why aren't you dating him?"

"Well, he hasn't asked me out, for one thing. And I don't think he's likely to, unfortunately. Not right now, anyway."

"Why not?"

"You know the cute lawyer I went out with last weekend?"

Bethany nodded. "The one that looks like a walking, talking Ken doll?"

"He's also Charlie's best friend."

"Oh. Well, that complicates things a little. But, you could just not go out with him again, right?"

"I already told him that I'd go with him to the Spinazolla event. But I think Charlie might be going, too."

"Really? Hmm, that sounds like it could be an interesting night. Do you have plans to see either of them before then?"

"Josh and I don't have plans before next weekend. Charlie mentioned that he might stop in tonight."

"Really? To see you?"

Was it to see her? "Not me specifically. I told him that Ivy is singing tonight and he said that he likes live music."

"Ah, well that explains it then."

"Explains what?"

"I thought there was something different about you tonight. You have a little more makeup on than usual, and you styled your hair differently."

Maggie was surprised that Bethany noticed. But she normally didn't wear much for makeup, just a bit of mascara if she remembered. But tonight she'd added a little eyeliner, rosy blush and her favorite dusty pink lip liner and gloss.

"I got a new curling iron, so I was just playing around with it." Maggie took her last bite of salad and felt a little silly for fussing with her hair and makeup so much.

Bethany stood. "Well, it looks lovely. I need to get back into the kitchen. I still need to have that ice cream."

CHARLIE WENT RUNNING SATURDAY AFTERNOON FOR THE first time in several years. He jogged for about three miles, all over his neighborhood and around Bear Lake, which was just over two miles. His calves were screaming by the time he made it to his driveway. He stretched for another ten minutes or so, then jumped in the shower and got dressed. His jeans and shirt were both new, from his trip to Lewiston, and fit perfectly. The shirt was a medium blue and he picked it out because it made his hazel eyes look bluer.

He figured that his eyes were his best feature. His face was starting to look a little less round, too. Unless he was imagining it, maybe he almost had a jawline. He was no Josh, but he didn't look too bad. He was looking forward to getting to Quinn's early enough to get a seat at the bar and having a chance to chat a little with Maggie when she wasn't busy with customers. And to hearing her sister Ivy sing.

His phone rang as he was pulling out of his driveway. He was surprised to see that it was Josh.

"What are you doing tonight?" Josh asked.

"I'm heading to Quinn's to listen to some live music. Are you still away?"

"Just got home, earlier than expected. I tried calling Liz, but she's not taking my calls. I think Maggie's working tonight. Why don't you save me a seat? I'm going to having something to eat and then I'll meet you there."

"Will do." Charlie ended the call and sighed. While he was glad for the company, he'd been looking forward to talking to Maggie again, without an audience. But, maybe he'd have a chance to chat a little before Josh arrived. And he was always good company.

It was almost seven when he pulled into Quinn's parking lot. The restaurant looked packed. It was prime time for dinner. When he walked inside, he was glad to see a few seats open up as a party of two that was waiting at the bar, was called for their table. Charlie slid into one of the empty seats and his eyes found Maggie instantly. She was at the opposite end of the bar, mixing what looked like an espresso martini. He watched as she drizzled chocolate syrup along the inside of the glass, making a swirly pattern, then strained the creamy mixture into it and dropped two chocolate-covered coffee beans on top. She delivered the frothy drink and then made her way to him, with a smile on her face.

"You made it! And just in time. Ivy's going on in about ten minutes. What can I get you to drink?"

Ironically, considering the business he ran, Charlie wasn't much of a drinker. If he went out to a bar or restaurant, he usually just had a beer or two. He did like some local micro-brewed beers, and he knew what Quinn's carried as he supplied it all.

"I'll have a Laughing Dog IPA."

"That's been popular lately!" Maggie went to get his beer and returned a moment later with a frosty glass. She opened the can of beer and expertly poured it in so that just the right amount of foam was on top.

"Josh is on his way. He's back in town early." Charlie took a sip of his beer and watched her face. There was a flash of something in her eyes. He'd like to think it was disappointment, but he suspected that was just wishful thinking on his part.

"Oh, I didn't think I'd see him this weekend." She looked like she was about to say something else, but someone waved her over for a drink. Charlie watched her work, admiring how she laughed and joked with the customers while moving quickly to make their drinks. Once everyone was all set, she spent some time chatting with him, while keeping an eye on the bar in case anyone needed anything.

"Do you have to work tomorrow, too?" Charlie asked.

"No. I always take Sundays off. I'd love to just be lazy, but I have plenty to do—laundry, grocery shopping. There's a new Jack Raven movie that just opened up that I'm dying to see. I might see if anyone is up for a matinee."

"Is that already out? I wanted to see that one, too."

Maggie grinned. "You should meet me there. It starts at two. I don't mind going alone, but it's always more fun with friends."

"Maybe I will," Charlie said as Maggie went to take someone's credit card. He was already looking forward to seeing her the next day.

"What are you smiling about? You're looking awfully happy?" Josh slid into the empty seat beside him.

"You got here fast." Much sooner than he'd expected.

"I decided to just grab something to eat here. Did you already eat?"

"No. I was planning to get a burger."

"That sounds good. I'll do the same.

When Maggie returned, she looked happy to see Josh, and took his order for a Jack and coke and burgers for both of them.

"Ivy's about to start singing." She set Josh's drink down and ran off to help several new customers that were lining up for drinks. There were no empty seats now at the bar, and most people were watching as Ivy stepped up to the mic and the music began. Charlie was quickly impressed. Ivy had a clear, soulful voice and a special quality that reminded him of his sister. He'd have to bring her by to hear Ivy when she was in town next weekend.

It didn't take long for their burgers and they were cooked perfectly. They ate while Ivy continued to sing. She took a break after a few more songs and Maggie said she'd be back in a while for a second set.

"She's really good. You were right." Charlie ate his last French fry and reached for his beer to wash it down. His glass was just about empty.

Maggie glanced at the glass, "Would you like another?"

"Maybe just one more. Thanks."

"So, where did you go again this weekend?" Charlie asked Josh.

"Up to my dad's place in the mountains. It's just sitting there empty, and he said I could go there anytime.

I thought it might be good to get away, do some fishing and relax. Clear my head."

"And was it? Relaxing?" Charlie hated fishing. He thought it was about the most boring thing imaginable.

"It was all right. I didn't catch a single fish and got a little stir crazy when I got back to the house." He reached for his beer and took a big sip. "I didn't think I'd miss her so much."

"Maggie?" Charlie was watching her pour a draft beer.

"No! Liz."

"Oh, of course."

"I think she's furious with me. She's not calling me back."

"Can you blame her? You dumped her."

"But, I didn't. Not really. I was happy with things the way they were. They were great."

"So, you've decided to marry her, then?" Charlie thought that was an excellent decision. He fully approved.

"What? No. I haven't changed my mind about that. I mean, maybe someday, but not yet. I'm not going to be forced into anything."

"So, what are you trying to do, then?"

"I just want things to go back to the way they were."

"Hm. It doesn't seem like she wants that."

"No. Not yet. But I'm optimistic that she'll change her mind and come around. Maybe she's missing me, too!"

Charlie shook his head. How could his smart friend be so dumb when it came to women? Not that Charlie was an expert, but it didn't seem likely that Liz would decide to change her mind.

"Are you doing anything special on your day off?" Josh asked Maggie. She was leaning against the bar, pouring herself a glass of water.

"Running errands, relaxing. I'm thinking about seeing a movie. What about you?"

"I don't remember the last time I went to a movie. I like to be more active. I might try to get some more fishing in. See if my luck is any better tomorrow. Do you fish?"

Maggie laughed. "No. I'm terrible at it. But it's supposed to be beautiful tomorrow. I bet it will be a great day. Hope you catch loads of fish."

Josh watched as Maggie went to welcome two new customers on the opposite end of the bar.

"She's really a great girl. Beautiful, too. Maybe when Liz sees me with Maggie, she'll realize what she's missing."

"Liz is going to Spinazolla?" Charlie hated to see Maggie caught in the middle of Josh's game-playing.

"She never misses it. She's the one that introduced me to it. I'm sure she'll be there with her friends."

"What if she brings a date?" Charlie said.

Josh scowled at the suggestion. "I don't think she'd do that. It's too soon."

"That didn't stop you. Oh, I'm bringing Hannah with me. She's coming home that weekend."

Josh perked up. "Great, we can all go together. I'll have my assistant book us a car."

"Sure, that sounds fun." Charlie rarely had more than two drinks, but recognized that it was smart to hire a driver, anyway. At tasting events, it was hard sometimes to know how much you'd actually had as the small sips they poured could add up quickly.

They stayed through Ivy's second set and by then Josh was yawning.

"I think the day has caught up to me, sitting in the sun all afternoon and then the long drive back. I'm going to head home." Charlie was ready to go, too.

Maggie brought them their check, and they both put enough cash down to cover the bill and give her a generous tip.

"See you next Saturday," Josh said as they stood to leave.

"I'm looking forward to it. And Charlie, I hope I'll see you tomorrow for the matinee?"

"I'll meet you there a little before two."

Josh raised his eyebrows at Charlie as they walked out. "You're going to a movie with Maggie tomorrow?"

"She didn't want to go alone. And it's a movie we both wanted to see. You don't mind, do you?" If he did, Charlie would call Maggie and cancel.

But Josh laughed. "No, of course not. I was just surprised. You know I hate going to movies. And you guys are friends. I know I don't have to worry about you moving in on my girl."

CHAPTER 6

Maggie woke Sunday morning feeling unusually cheerful. She tended to be a morning person, anyway. She liked getting up early and enjoying her coffee in the quiet peace of morning, before her day got underway. And on Sundays she could linger even longer, have a second or third cup of coffee, surf the internet and catch up on her friends' Facebook posts and the headline news.

She looked around her cozy condo and the kitchen that she was itching to remodel. She'd bought the condo a few years ago and it suited her well. It was walking distance to Quinn's pub and had two bedrooms, a living room that opened into the kitchen and a small patio that overlooked a grassy backyard and a small pond. She'd gotten it for a good price, but the kitchen badly needed updating. The cabinets were dark wood and the counters beige Formica.

Eventually, she'd like to paint or reface the cabinets to a lighter shade and upgrade the counters to granite or quartz. She really wanted honed marble. She loved the sleek look of it and the smooth feel, but everyone warned her that it was too porous and easily stained. To prove them wrong, she'd brought a marble tile home and tested it. Sure enough, everything made a mark. But she still longed for it, someday. She'd just have to be really careful.

While her laundry was in the dryer, Maggie tried out a new online yoga video, then showered and headed to the market for her weekly grocery shopping. Once everything was put away, she made herself a peanut butter and jelly sandwich and went to change into the perfect outfit to go see a movie with Charlie.

She'd been intrigued and excited that he was interested in seeing the same film and so quickly agreed to meet her there. She'd mentioned it to Josh before they left because she wanted to be upfront, so he wouldn't have any reason to be upset with her or with Charlie. After all, they were just two friends going to see a movie, right? Never mind that she wanted more than that.

Charlie was hard to read, though. Her heart had skipped a happy beat when he walked into Quinn's the night before. She'd been surprised and a little disappointed when Josh joined him. She kind of wished that she hadn't agreed to go out with Josh again as the spark just wasn't there for her, and she didn't think it was for him, either.

But, she was looking forward to going to Spinazolla,

especially as Charlie was going with them, too. He'd mentioned that he was bringing his sister and had said that he'd love to bring her to hear Ivy sing sometime. She knew that might give Ivy a nice boost of confidence.

She stood in front of her closet for a solid five minutes, debating and rejecting different options for what to wear for her non-date with Charlie. She finally settled on her favorite jeans that made her look a few pounds slimmer, and a light blue and white striped cotton sweater. It was pretty but casual.

For makeup, she just added a bit of mascara and a swipe of soft pink lipstick. And then she was off. The movie theater was right around the corner from Quinn's, so it was walking distance for her. It was sunny but slightly cool, typical April weather. She grabbed a light jacket and started walking.

When she arrived at the theater, Charlie was waiting outside and smiled when he saw her. He was wearing a brown leather jacket over jeans and a navy blue New England Patriots shirt. The blue of the shirt and the sunshine made his eyes appear very blue. She hadn't noticed that before. She also liked the way his smile made tiny laugh lines appear beside his mouth and eyes. When Charlie smiled, it lit up his whole face, and then when he spoke, his voice gave her the shivers.

"I didn't realize you lived close enough to walk."

She nodded. "I live less than a mile from Quinn's. As long as the weather is nice, I walk to work most days. Where do you live?"

"I'm near Bear Lake. I had a house built and moved in about a year ago. I love it out there. It's maybe ten minutes to downtown, but a little quieter and I have a nice, big yard."

"That sounds lovely." She smiled. "I hear the fishing is good on Bear Lake."

He laughed at that. "I wouldn't know."

They went inside. Charlie bought the tickets and Maggie insisted on buying their popcorn and drinks. They got a large with extra butter to share and two waters, then made their way into the theater. Charlie told her to pick the seats, and she led them toward the front and in the center. There were a few people waiting for the movie to start, but it wasn't crowded.

They settled into their seats and Maggie balanced the tub of popcorn on her lap. The previews started a few minutes after they sat down and soon they were engrossed in the movie. Maggie was still very aware of Charlie by her side, and now and then his hand brushed against hers as he reached for more popcorn

The movie was an edge-of-the-seat action suspense thriller and Maggie was a little embarrassed when more than once, she jumped in her seat when something unexpected happened and then Charlie softly chuckled. As they walked out of the theater when the movie ended, she apologized for being so jumpy.

"I probably should have warned you. That always happens. It's a good thing we didn't see a horror film or I might have jumped right into your lap."

He laughed. "Maybe I wouldn't have minded that."

She glanced at him and he winked at her. She knew he was just teasing her, but there was something about the way he said it that gave her hope that there might be some interest there.

"It's a beautiful day. Do you want to walk around a bit? I wouldn't mind getting an ice cream at Smith's," Maggie said.

"Sure. You never have to ask me twice about ice cream."

"Bethany was talking about her strawberry ice cream cravings the other day and I've wanted one ever since," Maggie admitted as they reached Smith's, the coffee shop that also sold ice cream and old-fashioned penny candy. The front door opened and an older couple walked out holding two ice cream cones.

"Well, hello Maggie and Charlie, right?" It was her mother and her constant companion, Harry Peterman.

"Nice to see you, Mrs. Quinn," Charlie said politely.

"We just came from seeing the new Jack Raven movie." Maggie answered her mother's unspoken question. She could tell her mother was dying to ask more, but it wasn't the time.

"Isn't that nice? We went to Quinn's for lunch after church, like we usually do. You should join us one of these Sundays, Maggie."

"It has been a while," Maggie agreed. She went to church in spurts. She was all in for a few months and then didn't go for a while. When she did, it was a given that Sunday lunch would follow at Quinn's and sometimes, she felt like she spent enough time there during the week and treasured the solitude of her Sundays at home.

"Well, we're off. I forced Harry to get an ice cream and the agreement is that we walk it off now by strolling through the park. See you tomorrow, honey."

"Your mom seems sweet. Is that her boyfriend?" Charlie asked once they were inside and looking at the array of ice cream options.

"She is. We're not entirely sure what Harry is. She's not admitting to anything, but they are pretty much inseparable. It's been over ten years now since we lost my dad, so we're all happy for her. They knew each other from years ago and reconnected recently."

Maggie ordered a small strawberry cone and Charlie got a classic hot fudge sundae with vanilla ice cream, whipped cream and nuts. They took their desserts outside and sat by a space heater that kept them warm while the cool-ish breezes drifted by.

"I know it's been a few years now since you lost your wife. I can't imagine how hard that must have been. How did you know when you were ready to date again?"

Charlie swallowed a bite of ice cream and thought about the question. "I haven't actually dated anyone yet. Since the accident. Josh has been pushing me for over a year to get out there. But, I haven't felt ready until recently. Now, I'm at least thinking about it. Meredith and I were together since we were kids. Neither one of us ever dated anyone else. So, I'm really not good at this," he admitted. His voice cracked a little and Maggie had to fight the urge to give him a hug.

"I think you'll do just fine. There's no shortage of women for a good guy like you," she said impulsively. His face turned red and he focused on his ice cream.

"That's really kind of you to say."

"It's true." She paused and then took a chance to let him know how she really felt. "If you'd asked me out before Josh did, I would have happily said yes."

"Really? Well, that's good to know."

"When he asked me out, I also had no idea that the two of you were friends."

Charlie laughed. "I think I was even more surprised when I saw that those flowers in the bar were from Josh. Last I knew, he was practically engaged to Liz Cunningham. How did he happen to ask you out?"

"He came into Quinn's one night for dinner, and he seemed really down at first. He was by himself and was furiously texting to someone. He had a few drinks and a sandwich and when the bar emptied out, he stayed around talking to me and cracking jokes. He can be pretty funny when he wants to. He was easy to talk to, and his mood seemed to change from being down to in a great mood. When he suggested dinner, I knew it would be an entertaining night. And it was."

"She gave him an ultimatum," Charlie said. "And Josh is used to things going his way, calling the shots. It threw him off. He didn't react well, and she ended things."

"He did seem a little preoccupied at times," Maggie said. She remembered how Josh kept glancing at his phone, as if he was waiting for a text message that never came.

"He's a great guy, and my best friend. I just hope he comes to his senses about Liz. I was surprised that he asked you out. I think he's trying to deal with losing Liz, and he's not going about it the right way. That didn't come out right." Charlie looked worried that he'd insulted her, but Maggie touched her hand lightly on his arm to reassure him.

"It's okay. I know what you meant." She took her last bite of ice cream and stretched her legs. Charlie's sundae was already gone.

"I think your mother had the right idea to walk this off. Shall we?" Charlie stood, and she followed him to the sidewalk. They strolled down Main Street for a while, then turned and made their way back on the opposite side. Maggie stopped in front of Paws, the local pet shop. There were several kittens in the window, rolling around and looking adorable.

"Do you have any pets?" Maggie remembered him mentioning that he had a big yard. Maybe he had a dog.

"Not really. I mean, not officially. There's a huge neighborhood cat that comes by every day and I'm not sure if he's feral or actually belongs to someone and just likes to make the rounds. I think he's feral, though, because he comes every day for food. And in the winter, he snuggles into a heated cat house that I got for him. I've invited him in, but he won't take that step.

"What's his name?" Maggie wondered.

"I have no idea. He doesn't wear a collar. I started

calling him Tank, because he's so huge. He doesn't seem to mind it."

"That's cute." Maggie looked back at the kittens. "I've been thinking about getting a new cat. It's been a few months since I lost my last one. I adopted Lucy from a shelter when she was six and had her for eleven years."

"Maybe you should get a kitten this time?" Charlie suggested as the littlest kitten, a fluffy gray ball of fur, pressed its nose against the glass and Maggie's heart melted.

"Hmm, maybe. We'll see." As tempted as she was, Maggie needed to think this through. She'd never had a kitten before and had always adopted older cats. She liked rescuing them as she knew it was harder for them to find good homes.

"You could always get two, an older cat and a kitten to drive it crazy." Charlie laughed as they continued walking toward his car. The air was starting to get cooler and Maggie shivered.

"That jacket doesn't look very warm. Why don't you jump in and I'll drop you at home. You've gotten enough walking in."

"I'll gladly agree to that." Maggie climbed into the passenger side of Charlie's car. It was an older Volvo sedan, with comfortable leather seats. A few minutes later, he pulled into her condo complex and she directed him to her unit. There were a dozen or so condos and she had one on the end.

"Thanks for suggesting the movie, and the ice cream," he said as she grabbed the door handle.

"I'm glad you were able to make it. See you on Saturday."

"See you then." Maggie walked to her door and looked back. Charlie was still there, waiting for her to go inside before driving off. She waved as her key turned in the lock. It had been a really nice day. It may not have officially been a date, but she was hopeful that soon, maybe that would change.

CHAPTER 7

Charlie picked his sister up at the Lewiston airport Friday afternoon. Hannah looked beautiful, but thinner than the last time he'd seen her.

"You've lost weight," he said after he hugged her hello and they stood waiting for her luggage in the baggage claim area.

"You have, too! You look great, Charlie. Look at that jawline." She took a step back and studied him closely. "So, who is she?"

Charlie looked away. His sister knew him too well. "I'm not dating anyone. I just wanted to get in shape. Dr. Finnegan read me the riot act at my yearly checkup. He reminded me that heart disease runs in the family.

"Hmmm. That's true. Well, you look wonderful, regardless."

"You do, too. So, why have you lost weight?"

She sighed. "The usual reason. I've been so busy, I just forget to eat sometimes. You know how it is."

He chuckled. "No, I don't, actually. I don't think I've ever missed a meal. But I know how you are. You lose yourself in your music."

She grinned. "You know me well."

He grabbed her suitcase when it came by on the carousel and they drove back to Quinn Valley. They hit quite a bit of rush hour traffic and it was almost six by the time they reached his house.

"Are you hungry?" he asked.

"I am, actually. I missed lunch."

"How does steak sound?" Her stomach rumbled in response and they both laughed. Charlie carried her suitcase to his spare bedroom and fired up the grill while she freshened up.

"Can I do anything to help?" Hannah asked when she came downstairs and into the kitchen where he was chopping a tomato to add to a bowl of lettuce.

"Do you want to open that bottle of wine? The opener is in the silverware drawer."

"You remembered that I liked the Josh cabernet," Hannah said as she carefully removed the foil from the top of the bottle, opened it and poured a glass for each of them.

"I wouldn't be very good at my job if I didn't remember my sister's favorite wine."

Hannah laughed. "Are we still on for breakfast with Mom tomorrow?"

Charlie nodded. "She said she'll be over around ten and she's bringing homemade blueberry muffins."

"My favorite. How is she? I talked to her yesterday and she sounds good."

"She is. I usually see her at some point during the week. Lately it's been breakfast or lunch because she's been going out more with her friends."

"Really? That's great. It's about time." Both Charlie and Hannah had been encouraging their mother to have more of a social life in recent years. Finally, she seemed interested.

"Steaks should be done. I'll be right in. Do you want to grab the container of potato salad out of the fridge?"

Charlie brought the steaks in and they fixed their plates and settled around his big kitchen island. It was in the middle of his kitchen and was a rustic, polished wood slab with six chairs around it. It could be a work station, but Charlie did most of his cooking on the grill, so it was mostly where he ate, and when he had friends over, where everyone gathered.

As they ate, Hannah told him funny stories of her life on the road, traveling from city to city. She had a small house in Nashville, where she'd moved years ago when she was trying to get her music career off the ground. Charlie looked at his tiny sister in awe. If you didn't know her, you'd think that she was fragile as she was so thin. Her eyes, the same hazel as his, looked huge and blue-gray as she spoke, gesturing with her hands for emphasis.

She looked very much like the creative artist that she

was, but his sister was anything but weak. He remembered the first time he'd seen her in full concert mode. She played a sold out show at Lewiston's biggest venue and held the crowd spellbound for several hours. It was her first big show in the North West and she was compared in reverential tones to Adele. Except her songs were a little more folksy. Hannah Keane was one of a kind. He expected that she'd have a long career, so her next words surprised him.

"I'm thinking about moving back to Quinn Valley."

Charlie put down his knife and fork. "You are? Why? Not that I wouldn't be thrilled to have you move back, but Quinn Valley?"

Her lips turned up slightly as she reached for her wine. "It's not a decision that I've made lightly. Let's just say that my manager is barely speaking to me. He doesn't approve. At all. But it feels right."

"Is it your throat again?" Hannah had to cancel the last few shows of her tour the prior year because of throat nodules. She'd rested and they'd eased up, but she'd been warned that if she overdid it again, she could do serious damage and might need surgery.

She nodded. "Partly. I just finished a tour and I wasn't sure I'd make the last show. My voice was feeling really rough. But I made it, just barely. So, there's that. But, honestly the traveling is wearing. The money is amazing, nothing like it. But, I've saved a lot now and my expenses are low. I've already put my house in Nashville on the market."

"Are you retiring then? What will you do in Quinn Valley?"

She grinned. "Bother you. No, seriously I have a plan. I want to teach, and to write and record new music. I can still do that without touring like I used to. And maybe I could do a limited tour, just a few nationwide stops."

"You could sell those seats at a premium, too. They'd sell out in record time if there's only a few chances to see you."

Hannah chewed her bottom lip and frowned. "I wouldn't do that. I don't want to gouge people. I want to keep the ticket prices reasonable."

"Prices have gotten crazy for some of these shows," Charlie agreed.

"I thought about doing songwriting workshops, maybe holding the events at Quinn Hotel, and including a few scholarships to students at Berklee and other places with music programs, as a way of giving back." Charlie could tell that she'd put a lot of thought into this and was passionate about it.

"I think it's a great idea. And selfishly, I'm all for you moving back to Quinn Valley. I miss having my sister around."

"So, enough about me. What have you been up to? Tell me more about this Maggie that is coming with us tomorrow night. And why is she Josh's date? What happened to Liz?"

Charlie laughed. "I have a lot to catch you up on."

CHAPTER 8

Maggie twirled in front of her bedroom mirror and assessed the blue cocktail dress. It still looked pretty good, even though she was still the exact same weight she was two weeks ago. Her plan to lose a few pounds had failed miserably. She supposed it could have been the strawberry ice cream, or the fact that her gym had actually sent her an email saying they missed her and would she consider coming in for a visit soon, to take a class or enjoy a smoothie. Nothing like being guilted by your gym.

At least her job was an active one. She was on her feet the entire time and on a busy night, it often felt like she ran from one end of the bar to the other. But, Maggie always had a weakness for delicious things. And it didn't help that Bethany was pregnant now and pushing comfort food for staff meals more than ever.

She supposed that holding steady wasn't such a bad thing, though. The dress was flattering, and her arms were nice and toned. The cut of the dress made her waist look smaller and her average size bust a bit curvier. And best of all, the dress was comfortable. She'd be able to indulge in all the food sampling without worrying about a belly bulge.

She did her makeup and curled her hair a bit, just to fluff it up and define the natural waves even more. Josh had said they'd be coming by at seven to pick her up. He'd hired a car for the night, so no one had to drive, which she thought was a smart thing to do, as it was almost an hour drive to Lewiston.

At a few minutes past seven, there was a knock on the door. She grabbed her coat and purse and opened the door.

"You look gorgeous! Are you ready to go?" Josh looked sharp in his tux.

"I'm ready."

Josh led her to the waiting limo. It was a sleek, black Lincoln Town Car and when she stepped inside, Charlie and his sister were sitting across from them. Charlie looked so handsome in his tux. He introduced her to his sister, Hannah, and Maggie shook her hand. It was tiny and delicate.

Hannah was much smaller than she'd imagined. Her hair was long, relaxed ringlets that fell to the middle of her back and the color was a rich, strawberry blond. Her eyes were the same blue-gray as Charlie's and her dress was strapless and a shimmery pewter color. She wore a feathery shawl in the same shade over her shoulders.

Josh entertained them with funny stories for most of

the drive. He was a general practice lawyer, handling everything from personal injury to criminal cases, though in a small town like Quinn Valley, the criminal cases were pretty minor. And some comical, like the recent attempted bank robbery by the not-too-bright Robby Benson who was caught running down Main Street with hundred-dollar bills sticking out of his back pockets.

Maggie did a double-take as the limo drove by her cousin Katie's house. As Robyn had mentioned, there was a black sports car in Katie's driveway. She wondered if Katie would be at Gram's Monday night. She sensed that there was a story there.

The drive to Lewiston flew by and before she knew it they pulled up to the elegant Rosemont Hotel. It was one of the biggest in Lewiston and lots of functions were held there. They went inside and dropped their coats at the coat check. Josh and Charlie had their tickets and they gave them to the woman at the entrance to the main ballroom. She handed each of them a wine glass and a small tray with a clip on the corner to slip the stem of the wine glass into, which would make it easier to sip and eat at the same time.

"Wow. This is something." Hannah looked around the huge room where there were rows of long linen-covered folding tables set up. Vendors stood on one side, offering tastes of wine or samples of different restaurant dishes. It was a way for both to advertise and lots of well known area restaurants and wineries were there.

"They should do something like this in Quinn Valley," Josh said.

Maggie laughed. "I love the idea, but there's less than ten restaurants in all of Quinn Valley. It wouldn't be the same."

He grinned. "True point. Well, where do we start?"

They made their way to the shortest line and for the next hour, strolled around, tasting various wines and trying bites of everything from beef Wellington to coconut shrimp, seafood bisque, braised short ribs, and so much more.

"We're going to go sample some scotch. Are you ladies interested?" Josh asked.

"I'm ready to sit down," Hannah said as she set her purse on an empty cocktail table.

"Me, too," Maggie agreed. "You guys go ahead. I'm not much of a scotch drinker."

Hannah laughed and made a face. "Neither am I."

They collapsed into the two empty chairs and watched the crowd. It was packed and everyone looked so festive in their tuxes and cocktail dresses.

"I'm glad you were able to come with us. I know Charlie was excited for your visit this weekend," Maggie said.

"I was looking forward to it, too. Charlie and I are pretty close. I'm thinking about moving home to Quinn Valley, actually. Please don't say anything, though. I haven't announced it officially, but I'm going to stop touring for a while."

"Oh, wow. I'm sure Charlie and your mom and sister must be thrilled that you're moving back here. Will you miss Nashville, though?" Maggie remembered that

Charlie had said that was her home base, though she was always on the road. She imagined it must get tiring.

"I will miss Nashville. It's a great city and it's how I got my start. But I can always go back and visit. I don't need to live there anymore. I haven't really been there much the past few years anyway because I've been traveling non-stop."

"I don't think I'd like that. I'm sort of a homebody," Maggie admitted.

"You'd never know it, but I am, too. I get terrible stage-fright."

"Charlie told me that. I found it hard to believe, though, as you're so successful."

"It's true. Once I start singing, I'm fine. It's just getting started that's hard." Hannah smiled. "I'm excited to move home. I'll still be active with music. I just won't be traveling all the time. I think it will be nice."

"My sister Ivy has been singing locally and she writes her own music."

Hannah nodded. "Charlie said he heard her play at Quinn's the other night and she was very good. I'd love to hear her while I'm in town if she's playing anywhere tomorrow or Monday."

Maggie tried to remember Ivy's schedule. "I think she's playing tomorrow night at O'Shea's."

"Do you have to work tomorrow?" Hannah asked.

"No, I'm off on Sundays."

"We should all go see her, then. I'm sure Charlie and Josh would be up for it."

"I'm not sure about Josh. This is only our second date

and, well…" How did she nicely tell Hannah she wasn't interested in a third?

But she seemed to understand. "We don't have to invite Josh, then. You, me and Charlie can go. It will be fun."

Maggie relaxed. "I'd like that."

"Charlie talks about you quite a bit. I think he enjoys your company." She smiled warmly and Maggie was pleased to hear it.

"I enjoy his company, too. Charlie is a great guy."

"I agree, even though I am his sister!"

"What are you two laughing about?" Charlie said as he and Josh strolled back to the table holding glasses of scotch.

"Oh, nothing. Is anyone ready to visit the dessert tables?" Hannah led the way to the long tables against the wall that were piled high with all kinds of desserts. Maggie was full, but they looked too good to resist.

"They're small. That means you can take two or three at least," Charlie said as he picked up a plate and selected a cannoli and a brownie.

"He has an excellent point." Hannah was next in line, and Maggie grabbed a plate and joined her. Maggie just took one cannoli, the Italian wafer cookie that was rolled and stuffed with a sweet ricotta cheese filling, then dipped in mini-chocolate chips. It was her favorite dessert. Impossible to resist.

"No dessert for you?" Maggie asked Josh. He was still sipping his scotch and looking around the room.

He smiled and lifted his glass. "This is my dessert. I'm not much on sweets."

Maggie took a bite of cannoli, then almost swallowed wrong when she heard a familiar and unexpected voice behind her.

"Maggie Quinn! Fancy seeing you here!" Maggie turned to see her grandmother and her posse of friends in their best cocktail dresses.

"Grams! I didn't know you were coming here?"

Her grandmother laughed. "I didn't either. But Ruby won tickets yesterday on the radio station. She was the lucky caller, so here we are. We took an Uber!" Maggie stared speechless at her grandmother. She didn't know she even knew what an Uber was.

"Isn't it marvelous?" Ruby said. "I can't believe we haven't done this before. And the dancing is about to start. We should hurry girls. We don't want to miss it."

"See you on the dance floor, Maggie!" Her grandmother whirled off, following her friends into the connecting ballroom where there was a big band and, evidently, dancing.

"Your grandmother is a hoot," Hannah said.

"She's full of surprises," Maggie agreed.

"Want to go sit in the other room and listen to some music?" Hannah suggested. "Maybe it will be good."

"I see someone that I need to go say hello to," Josh said. "I'll meet you all in there."

As they slowly made their way into the next room, Charlie was stopped several times to say hello to various vendors that knew him. He seemed to know a lot of

240 PAMELA M. KELLEY

people throughout the event which wasn't surprising, given his business.

"He really does love it," Hannah said as she watched her brother laughing with a wine vendor.

"He's a good businessman. He told me how the business has grown some in the past few years and he gave me some great suggestions for how to order better and what works well for his other customers."

"He's modest. The business has exploded since Charlie took it over. He's done a great job and people respect him. My dad had that same quality, but he didn't have the same business savvy. I'm really proud of him."

"OMG, it is you. It's Hannah Keane!" Three women swarmed around Hannah. Maggie was nervous for her, but Hannah just laughed and took a step back.

"You're from around here, aren't you?" one of the women asked.

"I am. I'm home visiting family."

"How lovely. Could we possibly bother you for an autograph?" One of them asked and they all looked hopeful.

"Of course." The women all handed her their programs and a pen, to sign with. Once Hannah signed all three, the women walked away happy and waving goodbye. And a moment later, a few more women came over asking for autographs. Hannah was gracious to everyone and Maggie watched it all with interest.

"Does that happen often?" she asked, when the women were finally gone.

"It does, yeah. I'm used to it now. I think I'm going to get a cup of tea. Do you want anything?"

"No, thanks. I'm too full."

Hannah wandered off and Maggie stood, people watching. Charlie was chatting away with a different vendor. She suddenly felt a tap on her shoulder and almost jumped. She turned and her brother David was standing there. She didn't know he was coming, but she wasn't surprised as he was in the food business, too.

"You're looking good, Mags. You here with Charlie?"

"Sort of. We all came together, me, Josh, Charlie and his sister, Hannah."

David stiffened. "Hannah is here? What is she doing slumming in Lewiston?" His tone surprised her. David wasn't usually so sarcastic.

"She's just home for the long weekend visiting her family. She's staying with Charlie. Do you know her?"

"We graduated together. She wouldn't give me the time of day in high school. It took me forever to get up the courage to ask her out, and then she didn't say a word. Just stared at me like I was a speck of dirt on her white dress. I slunk away in misery."

Maggie frowned. "That doesn't sound like Hannah. She's been lovely."

"Hmm," was all David said.

Hannah returned a moment later with her tea and stopped short when she saw David.

"Hi, Hannah," he muttered.

There was a long, uncomfortable moment of silence before Hannah finally spoke. "David. It's nice to see you."

She turned to Maggie, her face pale and said softly, "I'll be back in a minute. I need to run to the ladies' room. Will you hold this for me?" She handed Maggie her tea.

David watched her go.

"See, nothing has changed. One look at me and she runs out of the room."

"I'm sure it's not like that. She's been so much fun all night."

"Until she saw me," David said glumly.

Maggie looked at her older brother and shook her head. Her brother normally had women falling all over him. He had that dark, Irish look, with almost black hair and light green eyes, and he had the Quinn dimple. All the boys in the Quinn family had a deep dimple on one cheek and it added to their charm. "Get over yourself. I'm sure that had nothing to do with you and more to do with something she ate. We're going to head into the other room and listen to some music. Do you want to join us?"

But he shook his head. "No, This is really a working event for me. I have a lot of people I need to go talk to. I just wanted to come over and say hello."

"Okay. If you change your mind, you know where to find us."

David gave her a hug. "I'll see you soon."

A few minutes later, Hannah returned and took her tea back from Maggie.

"Are you okay? You took off so suddenly."

"I'm fine, my stomach just protested a bit. Too much cream, I think. Are you both ready to head into the other room?" Charlie had just walked back over, too, and the three of them made their way into the other room, which was filling up now that the band was playing. Charlie spotted one of the few remaining empty tables and made a beeline for it. They followed and took seats on either side of him.

The music was big band, smooth jazz and some of the couples who were on the dance floor were impressive.

"This reminds me a little of Dancing with the Stars," Maggie said as one of the men dipped his partner so low that her hair almost touched the floor.

"You two should get out there," Hannah urged. Charlie looked hesitant and Maggie guessed that it was probably the last thing he felt like doing. Not that kind of dancing, anyway. Maggie had taken dance lessons for years, when she was younger, so she loved to get out there, but she knew not everyone, especially most men, were up for it.

"We don't have to," she said quickly. Relief--or was it disappointment--flashed across Charlie's face. She smiled as she saw her grandmother coming over to their table with a determined look.

"What are you young people doing just sitting there? Young man, you really should take one of these ladies out on the dance floor. Take turns, it doesn't matter. But it's a shame to not enjoy this opportunity to dance!"

"Yes, ma'am." Charlie jumped up and held out his hand to Maggie.

She took it and and whispered in his ear as they

walked to the dance floor. "You really don't have to do this if you don't want to."

A slow smile spread across Charlie's face. "Maybe I want to."

He pulled her to him dramatically as they stepped onto the dance floor, and Maggie caught her breath. Charlie knew how to dance! He whirled and twirled her across the dance floor and even dipped her a few times and held her close when the music slowed. By the time the song ended they were both breathless. "Want to go again?" he asked.

They danced three more songs. The last song was a slower one, and she swayed in Charlie's arms and didn't want the music to end. Finally it did, and they slowly walked back to the table where Hannah was chatting with Josh, who'd joined them.

"How did you learn to dance like that?" Maggie asked.

"My sister Caitlyn was into dance and needed a practice partner. So, I got drafted."

"Well, that was amazing and so fun!"

He grinned. "It was, wasn't it?"

They sat back down at the table and Maggie noticed that Josh's eyes were stormy.

"Charlie, feel like taking a walk? I want to get some air." Josh was tapping his leg nervously and looked agitated.

"Sure." He glanced at his sister and Maggie. "We'll be back in a few minutes."

Once they were out of earshot, Maggie looked at

Hannah. "I wonder what's wrong with Josh. He seems upset about something."

Hannah hesitated, then carefully asked. "How interested are you in Josh?"

"I'm not. I mean, he's a great guy, but he's not the one for me."

"Okay, good. I didn't want to say anything if you did have hopes in that direction. His ex-girlfriend is here."

"Liz?"

"Yes. He tried to talk to her, but she gave him the cold shoulder. She's here with her friends, and she told him that she didn't want to go back to the way things were. That's what he proposed, evidently." Hannah shook her head in disgust.

"So, he's upset because he didn't get his way. She didn't fall back into his arms."

"No. Luckily, she's here with her friends. And she held strong. Maybe he'll come to his senses, hopefully before it's too late."

Fifteen minutes later, Charlie and a calmer Josh returned. Josh was distracted and quiet, and when Hannah yawned, Charlie asked if everyone was ready to head home. They all agreed and headed out to the limo that was parked outside waiting for them.

Josh was more subdued on the way home, but he perked up after a bit and had them laughing for the rest of the way. When they reached Maggie's condo, he jumped out and walked her to the door. And he apologized for his bad mood.

"I'm sorry I was such a grump earlier. It had nothing to do with you. I hope you had a good time tonight?"

"I did. I had a lot of fun getting to know Charlie's sister."

He smiled. "Hannah's a great girl. Have a good night, Maggie." He pulled her in for a hug and dropped a kiss on her forehead. Maggie smiled. It was a friendly kiss and it was over in a second. Which suited her just fine.

"Goodnight, Josh, and thank you."

CHAPTER 9

Charlie and Hannah slept in the next morning, and were just up and sleepily enjoying their first cup of coffee when their mother knocked and two seconds later, let herself in the front door. Charlie went to get up, but his mother waved for him to sit back down.

"I'll pour myself a cup and join you. Here are the blueberry muffins. They're fresh out of the oven." She hugged each of her children, then set a plastic container between them on the island, helped herself to some coffee and joined them.

"Help yourself. There's a few paper napkins in there, too, since your brother never keeps a proper napkin in the house. Paper towels are not the same."

"Thanks, Mom." Charlie opened the container and handed out the muffins. They were bursting with blueberries and still warm, as his mother had said.

"So, tell me all about this Spinazolla thing. Did you have a good time?"

"We did." Charlie told her all about it, and she shook her head over Josh's foolishness. Charlie was tempted to tell her about the ring that Josh had stashed away, but he'd been told that in confidence, so he kept quiet and hoped that soon enough, he'd be able to share that part of the story, too.

"I've heard so much about this Maggie lately. Maybe it's time for you to take her out?" his mother suggested.

"I agree completely," Hannah agreed. "I think they're both smitten with each other."

Charlie laughed at the absurd suggestion that Maggie was 'smitten' with him.

"Well, I'm definitely smitten and have been for sometime. I always looked forward to Maggie's weekly calls. We always chatted about much more than just her order. I will ask her out, when the timing is right." He took a sip of coffee and glanced at his sister. "Enough about me and Maggie, Hannah has some big news to share."

"Oh? What is it, honey? Are you expanding your tour? Releasing a new album soon?"

"Not quite. I'm going to come off the road for a while, and I've put my Nashville house on the market. I'm moving home to Quinn Valley."

His mother's face lit up like a Christmas tree being plugged in. "Hannah, that's the best news you could possibly give me. Well, other than that you're engaged or making me a grandmother." She cocked her head and studied her daughter. "Neither of those things are happening too, are they?"

Hannah almost spit out her coffee. "No! I'm not dating anyone and babies are far, far down the road."

Their mother looked both relieved and a bit disappointed. "Well, it's marvelous that you're moving home. Will you still be able to have the same career from here? I know how much you love your music."

"It's going to change a little, but hopefully in a good way. I'm tired of all the traveling. And it never gets easier stepping onto the stage. It terrifies me every time. I should be able to do an occasional show, hopefully, if people don't forget about me. That is a possibility I suppose. But, it's one I've considered, and I'm okay with it."

"You won't be forgotten," Charlie assured her. "If anything, touring less often should make your appearances even more in demand."

"Maybe. I hope so!" She told her mother the rest of her plans, about the classes she planned to teach and the events she hoped to hold at Quinn's hotel.

"Hannah will turn Quinn Valley into the Nashville of Idaho!" Charlie said proudly. He had no doubt that Hannah's venture would be a success.

"My head is spinning," their mother said happily when Hannah finished filling her in. "This is the most marvelous news. When are you thinking you'll be back?"

"Not for a few more months. I still need to get the house in Nashville sold and packed up, and meet with my manager to discuss options going forward. He's not at all happy about this."

"Hmmmm. Too bad," their mother said. Charlie and Hannah both laughed at her tone. Their mother was a force to be reckoned with when she wanted something done.

"What's new with you, Mom? How've you been? Charlie and I have been hogging the conversation."

"Oh, I'm not nearly as interesting as the two of you, but I have been getting out some lately. Spreading my wings, you'll both be glad to know." Charlie couldn't help but notice that his mother looked better than he'd seen her in years. She was well-rested and had a rosy glow about her that wasn't just makeup.

"I've been going to that new, fancy gym. The one you got me the membership to, Charlie. As you know, I wasn't too keen on it at first, but it's grown on me. The water aerobics class is fun, and I'm feeling more fit. I've lost a few pounds. And I've met the most interesting people there. They're very friendly. One in particular…"

"OUR MOTHER IS DATING NOW," HANNAH TOLD MAGGIE as they ate dinner with Charlie at O'Shea's. Although the food was pretty good, O'Shea's was more of a pub than a restaurant like Quinn's. Ivy was due to sing her first set soon.

"That's wonderful, isn't it?" Maggie asked.

"Yes! I think it is. Charlie does, too, right?"

Charlie didn't look as enthusiastic. "Yes, as long as the

guys are decent. Mom's out of practice. I worry a little that she could be taken advantage of," he admitted.

"She's more savvy than you know," Hannah said. "And she seems excited, so I think it's a good thing. She was a hermit for years after our father died. It's nice to see her finally coming out of her shell. The gym membership was a great idea, Charlie."

"Have you talked to Josh? Has he talked to Liz yet?" Maggie wondered.

"I haven't heard anything. I think Josh will get there, in his own time."

"Charlie says that you bartend and are a co-owner at Quinn's. Do you love it? Do you have to work every night?" Hannah asked and then immediately apologized. "Sorry for all the questions. I'm just so curious. I've never worked in a restaurant. It looks like hard work."

"It is," Maggie assured her. "But I do love it. We've grown up working in the restaurant. And both Ryder and I majored in business in college, which has been helpful. I make my own schedule, but as you can imagine, it's a lot of hours. I'm there almost every day, but never on Sunday. And I mix it up. I usually work the lunch shift on Monday, then Tuesday and Wednesday night. The rest of the week varies depending on what's going on."

"And Ivy works there, too?" Hannah asked.

"She does. She waitresses."

"It looks like she's coming on now," Charlie said as Ivy stepped up to the mic.

Maggie was proud of her sister as she sang song after song. She was getting so good and more comfortable in front of a crowd than she used to be. When she finished her set, she came over to see them.

"I didn't know you were coming in," she said to Maggie and then realized who was there with her. Her jaw dropped. "Hannah. I'm such a fan."

Hannah smiled. "Thank you. But I'm a fan, too. You were wonderful." Ivy sat, and she and Hannah chatted non-stop about music until it was time for her next set.

"Your sister really is good. And this is just a hobby for her? She seems pretty serious about it."

"It's just a fun hobby for her now. She gave up on her Nashville dreams when she was eighteen, due to an audition on a reality TV show."

"Oh, that was her? I remember," Hannah said.

"How long are you in town for?" Maggie asked. She and Hannah had become fast friends and she hated to see her leave. But, she was happy that she planned to return on a more permanent basis.

"My flight out is tomorrow. But I'll be back for a house-hunting trip soon. I hope that I'll see you both then."

"Definitely." Charlie and Maggie both spoke at the same time and laughed.

Maggie liked Hannah almost as much as she liked her brother. She glanced at Charlie. He was listening to the music, but when he saw her looking his way, their eyes met, and he smiled. She felt a strong sense of contentment, that she was exactly where she was supposed to be. She knew, deep in her soul, that Charlie was the one for her. Now, if he'd just ask her out.

"WHO WERE YOU JUST TALKING TO?" RYDER LOOKED AT his sister with a funny expression. It was Monday morning, a few minutes past eleven and he and Bethany had walked over to the bar as Maggie was finishing up her call.

"Just my weekly call to Charlie to place my order," she said happily. She was in the best mood ever, for a Monday.

"So you two are finally dating, then? It's about time." Ryder said.

Maggie looked at her brother in surprise. "We're not dating. Not yet anyway. We're just friends. I met his sister, Hannah this weekend. We all went to Spinazolla together."

"Well, if you're not dating, you should be. You look all dreamy-eyed when you talk to him, or even when you say his name."

"Leave your sister alone," Bethany said. But then she grinned. "It is true, though."

"It's totally true," Ivy added as she slid onto a barstool and started wrapping silverware sets into napkins. "They came to see me sing last night and if I didn't know better, I would have guessed that Maggie and Charlie were an old married couple. Although, maybe married couples don't smile at each other quite that much."

"It's really that obvious?" Maggie was a little horrified, considering that she and Charlie had yet to go on a real date.

Bethany and Ivy both nodded. "You look cute together," Ivy said.

"Are you both going to Gram's tonight?" Maggie changed the subject.

"I'm not. I'm meeting up with some friends downtown," Ivy said.

"I'll be there. I'm looking forward to it. I'm debating what to make. What do you think? Buffalo Chicken Mac and Cheese or meatballs in sauce?"

"I've never had Buffalo Chicken Mac and Cheese. That sounds interesting," Maggie said.

"I've never had it either, but it seems like it might be good. If I make it, you'll all be my guinea pigs. And if it works, we'll try it as a lunch special."

"Sounds good." Maggie looked up as the front door opened and a party of women came in for lunch. It was time to get to work.

Maggie carried a big bowl of salad into her grandmother's kitchen. She'd called earlier to tell her what she was planning to bring. Bethany's creamy pasta dish was rich, comfort food, so Maggie thought her kitchen sink salad would go well with it. It was just a bowl of mixed greens topped with everything she could find in her kitchen that seemed interesting—three bean salad, chick peas, chopped tomato, peppers and onions, sliced canned artichokes and steamed asparagus. She tossed it all with Italian dressing and sprinkled a bit of parmesan cheese over the top.

All the usual suspects were gathered in her grandmother's kitchen. The ladies who had all been at the gala, as well as Maggie's mother, several aunts, and cousins. Bethany was there too, taking her casserole dish out of the oven. It was browned and bubbling and smelled incredible.

Her grandmother came over to greet her. "There you

are! And just in time." She took the salad and set it on the counter, by a giant loaf of crusty bread and a platter of cheese and crackers.

"Time to eat! Everyone help themselves," she announced.

Over dinner, her grandmother told everyone how marvelous the Spinazolla event had been and then embarrassed Maggie by raving about her dancing with Charlie.

"The two of you looked like you'd been dancing together for years. Almost Dancing with the Stars worthy." Her friends all nodded in agreement. "So, is there anything we need to know yet about you and Charlie?" her grandmother and her friends leaned in closely.

"There is no 'me and Charlie', Grams. I was there with Josh, and Charlie brought his sister, Hannah."

"Hmmmm. Well, you should work on that. A man who can dance like Charlie won't stay on the market long," her grandmother warned.

Maggie smiled. "I'll keep that in mind."

LATER, DURING ONE OF THE COMMERCIAL BREAKS, Maggie joined Bethany and Robyn in the kitchen so they could chat without disturbing the others and so Bethany could have dessert. Maggie watched in amusement as Bethany put a fudge brownie on a plate and smothered it with a giant scoop of strawberry ice-cream.

"Want some?" she asked before putting the ice-cream

back in the freezer. Maggie and Robyn both shook their heads no.

"I was hoping Katie would be here tonight," Maggie said. "I drove by her house the other night, on the way to Lewiston, and I saw that car you mentioned."

"The black sports car?" Robyn asked.

Maggie nodded. "Has anyone talked to her?"

"I've left her a few messages but we haven't connected yet," Robyn said. "If I hear anything I'll let you know. How are you feeling, Bethany? Is your back better?"

"Yes. My appetite has kicked in, though. I'm always hungry. Ryder's been good about keeping me well fed, though."

"He seems so excited about the baby," Maggie said. "He keeps a copy of your ultrasound picture in his wallet. He was showing it off to me earlier today."

Bethany laughed. "He is excited. And willing to give me nightly foot rubs. Being pregnant isn't so bad."

"Do you want kids, Maggie?" Robyn asked.

"When I was a kid, I thought I'd have four kids by the time I was thirty-five. Now I can't imagine having that many, but I think I'd like at least one or two. I suppose I should find someone to have them with first?" She laughed, but it was interesting how the thought had crossed her mind recently. Ever since Bethany and Ryder announced that they were expecting, Maggie started noticing babies everywhere, and wondering if it would actually ever happen for her.

MAGGIE WAS SITTING IN HER KITCHEN TUESDAY afternoon, painting her toenails a pretty shade of coral when her phone rang and she was surprised to see that it was Charlie. She had the afternoon off and didn't have to be into work for another few hours. It wasn't like him to call her this time of day and she'd just called her weekly order in the day before.

"Hi, Charlie."

"Hey, Maggie, sorry to bother you. But I remembered that you're off today and I wasn't sure who else to call. I know that you've had cats." He sounded anxious and Maggie hadn't a clue what he was calling about.

"What's going on, Charlie?"

"It's Tank. I put one of those cat doors in a few months ago, so he could get into the basement when it got cold out, but he never used it, until now. And it turns out that he is a she and just had a litter of kittens in my basement. I'm not sure what I should do, if anything."

"Kittens? What's your address? I'll be right over."

Maggie jotted down Charlie's address, then jumped in her car and drove to Paw's, the pet shop on Main St. She stocked up on wet cat food, bought a litter box and some litter and a soft fleece blanket. She figured Charlie would have some old towels they could use, too.

She put his address in the GPS of her white Honda Civic and arrived at Charlie's house twelve minutes later. He heard her pull into the driveway and opened the front door as she walked towards it, carrying the bag of pet stuff. He took it from her and glanced inside it.

"Thanks for coming. What is all this?"

"Everything I could think of that you might need. Tank might not be up for leaving her babies anytime soon. So you'll need food, and a litter box. Do you have any old towels we can put down around them? I picked up a soft fleece blanket for them to snuggle on, too."

"This is great. I didn't think of any of this. Do you want to go see them?"

Maggie nodded and quietly followed Charlie into the basement. It was mostly empty except for a few big plastic storage containers and in one of them, a giant brown and white cat lay with six or maybe seven kittens clamped onto her, trying to nurse.

"Aw. They're so tiny. And their mother looks exhausted."

"She does." Charlie set up the litter box in a corner and went back upstairs and returned a minute later with two bowls, one filled with water and the other for the wet food. He also had a stack of old towels that he laid around Tank, along with the fluffy, fleece blanket. Tank rubbed her cheek against the blanket and purred. Charlie reached down, and lightly petted her head and scratched behind her ears. "You did well," he told her as she purred even louder.

Tank's eyes grew heavy and soon she was sound asleep, while her kittens continued to nurse. Charlie and Maggie watched for a few minutes reluctant to leave them. When one of the kittens rolled away, Tank woke immediately to check on her baby and nudged it back into place.

"I think she has things under control," Charlie said.

"I can't get over how tiny they are." The kittens were the size of mice. Squirmy, damp mice with eyes that were almost completely shut. They were so helpless looking. "It's hard to believe that they'll soon be running around."

"You sure you don't want a kitten? You'll have your pick to choose from!"

"Maybe it's a sign that I should take one," Maggie agreed.

"I don't think that it will be hard to find homes for them. I'll spread the word. There's always the shelter, but I've heard kittens are always in demand. Do you have time for a cup of coffee before you head into work?"

"Sure." Maggie followed him upstairs and into the kitchen. It was a sunny room, with lots of natural light streaming in through oversized windows. She liked the big center island and the creamy off-white cabinets and her jaw dropped when she saw that his counter tops were made of honed Calcutta marble. She ran a finger lightly across the smooth surface. It was absolutely gorgeous— mostly white with streaks of ash and gold running through it.

"This is exactly what I dreamed of doing in my kitchen. I've always wanted marble, but everyone says it's not practical."

"Oh, it's not. I was a little worried about that when I had it built, but my contractor said it would be fine as long as I kept wine away from it and wiped up any spills immediately. So far, so good." He grinned as he handed Maggie a mug of hot coffee.

"I have cream and sugar if you need it."

"Thanks, but I don't use either." Maggie watched with amusement as Charlie dumped at least four sugars into his coffee and gave it a stir. They sat at the kitchen island and sipped their coffees. Charlie looked like he had something on his mind, but they chatted about nothing in particular until Maggie finished her coffee and reluctantly realized she needed to head into work.

She stood and put her empty mug in the sink. "I should probably go."

"Thanks so much for coming. I think I panicked a little. We never had cats growing up, just dogs."

"It will be fun to watch them grow. Maybe you'll want to keep one, too?"

"The thought crossed my mind. I even considered keeping two, so they'd have a playmate." Charlie walked Maggie to the front door. He reached to open it and paused. "Before you go. If you're interested, I'd love to take you out soon, maybe dinner later this week?" The words came out in a rush and took Maggie by surprise, in a very good way.

"I'd love that. I'm off Friday night and of course on Sunday."

"Okay, good. I want to talk to Josh first, to give him a head's up. I'm sure he won't mind."

"Sounds good. I'll see you soon then."

Charlie opened the door and Maggie walked by him on her way out. They were standing so close that she could feel his breath on her face. They both stopped and for a moment, she thought he might kiss her, but then he stepped back to let her pass by and the moment was gone.

"Bye, Maggie."

As soon as Maggie drove off, Charlie grabbed his phone and called Josh. He picked up on the second ring.

"Josh Winters." He sounded busy and distracted.

"Josh, it's Charlie."

"Oh, hey, Charlie. I'm sorry. I'm just swamped and didn't look at the caller ID. You know how it is. What's up?"

"I won't keep you, just had something I wanted to talk to you about. First of all, have you talked to Liz?"

"That would be a no. I've called Liz twice since Spinazzola. Left her a message each time and haven't heard back from her yet. Looks like it's over for real."

"Oh. I'm sorry to hear that. Maybe you should try going to see her?" Charlie suggested.

"She should answer her phone!" Josh was clearly in a mood. Charlie debated waiting a day or two to talk to him about Maggie. But, he didn't want to wait any longer.

"I'd like to ask Maggie out. As long as you don't have a problem with that?" Charlie asked. His only answer for a very long minute was complete silence. Finally Josh spoke.

"You want to ask out Maggie? My Maggie?"

"I wouldn't exactly call her your Maggie. Have you asked her out since Spinazzola?"

"Well, no. Not yet. But I was planning on it. Espe-

cially since Liz seems to want nothing to do with me.
Maggie's much nicer. And she's already gone out with me
twice. I'd say my chances are pretty good."

Charlie sighed. This wasn't going the way that he'd
hoped.

"So, you don't want me to go out with Maggie?"

"Are you serious, Charlie? Of all the women in Quinn
Valley, you want to go out with her? Your timing really
stinks. I'm not ready to give up on Maggie yet. Can you
find someone else? Please?" He sounded annoyed and
spoiling for a fight and Charlie wasn't up for it. He could
tell that Josh was in a mood and it wouldn't go well.

"All right. I'll back off. For now. Let me know if
anything changes."

"I wouldn't hold your breath on that."

Charlie ended the call and sat fuming for almost ten
minutes. Finally, he decided to go for a run and burn off
the anger and frustration that was coursing through him.
The last thing he felt like doing was calling Maggie and
canceling their date. But he didn't see that he had another
choice.

HE CALLED HER THE NEXT AFTERNOON, AND SHE SOUNDED
happy to hear from him.

"Hi, Charlie! I'm looking forward to our date this
weekend. Did you want to go out Friday night or
Sunday?"

Charlie sighed. "I wish we could go out Friday night.
But I have some frustrating news. I called Josh after you

left, to let him know that I wanted to see you and well, he didn't take it well."

"What are you saying?"

"That Josh is going through something right now. He's not himself. This thing with Liz is wearing on him."

"The 'thing' with Liz is entirely his fault and he could clear it up immediately if he just talked to her."

"I agree, but she's not taking his calls at the moment."

"And until she does, he won't let you date me? That's silly."

"It is. But Josh is my best friend and he's hurting right now. I just don't want to make things worse for him. You have no idea how badly I want to take you to dinner. But I think we need to wait a little until this works itself out or dies down. He'll come to his senses soon."

"And if he doesn't?"

"Well, we'll cross that bridge when we get to it, I suppose."

"Okay. But, if he calls me again I am not going out with him!"

"I would hope not!" Charlie laughed, then added softly. "I'm really sorry about this Maggie."

"It's all right. You're just being a good friend."

"I'll keep you posted."

CHAPTER 11

"So, you haven't heard from Josh, or Charlie, and Josh won't allow Charlie to ask you out?" Bethany dipped her spoon into a big bowl of strawberry ice cream and shook her head at the ridiculousness of the situation.

"That's about the gist of it," Maggie said. It was Friday afternoon and she and Bethany were sitting in the back room, while Maggie counted the money in her drawer to make a deposit. They were both almost done for the day. Bethany was just waiting for Ryder to finish up and then the two of them were going home to shower and head out for their regular Friday date night.

The weekend stretched out in front of her, long and empty. She'd been looking forward to seeing Charlie Friday night but now she was going to be staying home alone.

"I don't even have a cat to keep me company," she complained. She was feeling pretty sorry for herself.

"Well, that's dramatic. You have loads of friends. Is no one around to go out with tonight?" Bethany asked.

"Oh, probably. I'm just not feeling up to going out with the girls tonight. I'm tired and I want a long, hot bath, a good book and some of that ice cream."

"That sounds like a pretty good night to me," Bethany said.

"It doesn't sound too bad, actually. It's just not what I originally had in mind. I was really looking forward to seeing Charlie."

"I know you were." Bethany's eyes were sympathetic and Maggie felt her own eyes water. She was feeling so emotional. It was silly. She tried to push the sad feelings aside and to think of something positive instead.

"There's a new romantic comedy that just opened today. Do you maybe want to catch a matinee on Sunday?" Maggie knew that Bethany shared her love for fun, romantic movies.

"I'd love to."

Maggie was in a mood Monday morning when she strolled into Quinn's for her lunch shift. Her mother was already there, making the coffee and setting out a plate of hideously green muffins. They did not look appetizing. Maggie helped herself to coffee and ignored the muffins.

"Oh, you have to try one," her mother urged. "It's a new recipe. Pistachio, like the ones we liked from the bakery. I think they came out good."

Bethany was sitting at the bar, making notes on her food order for the week. She took a bite of a muffin and looked like she was in heaven.

"See, Bethany likes them," her mother said.

"Bethany likes everything right now," Maggie laughed.

"It's true. I do," Bethany agreed. "These are very good, though."

To appease her mother, and because she knew she'd never let up until she tried one, Maggie took a muffin and ripped a chunk off and ate it. She knew that she was in a bad mood because it actually made her mad that the muffin was good.

It had just been a long weekend. Even though Friday night had been relaxing, she couldn't help thinking more than once that she could have been spending it with Charlie if he'd been firmer with Josh. She understood. She just didn't like it.

As soon as she finished her muffin and waved goodbye to her mother as she went off to run errands, Maggie picked up the phone to call Charlie and put her weekly order in. He answered on the first ring.

"Hi, Maggie, it's great to hear your voice. Did you have a good weekend?"

"Hi, Charlie. It was fine." Her tone was short and she couldn't seem to keep her frustration out of her voice. "Are you ready for my order?"

"Of course. Whenever you're ready."

Ten minutes later, they were done discussing her order and the conversation suddenly halted. There was an awkward moment of silence before Maggie asked, "How are Tank and the kittens?"

"Oh, they're good! They're already getting bigger."

"That's great." She paused for a moment then asked the question she needed to know. "Have you talked to Josh? Has anything changed with Liz?"

There was a long moment of silence before Charlie spoke. "I haven't heard from him."

"I see. Well, I have to get going. Goodbye, Charlie." Maggie hung up the phone and sighed. Time to focus on work.

CHARLIE COULDN'T RELAX AFTER HIS CALL WITH MAGGIE. The frustration in her voice echoed his own and it had only grown worse after what had been a very long weekend. One he'd hoped to spend with Maggie. He'd thought for sure that he would have heard from Josh by now. He entered Maggie's order in the system and decided to take matters into his own hands. He was tired of waiting.

He drove downtown, to Josh's posh office and greeted Estelle, Josh's receptionist, warmly. She was about his mother's age, and she was always elegantly dressed with her hair curled and a double strand of pearls over a cashmere sweater.

"Any chance I could steal ten minutes from Josh's schedule?"

She glanced at her computer screen. "He just hung up a call and doesn't have anything for another twenty minutes. You can go on in."

Charlie tapped lightly on his office door, that was slightly ajar and then walked in. Josh looked up in surprise when he saw him.

"Hey, there. What are you doing downtown? Is everything all right?"

"Everything is fine, or at least it will be. We need to talk about Maggie."

Josh scowled. "I thought we already did."

"No, I told you what I wanted to do, out of courtesy since you're my best friend. But you're not serious about Maggie. There is absolutely no reason why I can't ask her out. Except that you don't want me to because you're miserable about Liz. What have you done about that?"

"I've called her and left messages. I don't know what else you think I should do."

"Do I really have to spell it out for you?" Charlie asked. And because Josh stayed silent, Charlie told him what he thought he should do.

"You really think that will work?"

"Probably. Maybe not. You'll never know, though, until you try. She's worth it right?"

"Of course she is," Josh snapped.

Charlie grinned. "Well, then, take action. Go see her tonight and call me after."

"All right. I will. And Charlie, I'm sorry. I've been so wrapped up in myself that I didn't realize how interested you were in Maggie. It must be pretty serious if you came all the way down here to see me. You have my blessing and good luck."

"Thanks. And good luck to you, too."

CHARLIE CALLED MAGGIE AS SOON AS HE WALKED outside. She sounded surprised when she answered the call.

"Hi, Charlie. Did I forget to order something?"

"No, I don't think so. But I just wanted to let you know I just left Josh's office and told him that I'm going to ask you out and he needs to be okay with it because it doesn't matter what he wants anymore."

"You really did that?"

"I did. Is our schedule the same this week as it was last week?"

"It is."

"Would you like to have dinner with me Friday night?"

"I would like that very much."

CHAPTER 12

Maggie's mood improved instantly and she spent the rest of the week in eager anticipation for Friday night. She went shopping Thursday afternoon before work and bought a pretty new white and gray sweater to wear with her favorite jeans and bright pink cowboy boots. She was ready when Charlie came by at six thirty to pick her up.

When she opened the door, he stood there, smiling and holding a bouquet of vividly-colored wildflowers in a clear glass vase. He handed them to her.

"I saw these, and they reminded me of you. I thought they were beautiful."

"They are. How thoughtful. Thank you." She took the flowers and set them on the counter, then grabbed her purse and went to walk out the door. But Charlie took her hand and pulled her toward him.

"Before we go, there's something I've been wanting to do for a while. I hope you don't mind."

Maggie caught her breath as Charlie leaned and his lips lightly touched hers. The kiss caught her by surprise and was even better than she'd imagined.

"I had to do that," he said a moment later.

"I didn't mind," she assured him.

He took her to Mamma Mia's in Riston, the next town over. Maggie had been there before, but not for a long time. It was better than she remembered. The service and the food were amazing, and she and Charlie talked and laughed all through dinner.

"I can't believe that Josh actually bought a ring after his first date with Liz. And held onto it for so long. What made him wait do you think?"

"Fear of change, maybe? Things were going so well with Liz that I think he was just afraid to mess with it. But he finally came to his senses, went to her house, apologized profusely for being such an idiot and then showed her the ring. She burst into tears when he told her how long he'd had it. And then she said yes."

"I'm so glad, for both of them."

Charlie looked over at Maggie. "I don't want to wait three years."

Maggie's heart skipped a beat. Was Charlie already thinking about marriage?

"Three years is a long time," she agreed.

"I've only ever loved one other person. And we pretty much knew right away. I didn't think I'd find that kind of connection again. But I feel like we might have that. We talked on the phone for a long time before we met, and I feel like we really got to know each other. I never spent that much time taking anyone else's order."

Maggie laughed. "I might be jealous if you did."

Charlie looked deeply into her eyes.

"Do you think it's possible to fall in love over the phone? Because I think I was head over heels before we actually met."

"You kept rescheduling our lunch meeting, so I wasn't sure what to think. I suggested it because I was falling in love with you, too. I didn't really want to date anyone else. You have a mesmerizing voice. I wanted to stay on the phone longer just to listen to you talk and it was more than your voice, it was you."

"I rescheduled our lunch meeting because I was worried that you wouldn't be interested once you met me in person. I don't look like Josh."

Maggie reached out and took his hand. "I'm not attracted to Josh. He's handsome, but he's not you. He doesn't have your eyes, your smile, your soul."

"If it wasn't entirely crazy, I'd propose to you now and suggest we run off to Vegas to get married. But I don't think either of us is that crazy? Are we?"

"It's tempting, but no. I don't think we are."

"I don't want to wait long, though. Is two months long enough?"

"That seems like a respectable time to me."

"Two months it is, then. If things are still going well, we can get engaged, elope, do whatever feels right."

"That sounds quite sensible to me."

"So, how's this, then. Let's make a toast?" Charlie lifted his glass. "To almost being in love."

"We're so close!" They tapped glasses, and Maggie dipped her fork into the oversized cannoli that they were sharing for dessert and took a bite. It had been an absolutely perfect night.

SIX WEEKS LATER

Maggie arrived at Charlie's house Sunday afternoon. They were planning an afternoon of playing with the kittens and watching movies. She couldn't believe how big the kittens were and how lively. They were into everything.

"That's their latest game," Charlie said as two of them tried to climb up the drapes in his living room.

"Have you decided which one you want yet?" The kittens were almost eight weeks old, the age that would be safe for them to be adopted.

"I'm not sure. I keep going back and forth between the big black one or the wild gray one. I'll probably end up keeping both. What about you?"

"The littlest one, I think." The runt of the litter was three quarters the size of the others and seemed drawn to Maggie. The little kitten liked to snuggle in the crook of her neck. Maggie didn't mind, except that when she relaxed the kitten's purr was so loud. It was hard to figure how such a loud sound came from such a tiny animal.

They had plans to meet up with Josh and Liz later on

for dinner downtown. But until then, they enjoyed being lazy on Charlie's plush black leather sofa and having a movie marathon. After they watched two films back to back, Charlie eased himself up and went into the kitchen. Maggie heard a familiar popping sound and smiled when he returned holding two flutes of bubbly champagne. He handed one to her and she raised her eyebrows.

"What's the occasion?"

"It's been six weeks since our first official date and exactly two months since we first met in-person."

"Oh!" Maggie's jaw dropped as Charlie got on one knee and pulled a small velvet box out of his pocket.

"I'm all the way in love with you now, Maggie Quinn. My feelings get deeper and stronger for you every day, and I don't want to wait any longer. Will you marry me?" He opened the box and a gorgeous, cushion-cut diamond sparkled.

Maggie didn't have to think about it. "I was almost all the way in love with you before we even met. I think I was just about there on our first date, but there's no doubt that I'm all the way there now. I love you, Charlie Keane. Let's get married."

I hope you enjoyed Maggie and Charlie's story! If you'd like to receive an email when my next book is released please join my mailing list.

Have you discovered Wall St. Journal and USA Today bestselling series that begins with, The Nantucket Inn.

ABOUT THE AUTHOR

Pamela M. Kelley lives in the historic seaside town of Plymouth, MA near Cape Cod and just south of Boston. She has always been a book worm and still reads often and widely, romance, mysteries, thrillers and cook books. She writes contemporary women's fiction and suspense and you'll probably see food featured and possibly a recipe or two. She is owned by a cute little shelter kitty, Bella.

MOM'S BLUEBERRY MUFFINS

Recipe

Mom's Blueberry Muffins
My mother's special recipe—she used to make a batch almost every Tuesday, her favorite day of the week—when she'd spend the day with my twin nieces, Taylor and Nicole.

1/2 cup butter
2 cups flour
1 1/4 cups sugar
2 eggs
1/2 cup milk
2 tsp baking powder
1/2 tsp salt
2 cups blueberries
2 tsp sugar on top

Cream sugar and butter until fluffy. Add eggs one at a time until blended. Alternately add dry ingredients and milk. Stir in blueberries. Sprinkle sugar on top. Grease muffin tins. Makes 12 big muffins.

Bake for 25-30 min at 375.

HANNAH'S HOME

Hannah Keane is tired of being on the road. She's eager to move home to Quinn Valley and live a quiet life, writing music and teaching workshops and classes at the local kids' center. But there's also another reason she doesn't want anyone, especially the media, to know where she is.

David Quinn is the last of Marcia Quinn's five children to settle down and he doesn't seem to be in any hurry to find love. The very last person on his list would be Hannah Keane, who seemed to look down her nose at him the last time she saw him, like she did back when they were in high school. But as he begins to realize that maybe he was wrong about Hannah, he also starts to worry that something else is going on, something that Hannah is running from and that she won't be able to stay in Quinn Valley after all.

CHAPTER 1

Okay, it's all yours now." Missy Roring, Hannah Keane's bubbly, thirty-something realtor, handed her the keys to her new home. The closing for her home was finished, all the paperwork completed. They said their goodbyes to the attorneys and walked out of the law office together.

"Thank you for all of your help. I can't wait to get settled in." Hannah was eager to get into her new house and start unpacking. The movers were due to arrive in a few hours and she had a carload of suitcases and new stuff she'd bought as well.

Missy shook her head and smiled. "I can't believe you really want to move back to Quinn Valley after living in Nashville and Hollywood! Are you sure you won't be bored?"

Hannah laughed. "I'm sure. Quiet is exactly what I'm looking for."

Missy still tried to make sense of it. "I suppose that's good for writing more songs?"

"I hope so." Hannah was looking forward to hunkering down and losing herself in her music and a few other projects she was excited to get started on.

"Well, if you decide to move back to Nashville once you get your songs written or whatever, I hope you'll give me the chance to work with you again?"

"I'll keep that in mind." Hannah's phone beeped with a text message she'd been waiting for. Before she gave it her full attention, she needed to get rid of Missy. "Thanks so much, Missy." She smiled and hoped the other woman would get the hint. Missy looked as though she still wanted to say more, but finally seemed to realize the conversation was over.

"All right, then. Enjoy your new home! And again, if I can be of any help, don't hesitate to call!" Missy turned and flounced off, her blonde hair bouncing around her shoulders and in shoes with heels so high, Hannah wondered how she was able to walk around town in them.

The text message from her assistant, Mary, simply said 'call me', so she did.

"How did it go?" Hannah asked when Mary picked up. "There's nothing they can do, is there?" She felt her chest tighten with anxiety as she thought about the situation she'd been trying to pretend wasn't happening.

"The officer that came out to the house to take the report was a nice young man. I swear he looked about sixteen, but I suppose he's old enough if he's actually doing the job. Anyway, he took all the information. I forwarded him the emails, and he said he'd check with his team, but he didn't think it was likely they'd find anything. He said if it happens again, if it escalates, to be sure to let them know. He also said if it happens to anyone else that might help them too, if they could find a pattern."

Hannah sighed. "Somehow I doubt a stalker will send the same messages to multiple people, but I suppose you never know."

"And no one knows you're moving back to Quinn Valley, right? As long as it's not made public, you should be safe. There's probably nothing to it anyway," Mary tried to reassure her.

"I really don't think there is. But it's still unsettling. Thank you for meeting with the police."

"Of course. I still wish you weren't moving. We could manage the threat here and it really is better for your career to be in Nashville." Hannah smiled. Mary had been her assistant since the beginning and was protective of her.

"You know that's not why I'm moving, though it does seem to confirm my decision. It's just time. I'm ready to pull back from living so publicly. I know the money is fantastic when I tour, but I only need so much and I've managed to save quite a bit." Hannah had been touring almost non-stop for the past few years and had little time to spend all the millions she was earning. And she had other ideas for that money now.

Twenty minutes later, Hannah pulled into the driveway of the house she'd fallen in love with at first sight. She had to admit, Missy was good at her job. She'd lined up a number of houses for Hannah to see. They were all fine but nothing special until Missy turned onto Edgewater Drive and Hannah sucked in her breath as the house immediately came into view. The sun had shone down brilliantly that day, dancing on the water behind the house and casting a rosy glow over the cream-colored farmer's porch.

The porch wrapped around to an expansive deck in the back that overlooked the lake and there was a boat dock, too. Not that Hannah had a boat, but it might be fun to pick up something very small that she could ride around in.

The inside of the house was perfect for her too. It was roomy and cozy at the same time, with three bedrooms and an open layout downstairs that had gorgeous water views. The living room had a brick fireplace, and the kitchen had an island with the cooktop in it, so she could cook and look out at the lake at the same time. Hannah hadn't done much cooking in recent years, but she liked to play around in the kitchen and she was looking forward to trying out some new recipes and having her brother Charlie and his girlfriend Maggie over for dinner.

Hannah was thrilled for her brother as she'd liked Maggie Quinn right away. Especially since it was obvious how much she cared for Charlie. The last time Hannah was in town, they'd all gone to a charity event and it had been a wonderful night, until Maggie's brother David showed up. He still had a chip on his shoulder for something that had happened when they were in high school.

He'd asked her out, and she'd just frozen, unable to speak with no doubt a look of misery. But he'd misunderstood and thought she was horrified at the thought of going out with him. When actually, she was just so nervous that by the time her words came to her, David was long gone. She'd always felt terrible about it. People often assumed that because she was a performer that she was outgoing, but it wasn't so.

Hannah was a true introvert, and it was only the music that allowed her to step out of her shell. Very few people knew it, but she still had horrible stage fright every time she went onstage. Once she started singing her nerves went away. It took a toll on her though, every live performance, because there was also the meet and greets with fans and press after the show. By the time she got home, she was always so drained and ideally needed a day or two to recharge. That usually wasn't an option though, with back-to-back shows in most cities. She was looking forward to slowing down and was excited for her next chapter in Quinn Valley.

CHAPTER 2

Marcia Quinn looked around the table at Quinn's Pub and smiled. Every Sunday, whoever was available in the family would meet for a late lunch or early dinner. Today, all but two of her five children were there. Ivy, her youngest lived in Nashville with her husband. David, her oldest, was working. He ran a successful food supply company and sometimes liked to go in on Sundays and get a head start on the week.

Sunday was also the one day that everyone in the family that worked at Quinn's took off. Her son Ryder and her daughter Maggie co-owned it now, Ryder handled general management and Maggie oversaw the bar. Ryder's wife, Bethany, was the head chef and Maggie's husband, Charlie, was their liquor distributor. After founding and doing all the cooking at Quinn's for many years, Marcia now did as little cooking as possible, other than major holidays or occasionally trying out a new muffin recipe and bringing it into Quinn's for morning coffee with her kids. She liked to stop in on most days, have coffee and then be on her way.

Her other son Carter, and his wife Avery were chatting with Gertie, their grandmother, and Marcia's mother-in-law. The gentleman on Marcia's right, Harry Peterman, leaned over and whispered, "she's up to something."

Marcia had also noticed that Gertie had an interesting gleam in her eye as she reached for the butter and tore open a roll. She waited until she had everyone's attention before speaking.

"So, I wonder how David feels about his new neighbor? Has he mentioned anything?" Gertie glanced around the table at a sea of blank faces.

"What new neighbor?" Marcia asked.

"None of you have heard? Hannah Keane bought the big house on the lake. It's just a few doors down from David. He really hasn't said a thing?"

"I'm not sure he knows," Maggie said. "I just saw him yesterday, and he didn't mention it."

"How do you know about it Gram?" Ryder asked.

"Well, Ruth's daughter Missy is a realtor, and she told us all about the listing recently. She also mentioned that she was going to be showing some homes to Hannah. I may have suggested that the lake house could be good for her. Seems she agreed!" Gertie seemed quite pleased with herself as she bit into her roll.

"Are you playing match-maker again, Gram? I'm not sure this one is a good idea. I saw David talking to Hannah at the charity ball recently and I don't think he's a fan. He might not like that she's living so close." Maggie looked a bit concerned.

"He doesn't always know what's good for him," Gertie said. "I have a good feeling about Hannah."

"She's really moving back to Quinn Valley?" Marcia asked. "She's such a big success now, I would have thought she'd want to be in Nashville or Hollywood."

"No, it's true. I knew she was going to be moving back here, just not when. She said she misses Quinn Valley and wants to get out of the spotlight," Maggie turned to Charlie who was Hannah's brother. "Maybe Charlie can tell us more?"

He nodded. "It's true. Hannah just called yesterday to say she would be closing on the house this week, and it is on the lake. I didn't realize it was that close to where David lives though." He didn't look thrilled by the news.

But Gertie was undeterred. "It will be fine. It's David's time to settle down."

Gertie was right about that. David was the last of Marcia's children to find love. And it didn't seem like he was in any hurry to get there. He was a bit of a workaholic. He lived and breathed his business and it was quite successful. It wasn't that he didn't date. David actually dated often, but it never seemed to get serious.

When Marcia once asked him what he was waiting for, he just smiled and said that work was his priority and that when he met the right one, he'd know. Gertie had a good track record so far with her matchmaking but Marcia wasn't too keen on her latest attempt as David and Hannah already knew each other and it was pretty clear that she wasn't 'the one' for him.

CHAPTER 3

David Quinn slowed his car as he came around the corner and saw an alarm company van in front of 42 Edgewater Drive. So, the new owners had arrived and were installing an alarm system. That told him that they were likely not from the area, because almost no crime happened in Quinn Valley. Most people he knew didn't even lock their doors at night.

He was curious about these new neighbors and a little bitter because he'd wanted that house for himself. It was his dream location, and he'd had his eye on it for years, but it had never gone on the market. He finally did the next best thing and bought a house a few doors down when it came available.

His house was nice enough, but it wasn't right on the lake, and David loved to fish. He liked the area because of the lake. There was a neighborhood boat ramp that he used for the boat he kept trailered in his yard. He'd mentioned once to the older woman that had owned the house that if she was ever thinking of selling to please, let him know.

But when she died recently, everyone assumed her family would sell the house. David waited patiently for the for sale sign to go up, but it never did. Someone swooped in and bought it out from under him. He never even had a chance to make an offer. He knew it wasn't the new owners fault and they were probably nice people, but he wasn't feeling overly neighborly towards them at the moment.

He felt even less so when he saw the front door open and a petite woman with long caramel colored hair walked to her car. He watched her open her trunk and pull a box out of it. When she turned back to walk into the house, he got a good look at her face and his jaw dropped. Hannah Keane had stolen his dream house.

He'd once had such a crush on Hannah and when she didn't even respond when he asked her out in high school, he'd been devastated. She'd just stared at him as if she thought he was repulsive. He'd moved on of course, but when he ran into her recently at a charity event, she wasn't any friendlier. She was with his sister, Maggie and Charlie, who was also Hannah's brother. For a moment, he felt like he was back in high school and it wasn't a good feeling. He knew Hannah lived in Nashville and hadn't expected that he'd run into her again so soon. And now they were neighbors. It was not a good way to end his day.

HANNAH WOKE SATURDAY MORNING, STRETCHED AND
sighed with happiness as sun streamed through her
bedroom window. She could see the water rippling on the
lake and leaves dancing in the breeze. After a moment,
she eased out of bed, pulled a sweatshirt over her pajamas
and stepped through the French doors in her bedroom
onto a small deck. She took a deep breath of the fresh,
clean air and enjoyed the view. There were already a few
small boats on the water and people fishing. The air was
slightly chilly, but she knew it would warm up in a few
hours.

Her first week in her new home had gone well. She
didn't go far, except to the grocery store and to visit her
mother. She needed to go shopping again this morning,
and to the local butcher to get some nice strip steaks.
Charlie and Maggie were coming over for dinner. She
wanted to stop at the hardware store too to pick up a
small hammer and some nails to hang her pictures.

There was also an association meeting in the afternoon that she thought she'd attend. Her home was part
of a small neighborhood association and they had a
shared clubhouse with a pool and use of a boat ramp.
Hannah wanted her neighbors to get to know her, and to
see her as a normal person instead of a celebrity.

She went downstairs and made herself a cup of coffee
and a few slices of sourdough toast with butter. She
wasn't much of a breakfast eater but knew she needed
something in her stomach if she was going to be running
around all morning. She sat at her kitchen island and
glanced around the room. It was starting to look homey

and the way she'd envisioned it. Almost everything was unpacked and put away, except for a few boxes in the basement that she wasn't sure about. She might still donate more stuff to the local thrift shop.

Only thing left to do was to hang her pictures. She had lots of pretty watercolor paintings and prints as well as some photographs she'd taken herself over the years and had enlarged and framed.

An hour later, she was at the local hardware shop, strolling the aisles looking for the picture hanging tools. Her head was down and she almost ran right into someone. An annoyed, 'watch out', got her attention, and she stopped short in her tracks and immediately apologized.

"I'm so sorry!" She said the words before looking up and when she did, she felt even worse. Of all people to almost run into, she'd nearly walked right into David Quinn. He stared down at her from his six two or so height, almost a foot taller than she was at barely five three.

"No harm done. You should pay attention though to where you're going."

Hannah felt her face flush. He was completely right. "Yes, I'm sorry. I was just so intent on finding what I need to hang my paintings."

"I just saw the paint hanging kits in the next aisle. That's probably what you're looking for?"

"Yes, I think so. Thanks." Hannah went to scurry away, but his next words stopped her.

"So, how did you manage to get that house, anyway? I never saw it go on the market. I was waiting."

Oh no. David had wanted her house! Just one more reason for him to dislike her.

"Um, I'm not sure. Your grandmother actually referred me to Missy Roring, and she lined up a bunch of houses for me to see. I fell in love with the one on Edgewater immediately."

"My grandmother referred you?" David sounded confused.

"Well, not directly. I asked my brother and Maggie. Maggie said she was going to the weekly gathering where all the Quinn women meet to watch Dancing with the Stars and that she'd ask there. She said that her grandmother made the suggestion and was actually pretty insistent that I call Missy. So, I did."

David continued to give Hannah a strange, considering look.

"Well, I guess I can't blame you then. It is a great house."

Hannah relaxed a little. "I really do love it, and the area too. Do you live nearby?"

He nodded, "Yeah, I live at 46 Edgewater."

Hannah's jaw dropped. He was just a few doors down from her. She wasn't sure how she felt about that. She knew David was a good guy, he just didn't seem to have a very good opinion of her. Maybe this was her opportunity to change that.

She smiled. "Well, I guess that means we're neighbors then. Will you be going to the association meeting later today?"

"I'll be there." His cell phone buzzed, and he glanced down at it.

"I'll see you there then." Hannah scooted around him and went off to the next aisle.

DAVID STILL WASN'T SURE HOW HE FELT ABOUT HANNAH Keane. He'd been prepared to continue disliking her, especially as she'd stolen what he'd thought of as his house. But she'd actually been friendly at the hardware store. It was the most that she'd ever spoken to him. Especially now that his sister was married to Hannah's brother, he supposed he could try a little harder to get along with her. And they were likely to be running into each other more often.

He couldn't help noticing that she looked just as good, actually maybe even better than she had in high school. Hannah was petite and her long, wavy hair was so pretty and when she walked by him, he caught the faintest hint of something sweet like vanilla or sugar. But, he also knew it was best if he didn't notice those things and kept his distance from Hannah. He couldn't imagine that she was planning to stay long in Quinn Valley, and when she decided to move on, he'd be first in line for her house.

CHAPTER 4

B efore she made her way to the association
meeting, Hannah did an online yoga class. She
did yoga almost every day, usually one of the
Yoga by Adriene classes on YouTube. There was a huge
selection of them and today she did the one for anxiety
that she usually did on show days. It helped to calm her,
and she was nervous about this meeting. She wasn't sure
how many people would be there, but it was an odd
feeling to know that most would recognize her. She did
look forward to getting to know her neighbors though, so
the meeting was the best first step in doing that.

She showered after yoga and changed into her
favorite jeans and a pale blue sweater. At about ten of
three, she made her way to the clubhouse and took a deep
breath before she pushed open the door. She could hear
voices inside and about thirty faces turned toward her as
she walked in. Some were smiling and most looked curi-

ous. An older woman with a white chin-length bob and a friendly smile, came over to welcome her.

"Hello, I'm Jeannie Morgan. You must be our new neighbor?"

Hannah smiled and shook her hand. "Yes, I'm Hannah Keane. It's lovely to meet you."

Jeannie nodded. "I heard a rumor that you'd bought Estelle's place, but you never do know if these things are true. Follow me and I'll introduce you around."

Hannah shook many more hands as Jeannie introduced her to all the neighbors. She knew she'd never remember all the names, but she tried to pay close attention and everyone was friendly. She didn't see David yet, but people were still strolling in. She took a seat by Jeannie and just as they were about to call the meeting to order, David rushed in and sat in the back row. Hannah guessed there were about fifty residents in attendance and for the next forty-five minutes, the board of directors discussed old and new business.

It was typical association issues, should they try a new landscaper, did they budget enough for snow removal given that the winter forecast was stormier than the year before? Once the meeting adjourned, everyone helped themselves to fresh baked brownies and other snacks that were along a side table.

"So, what will you be doing here in Quinn Valley?" Allison, a pretty woman about Hannah's age asked. Like Missy she seemed baffled as to why Hannah would want to live in such a sleepy town.

"You're not retiring so soon?" Jeannie asked.

"No, just cutting way back on touring. I'm going to put some songwriting workshops and classes together. I thought maybe I could do something to help with the youth Center for the Arts, maybe a class possibly."

"Oh, that would be wonderful! David Quinn is the chair of our annual fundraising gala. Maybe you could perform. That would be quite a draw for ticket sales."

"I'm happy to help but I'm not sure about performing." The last thing Hannah wanted to do was to draw media attention to the fact that she was living in Quinn Valley.

David looked disappointed. "It really would help ticket sales considerably if you were able to perform even just a few songs. But, if you don't want to…."

A sea of expectant faces stared at her and Hannah felt her heart race. How could she explain to all these people about her stalker? She didn't want them to worry or worse yet feel unsafe in the neighborhood. And she was still pretty sure that it was nothing.

"I'm sure I can find a way to make it work for a few songs," she said.

David smiled. "That's great, Hannah. The kids will be excited and it is much appreciated."

David couldn't figure Hannah Keane out. For someone who said she was eager to help support the youth center, she'd been clearly reluctant to step up to perform. She'd agreed, but he could tell she wasn't keen on the idea. Maybe she was one of those people who preferred to write a check instead of getting involved. He'd be happy to take her check too, it was just surprising that she hadn't seemed more willing to sing a few songs. Most people were always thrilled to do it.

CHAPTER 5

You agreed to perform? I don't like it, Hannah."
Charlie frowned as he set down his glass of
wine. "It seems too soon and the whole point of
you being here was to keep a low profile so whoever has
been emailing you doesn't know where you are. You do
this and it puts a bulls-eye on the map."

"I'll talk to David," Maggie said. "He'll understand
why it's important that you don't do this. He just didn't
know."

Hannah reached for a slice of cheese. They were
sitting in her kitchen having some cheese and crackers
and enjoying a glass of red wine while the steaks were
resting after coming out of the oven. She was more
relaxed about her decision now.

"I'd rather that you don't say anything to him. I think
it will be fine. And it's too late to back out now. The cat's
out of the bag."

"What do you mean?" Maggie asked.

"Just that word is already out that I'm here. My manager messaged me about an hour ago. It's all over social media. Some neighborhood kids and parents too, have posted, and it's gone viral. So, since the world knows I'm here, there's no harm in helping out the kid's center with a few songs."

"Hmmm. I still don't like it," Charlie said. "I'll talk to David about having extra security."

"I'll have my manager send a few guys too. They're used to the drill now."

"They're at your concerts?" Maggie asked.

Hannah nodded. "Yeah, there's a security team that travels with us, in addition to whatever each venue provides."

"It's sad and scary that you have to worry about that." Maggie took a sip of her wine.

"It is," Hannah agreed. "There's a lot that goes into touring. I am looking forward to taking a break."

"Well, your house looks great. You've been busy this week," Maggie said as she looked around the room.

Hannah smiled. "Thanks. It's starting to feel like home now. My mother helped with some of the decorating, she's good at that."

"She is," Charlie agreed. "She rearranges things whenever she comes to visit me too, and it always looks better."

"Do they have any updates on your stalker?" Maggie's concern was evident.

"No. There's really not much they have to go on, just

a few anonymous emails. My gut tells me that it's nothing serious."

"Hopefully not," Charlie agreed. "But I wouldn't relax too much. There are a lot of nuts out there. Your security system is good?"

Hannah nodded. "Yes, I think so. I have cameras at the front and back door and sensors on all the downstairs windows."

"Is it hard to use? I'd be nervous I'd set off the alarm," Maggie admitted.

"It's actually really easy and I can control it from an app on my phone. But I have set it off twice so far. I've forgotten to turn it off when I go out. I've caught it immediately though. It's actually funny what the cameras pick up. They are very sensitive."

"Oh, like what?" Charlie asked.

"Cars that drive by, people walking their dog, even a spider spinning a web." Hannah jumped up to plate the steaks, and they brought their dinners to the large round table that had a gorgeous view of the lake.

"It's so peaceful here," Maggie said as she glanced out the window. A trio of sailboats looked like they were racing to the opposite end of the lake.

"It is. And there's always something to look at on the water. I do feel bad though. I didn't realize that David wanted this house too."

Maggie seemed surprised. "He did? Did he tell you that?"

Hannah nodded. "He asked me how I managed to find out about it before the listing hit the market."

Maggie raised her eyebrows. "How did you?"

"Your grandmother put me in touch with Missy. She knew it was coming on the market evidently."

"How interesting. My grandmother seems to know everything that goes on around here. I don't think she knew that David wanted this house though. It makes sense that he would though. He probably wanted it for the private dock."

"He mentioned that he keeps his boat trailered in his yard," Hannah said.

"He's always asking me to go fishing with him," Charlie said. "I like to fish now and then, but David goes almost every weekend it seems."

"I've never gone fishing. I'd love to try it though. I was thinking about getting a small boat too, so I could zip around the lake." Hannah noticed that Charlie and Maggie glanced at each other and then Charlie smiled.

"That's a great idea," he said. "I'd be happy to help you look for one. I can ask around too and see if anyone knows of any for sale. A used one might be a better deal. Not that you need to worry about the money."

Hannah laughed. "No, but I still like a good deal. I'd love your help."

CHAPTER 6

David stopped by Quinn's pub for a burger after work and was glad to see that Charlie was there too, sitting at the bar chatting with Maggie. David slid into the chair next to Charlie and watched as Maggie made one of Quinn's signature drinks for a customer.

She spread a generous amount of marshmallow fluff around the rim of a giant martini glass, dipped the rim in a dish of crushed graham crackers, then used a small crème brûlée torch to brown the marshmallow. A moment later she poured in the freshly made cocktail and gave it to Tina, one of the new waitresses, to deliver to her table.

"I'd never in a million years drink that, but you make it look good," David said as Maggie set a cold draft beer in front of him.

She smiled. "Your usual? Bacon burger, no cheese, crispy bacon?"

"Yes, please!"

"That sounds good. I'll have the same," Charlie said.

Maggie went off to put in their orders as David glanced around the bar. The restaurant was busy, but the bar wasn't too crowded. David knew it would get busy later when team trivia started though.

He and Charlie chatted about business while Maggie worked. They shared a lot of the same customers. David supplied them with their food and supplies while Charlie kept the bars stocked with all the in demand wine, beer and liquor. Eventually, their discussion turned to plans for the weekend.

"You up for some fishing this Saturday?" David asked Charlie. "I haven't been for a few weeks, so want to get out there first thing."

Maggie walked over with their burgers as David finished talking and exchanged glances with Charlie as she set their food down.

"I'm busy this weekend, but my sister Hannah mentioned the other night that she's never been fishing and wants to try it."

The idea of teaching Hannah how to fish both intrigued him and put him off at the same time.

"I'm not sure that Hannah would welcome fishing lessons from me. She didn't exactly seem enthused about singing to help the kid's center out. She actually said no at first."

"There's something most people don't know about Hannah," Charlie began. "She's actually very shy. She gets crippling stage fright before every performance."

"I didn't know that. Is that why she's stopped touring?" It made sense, if it was. And it would explain why she was back in Quinn Valley. Maybe Hannah would be sticking around longer than he thought.

"Yeah, that's part of the reason." Again, Charlie and Maggie seemed to exchange glances. Their eyes met and something unspoken passed between them.

"She told me that she's ready for a break. She might do an occasional show but not a heavy schedule like she used to," Maggie said. She reached under the counter and pulled out a new bottle of ketchup and set it in front of David. He'd just been about to ask for it.

"You're a mind reader." He opened the bottle and dumped a pile of ketchup on his plate.

"She had no idea that you wanted that house," Maggie added. "I'm surprised that Gram didn't tell you about it. Did she know you were interested?"

"In that house? I don't think I ever mentioned it to her. I'm sure if I did she would have given me a heads up, right?" Their grandmother was quirky but David knew she adored her many grandchildren.

Maggie looked thoughtful. "Right. I'm sure she would have. I'm actually glad that you're living close by though, for Hannah's sake." There was something in Maggie's tone that seemed a bit off.

"What do you mean, for Hannah's sake?"

"Just that it's bound to be an adjustment for her, after living in Nashville where things are livelier and from being on the road so much these past few years."

"Yeah, I can't imagine Quinn Valley is going to offer

the excitement that she's used to. She'll probably head back to Nashville or Hollywood. Maybe if I'm nice to her, she'll sell me the house when she goes," he joked.

"I wouldn't hold your breath on that," Charlie said. "You don't know Hannah. She's not a big city type. Quinn Valley is much more her speed. I think she wants to put down roots."

David frowned. That wasn't what he'd hoped to hear. He still wasn't convinced that it was true. The Hannah he thought he knew seemed as though she wanted to be anywhere but near him, or Quinn Valley. After living in Nashville, she was bound to be disappointed.

"Davidd, do you have a minute?" Sabrina, his assistant, stood in the doorway of his office looking perplexed and a bit stressed.

"Sure, come on in." It was a week after the association meeting and as usual, David was in his office early. Sabrina usually arrived a little after eight and checked in with him once she was settled at her desk with her morning coffee. She brought her coffee mug into his office and sat in one of the two leather chairs across from his desk.

"I just checked the numbers for the charity event. I probably should have checked them sooner. I just never expected this." She chewed her bottom lip as David waited for her to continue. She took a deep breath and went on. "We're almost completely sold out. It's because of Hannah. We've never sold even half this many tickets for past events." Sabrina was handling all the administrative work that went along with coordinating the charity event for the children's center.

"Really? Well, that's good right?"

"Yes, but, well, if you're able to change the venue, we might be able to raise even more money. The bulk of the sales came in yesterday as word is getting out that Hannah is performing. I predict that by lunch today, every ticket will be sold."

David mulled that over for a minute. The event was scheduled to be held at Quinn's Hotel, the family run business that was the largest hotel in the area. As they always did, the Quinn's had donated the space. So, it wouldn't be an issue if David found somewhere else, somewhere bigger to hold the event. But was it possible to switch things at this late date? The show was scheduled for two weeks out. And would Hannah even agree to do it? Singing locally in front of a small crowd was one thing, but at a bigger venue? It was exactly what she was trying to stop doing.

But, the difference in funds raised for the center could be significant. He supposed it wouldn't hurt to make a few calls and see if another venue was even possible.

"Thanks, Sabrina. Let me get back to you on that. I'll need to investigate what other options we have, and if Hannah will even consider moving venues."

Sabrina nodded and stood. "Okay, let me know what you find out. And good luck."

When she left the office, David checked the date on his calendar. He wasn't sure, but it didn't seem like a date that would be in high demand. An ex-girlfriend handled bookings for the Lewiston arena, which was the biggest venue in the area. Maybe too big. He didn't know if Hannah would go for it, but he figured it didn't hurt to see if it might be available.

Stacy answered on the first ring.

"Well, this is a surprise! How are you David? It's been a long time." Her voice was amused and intrigued. He could picture her as she spoke. Stacy was always so well put together, with her sleek blonde hair pulled into a low ponytail, stylish glasses and elegant clothes. She was a pretty girl, and they'd dated for a few months. He'd enjoyed Stacy's company, but they were both busy people and eventually seemed too busy to get together. They'd laughed about it at the time as both realized that if it had really mattered, they would have somehow found the time. In many ways, they were very much alike.

"I'm good, Stacy. How are things with you?"

She laughed. "Busy as usual, but somehow I managed to get engaged. Rick's a great guy. He's an attorney here."

He smiled. "I'm happy for you. He's a lucky guy."

Her voice softened. "Thanks, David. That's nice of you to say. What about you, has anyone captured your heart yet?"

"Not yet. Not fast enough for my mother, anyway."

"I can imagine. So, what can I help you with?"

"I have a favor to ask. It's a long shot as I doubt the date is even available, but if by any chance it is...here's the situation." He told her about the event and that Hannah was singing. When he finished, Stacy was quiet for a minute.

"Hold on a sec. Let me check the booking calendar." He heard the clacking of keys as she typed on her computer keyboard.

"Well, you're in luck. We had that date booked for almost a year, but the group had to reschedule just a week ago and it's free now. It's yours, if you want it." They discussed the particulars and David said he'd be back to her to confirm as soon as he connected with Hannah.

He decided to go home at lunch, and to stop by Hannah's house after. Something told him the conversation needed to be in person. It would be too easy for her to say no over the phone.

He inhaled a quick sandwich at his house, then walked a few doors down to Hannah's place. Her car was in the driveway, so he was pretty sure that she was home. He knocked on the door and rang the doorbell. He also noticed a small camera above the door and wondered if Hannah was checking to see who was at the door before she answered it. He hoped so.

A minute later, the door opened slowly and Hannah stood there in bare feet, old jeans and a faded blue college sweatshirt. Her hair was gathered on top of her head in a messy bun and she was wearing thick glasses instead of her usual contacts. She looked adorable and a bit confused when she saw him.

"Hi David, is everything okay?"

He smiled. "It's fine. I just came home for lunch and there's something I needed to talk to you about. I thought it might be easier to stop by if you were home. Do you have a minute?"

"Um, sure. Come on in." She opened the door wide and he stepped in and followed her to the kitchen where he saw a plate of cookies and a mug of hot tea.

"I hope I didn't interrupt your lunch?"

She laughed. "You didn't. Unless you call cookies lunch, which I guess maybe it is now that I think about it."

"I like that. Cookies for lunch. You must have a sweet tooth?"

"Guilty. Want one? I baked them yesterday. Peanut butter chocolate chip."

"Sure. That sounds good." She handed him the plate and he took a cookie and bit into it. "I can see why you'd want to make a meal out of these. This is delicious."

Hannah looked pleased with the compliment. "Thank you. So, what is it that you wanted to talk about?"

"I have some good news and some maybe not so good news, depending what you think that is. The good news is our ticket sales for this event have never been so good, thanks to you."

"Oh, that's wonderful news!"

"It is," he agreed. "But we have an interesting problem. As of eleven today, we sold our last ticket. And the demand is still really strong. Sabrina has been fielding calls from people looking for tickets. If we were to move to a bigger venue, we could probably sell more tickets and raise a lot more money for the center." He paused to see how she'd react.

"Oh, wow. Well, it would be impossible to get a bigger venue on such short notice I would think."

"Ordinarily it would be. But I'm friends with the booking coordinator at the Lewiston arena and they could do it. The date's available thanks to a cancellation. But, I didn't want to say yes until I checked with you, to see if you'd be okay with a bigger venue. I know you said you were looking to cut back on that kind of thing."

A look of something, surprise maybe, flashed across Hannah's face.

"How big is the arena?" She asked.

He told her and her jaw dropped.

"That's pretty big," she said slowly. "You really think you could sell enough tickets for it to be worthwhile?"

He nodded. "I do. The phone has been ringing off the hook, Hannah. Now that word is out that you're singing."

She was quiet for a long moment and then finally said, "Okay, I'll do it. Since it's for a good cause."

She seemed hesitant though and David felt a little guilty. He didn't want her to feel forced into doing something.

"Are you sure? I heard that you're somewhat introverted and that you get nervous in front of crowds."

She nodded. "It's true. I almost feel like throwing up before I go on stage—every single time, and the bigger the venue, the worst it is. But once I start singing, it all fades away. I really would like to help."

She sounded sincere and determined and David appreciated it.

"Thank you. It will mean so much to the center and the kids." He glanced out the window and saw the dock in the distance and the large back deck. Hannah followed his gaze.

"It's a gorgeous day out. Warm for this kind of year, do you want to walk out on the deck for a minute?"

"I'd love that." He followed her outside and to the end of the expansive deck which led down to the dock. The air was so still that the water barely rippled in the slight breeze. A small boat motored by and got Hannah's attention. She looked closely at it as it went by, then turned to David.

"Charlie is going to help me find a small boat. I'm dying to get out there myself and maybe even try fishing. It looks so relaxing and fun."

"It is. What are you doing this Saturday? I want to go fishing and it's always more fun with company. I'd be happy to teach you how to fish. It's the least I can do since you agreed to sing at the new venue." He grinned and found himself holding his breath as he waited for her to decide.

"This Saturday? Ok, I can do that. I look forward to it."

He grinned. "Great, I'll be by around nine or so, if that's not too early?"

"It's not too early. I'll see you then. Oh, and I'd like to see the venue this week if possible too, just so I can check out where everything is and prepare for it."

"Of course. Maybe tomorrow end of day I can run you over there and we can get a good look at the stage and the function rooms?"

"Perfect."

CHAPTER 8

Hannah changed outfits three times the next day, trying to find just the right thing to wear. She reminded herself that it was ridiculous as this was not a date. Just a meeting to check out the Lewiston arena. But still, she had that nervous feeling one sometimes got on a first date. Which was so silly. She knew this, yet still couldn't decide what to wear. And she took extra care with her hair, curling it into long, loose curls that spiraled down to the middle of her back.

At a quarter past five, she heard David's truck pull into her driveway and the alarm company app on her phone showed her the live camera footage of David standing outside her front door. She turned off the alarm and opened the door, grabbing her purse and jacket.

"Hey, there. Are you ready to go?" David asked when he saw her.

"I'm ready." She followed to his truck and was impressed that he politely opened her door for her. She climbed into the passenger side and settled on the soft leather seat. David hopped in and they were on their way.

Lewiston was just under an hour away and they chatted and listened to Hannah's favorite local country music station. She was pleasantly surprised when one of her songs came on and David sang along on the chorus.

"You like this one?" She somehow hadn't pictured David liking her music.

He laughed. "Are you serious? Everyone likes your music, Hannah. I have your latest CD. I think Maggie does too."

"I'm still not used to that. To people actually recognizing my music. I should be, I guess."

He glanced her way and smiled. "Yes, you should be. Will you still be making new music?"

"Yes. I hope so. I'm excited to focus on writing for a while, instead of performing. And teaching. I'm really looking forward to that."

"What will you teach? Singing?"

"No, I'm not a vocal coach. I'm planning to offer some workshops on songwriting and maybe work with kids at the center who might want to learn how to do that."

"I think that's a great idea and an incredible opportunity for them." He sounded so complimentary and sincere that Hannah felt herself blush.

"Thank you. I'd just like to be able to give back a little. I was fortunate to have some wonderful teachers that encouraged me when I was younger."

"That is so important," David agreed. "I had the

same, though not for music. I had a few teachers in high
school and college that nurtured my interest in business.
And of course it started with the family business, Quinn's
Pub."

"You weren't interested in taking over the pub, with
Ryder and Maggie?" Hannah was curious about that.

"No. That's their thing. I was always more interested
in the big picture of running the restaurant and where
everything came from. They worked with a few suppliers
that weren't great and I had ideas on how things could be
done better."

"And you were right. I hear your business is doing
great."

"It's doing ok," he admitted. "I enjoy it."

Hannah smiled. She knew from what Maggie had
proudly said, that David's company had grown to be the
top restaurant supplier in the region. He'd done very well
for himself and he clearly loved the work. She was happy
for him. She knew how lucky she'd been to earn a living
doing what she loved.

Another song came on that they both knew and they
sang along to that and a few more as they drove along.
Before she knew it, they were at the arena. David led her
in and introduced her to his friend Stacy, who was beautiful. Hannah sensed something, a certain familiarity
between David and Stacy, who seemed happy to see him.
But she also noticed that Stacy was wearing a gorgeous
engagement ring and chatted about her fiancé and their
upcoming wedding as she showed them around.

It was a very large venue. Bigger than Hannah would

have expected for Idaho, but Lewiston was a growing city. It just hadn't been on any of her tour schedules. Everything looked good though. She would forward the information to her security team and they'd do a check as well a few days before the performance.

"I'm so excited that you're going to do a show here," Stacy said as they walked out. "I'm actually a huge fan, and this is such a great cause. Rick and I are going to get tickets."

"We can give you complimentary tickets," David immediately said but Stacy shook her head. "That wouldn't feel right. I want to contribute to a good cause."

He grinned. "All right then. We will happily take your money."

The ride back to Quinn Valley seemed to fly by as they chatted easily. Hannah was happy to discover that David was surprisingly easy to talk to. He seemed to enjoy the conversation too.

"I have to admit, I was wrong about you," David said after they sang along to a Blake Shelton song that they both loved.

"What do you mean?"

"I had it in my head that you were stuck up, snooty and didn't want to have anything to do with the likes of me. That goes back to high school though, a long time ago."

Hannah sighed. "I understand why you thought that. I'm sorry that I gave you that impression. I was always painfully shy. I'd freeze up when people talked to me sometimes. They'd think I was rude or stuck up and it was just nerves. It took me a while to find my voice."

"You mean you weren't just disgusted when I asked you out? I have to admit, it crushed me a little."

"It wasn't you at all. It was just me being shy. By the time I found my voice, you were gone."

"Really? You mean if I'd stuck around, you might have said yes?"

"I might have."

"Well, isn't that something?"

They were both quiet for a moment, listening to a slow song about love lost and found again, that came on the radio. When they reached Quinn Valley, Hannah was mortified when her stomach growled loudly. But David just laughed.

"I'm hungry too. Do you want to grab a bite somewhere? Or I actually have a cooler in the back with some steak samples from one of my vendors. We could cook them up at my place or yours?"

"That sounds good. I have some mashed potatoes we could have and salad too."

"Perfect. I'm not much of a cook, but I have mastered cooking steak on the stovetop. Secret is to baste it in butter."

Hannah laughed. "Butter makes everything taste better."

"Do you like red wine? I think I have a bottle of cabernet too. Charlie actually gave it to me the other day and I forgot to bring it in."

"I love Cabernet."

CHAPTER 9

D avid was feeling something he hadn't felt in a long time, a magnetic pull towards someone and a hint of uncertainty as to whether they felt it too. He was encouraged by what Hannah had said. Blown away by it actually. To learn that she hadn't rejected him in high school and that she might even have said yes, if he'd been just a little more patient. It was quite a revelation.

But high school was many years ago and now Hannah was a superstar, way out of his league. Was he imagining that there was some kind of vibe there on her side too? It was too soon to know, but he was definitely intrigued by what he'd learned and what he was feeling. Most of the women he'd dated made it very clear that they were interested, but he was never sure if the interest was in him, or his company.

David wasn't a billionaire, but he was well off and

326   PAMELA M. KELLEY

successful, especially for someone his age. He smiled
thinking of his sister Maggie and how she often reminded
him that he was a 'catch' and that he needed to be super
picky to find someone that really loved him. He appreciated her concern, but it hadn't really been an issue
because David wasn't actively looking. He'd been happy
to focus on work and date lots of interesting women and
see where things went. He liked to keep it light and so far,
he hadn't met anyone that he'd wanted to get more
serious with. He wasn't at all sure of his feelings for
Hannah, but he was interested in exploring them, if
she was.

"Are you sure you don't mind cooking?" Hannah
asked when they reached her fancy stove in the kitchen. "I
could put the steaks in the oven," she offered.

He laughed at the thought. "I don't mind at all. Once
you've had my butter basted steak, you'll never cook them
in the oven again."

"Okay then. What can I do to help?"

"You could open the wine and pour us each a glass."

He handed her the bottle. It was a very good Cabernet. Charlie had excellent taste of course and knew his
wines. She got a saute pan out for him and a stick of
butter. While he started melting it in the pan, she
opened the wine and poured two glasses and handed
one to him.

She took a sip and closed her eyes for a moment,

savoring the taste. "I haven't had this one before. It's good. Really good."

David took a quick sip and agreed. "It's excellent."

Hannah watched as he swirled butter in the pan and then added the steaks. While they cooked, she tossed a salad together and heated up some leftover mashed potatoes. The steaks didn't take long, and once they were done, David set each on a plate and drizzled the buttery sauce over it. They helped themselves to the mashed potatoes and salad and brought their plates to her kitchen table.

It was still light out, but the sun was getting ready to set and as they ate, they watched it slip out of sight, leaving a breath-taking rosy pink sky.

"The views from here are incredible," David said.

"They really are. And your steak is too. I never would have thought to cook it like that on the stove."

He smiled, pleased with the compliment. "Thanks. It's a trick I learned from my mother actually, growing up working in the restaurant."

"She used to do most of the cooking there?"

"All the cooking. My parents started the restaurant together. My father was the business side of it and my mother handled the food. She's an amazing cook."

"She's retired now?" Hannah knew that David's father had died of a heart attack ten or so years go.

"She is. I think it was hard for my mother to be there after my father died. She stayed on until a few years ago though. Ryder and Maggie bought it from her and now she's doing whatever she feels like. Most days that means she stops by Quinn's in the morning to have coffee and visit before the day gets started."

"Is she dating someone now? I thought I saw her with someone last week at the coffee shop downtown."

"She is. An old boyfriend looked her up not too long ago and they've been pretty much inseparable since. He seems like a decent guy and she's really happy, so it's all good."

"Oh, that's wonderful. And what about you?"

He smiled slowly and it took her breath away when his eyes met hers. There was a hint of amusement and something else there. "What about me?" he said.

"Is there anyone special in your life?" She felt rather forward asking, but she was curious to know.

"No, there's no one now. What about you?"

"Me? No, no one. I've been too busy touring. My last relationship didn't last because of it."

He nodded. "I can imagine that must be hard unless the person toured with you, which most couldn't do."

"Right." She suddenly felt self-conscious talking about her dating status and changed the subject as she got up to clear their plates. "Do you feel like a little dessert? I have some fresh strawberries and whipped cream. No short-cake though." The berries were really ripe and delicious.

"Sure. There's always room for something sweet."

Hannah put the dishes in the sink to deal with later and got the strawberries out of the refrigerator, along with a can of whipped cream. She filled two dishes and handed David the whipped cream to add however much he liked.

They were just about done eating and Hannah was thinking what a perfectly lovely night it had been, when her phone dinged to announce a new email message. She glanced at it as she brought their bowls to the sink and had to grip the kitchen counter to steady herself as she reread the message.

"HANNAH, WHAT IS IT? ARE YOU OKAY?" DAVID couldn't help but notice that Hannah's face had lost all color as she read something on her phone. And that a mask slipped over her face when he asked the question. She turned to face him and smiled as if everything was perfectly normal.

"Oh, it's nothing. I misread something, that's all." She yawned as she rinsed the bowl and David took that as his cue to leave. He stood and walked over to her.

"This was fun. Thanks for checking out the venue with me and for sharing dinner." He wanted to pull her into his arms and brush the hair off her face and ease the worry that he saw there. He didn't know what was troubling her, but it was pretty clear to him that something was. The vibe that he'd felt earlier was gone and he wasn't sure if he'd imagined it or not earlier.

"It was fun," she agreed. "Thanks for bringing the steaks and the wine."

"Anytime. Are you still up for fishing on Saturday?" He hoped that she'd been serious about wanting to learn.

"Yes, I'm looking forward to it." She walked him to

the door and he noticed that as soon as he stepped outside and she closed the door, that he almost immediately heard a computerized voice say, 'Armed stay', meaning her house alarm had been activated. He wondered again what it was that had made her so jumpy.

CHAPTER 10

Hannah woke earlier than usual Saturday morning. She was excited and a bit nervous about her fishing lesson. She'd sensed something from David at dinner, a fleeting hint of interest that she wasn't sure was real. Maybe it was just wishful thinking on her part. She'd always found David Quinn very attractive. He was tall, and handsome with dark hair and piercing blue eyes that seemed to notice everything. He was smart and successful and was close to his siblings and his mother. So, if she was looking—he ticked all of her boxes. And when he'd stopped being a grouch, he was surprisingly fun to be around. Their ride to Lewiston and back had flown by as they'd laughed and sung along with the radio. It was easy to be with him, when she wasn't thinking about how attractive he was.

When she thought about him as a potential boyfriend though, she felt a confusing mix of emotions ranging from excitement to apprehension. She also knew that

David didn't have a great track record in that he'd never had a very serious relationship. And Hannah wasn't interested in anything casual. It was common in her industry for people to have flings on the road, but the thought of it made her shudder. It just wasn't how she was wired. She cared too much, felt too deeply and hurt too easily. So, all of her protective senses were warning her to keep David as a friend and not to cross that line because she knew how easy it would be to fall fast if she did.

So, she chose something that was more practical than cute. A pair of old jeans, rubber heeled shoes so she wouldn't slip on the boat, and a long-sleeved pink t-shirt with a navy fleece pullover. The air was cool when she stepped out on the deck, but she knew the sun would warm it up quickly and she'd be glad for the layers. She sipped her coffee and nibbled on some toast while she waited for David to arrive. And she dabbed a bit of sunscreen on her nose and found a baseball cap to keep the sun off her face. When she caught a glimpse of herself in the hallway mirror she laughed. Her hair was in a ponytail and with the hat on, she almost looked college aged.

She was just putting her empty coffee mug in the dishwasher when the front doorbell rang. A glance at the camera on her cell phone confirmed that David was waiting outside. She used her phone app to turn off the alarm system and went to let him in. When she opened the front door, she saw that his truck was parked out front and the boat trailer and boat attached to the back.

He grinned. "Are you ready to go?"

"As ready as I'll ever be." She locked the door behind her and followed him to his truck. Once they were both in, he backed it down the boat ramp, then jumped out to crank the boat into the water and tied it to a post. Hannah waited nearby while he moved his truck back to the house.

He jogged over a few minutes later and helped her to climb into the boat, then untied it and hopped in himself. She noticed that there was a cooler on the boat and several fishing poles laying next to it. The boat was a sleek Boston Whaler, with two bucket seats up front and two benches in the back. She guessed that it could hold up to six people.

David backed the boat up slowly, then turned it around and headed out into the lake. It was early enough that there was little boat traffic aside from a few others out fishing. They waved as they passed the other boats and about ten minutes later, David slowed the engine and they drifted into a cove of sorts. It was a quiet spot with no visible homes in the area just lots of woods.

"Is this a tested spot?" She teased him.

He laughed. "Yes. This is one of my favorites. I've had the best luck here recently."

She watched as he got everything ready. He pulled out a small radio and set it on a built-in table.

"Are you thirsty?" He reached into the cooler and pulled out two bottled waters.

"No, not yet, thanks." He put one back and opened the other, then set it on the table by the radio.

"Do you want to find us a good station?"

She flipped through the stations until she found one that came in and had some good music playing. Meanwhile David opened his tackle box and pulled out two lures. One was a bright pink, the other a reddish orange.

"These are my favorite spinners, the Yakima Bait Wordens original Rooster Tail. Which color do you want?" The two lures had fluffy tails and were identical, the only difference was the color.

"I'll take the pink one."

David showed her how to attach the lure to the fishing rod and demonstrated with his own pole how to cast it out into the water.

"Want to give it a try?"

"Sure." She grabbed hold of the pole and carefully swung it so that the line cast out over the water. When it splashed in a few feet away from David's she breathed a sigh of relief. She'd done it!

"Nice job! You sure you haven't done this before?" He teased her.

She laughed. "So, now what do we do?"

"Now we wait. When you get something on the line, you'll feel it move and then we reel it in. If we're lucky, we'll land a trout or two and eat well for dinner."

"Is that mostly what you catch here?" She'd wondered about that.

He nodded. "With these lures it's mostly rainbow trout. There's large-mouth bass around but I use different lures for those. I prefer to catch trout. It's my favorite eating fish."

"How long does it usually take to catch one?"

Hannah knew that her brother was often gone for hours when he went fishing.

"It's hard to say. Sometimes it's hours and we catch nothing. Other times they're biting right away. If we don't have any luck here, we'll try another spot further down."

Just ten minutes later, Hannah felt a tug on her line and got excited. She stood and looked at David for guidance.

"Slowly reel it in and hold on tight. Some of these fish are strong. If you let go, you could lose your pole."

Hannah did as he said. She held on and excitedly reeled the line in. She held her breath as the lure flew up and out of the water, but instead of a fish on the other end, it was a leather sandal that was tangled in the lure. She laughed when it flopped onto the boat. David grabbed it and untangled it from the line and tossed it back over the side of the boat, on the opposite side.

"False alarm," he said and grinned. "I forgot to mention that sometimes you catch other things. Cast it over again."

She did and settled back down. They stayed like that for well over an hour with neither pole budging. It was relaxing though, drifting along, listening to the radio and basking in the warmth of the sun. After a while, it got so warm that Hannah took off her sweatshirt and David did the same. She almost fell asleep at one point as her eyes grew heavy with the sun shining down and the soothing sound of the water lapping against the side of the boat.

But then sudden movement from David jerked her

wide awake and she opened her eyes to see him standing and excitedly reeling his line in.

"Hopefully it's not another sandal," he said and she laughed as a wriggling fish flew into the air, then landed with a splat in the back of the boat. She was surprised to see David carefully remove the lure from the fish and then gently toss it back into the water.

"It was too small to keep," he explained. "Do you want to reel yours in? Let's try our luck at that other spot I mentioned."

She did and they traveled for another fifteen minutes or so, to the opposite side of the lake. There were two other boats in the area, which David explained was a good sign that the fish might be there too. They cast their lines out again and Hannah grabbed the water that she wasn't ready for before. She noticed two sandwiches in the cooler and a big bag of potato ships.

"I figured we'd be out here for lunch, so I packed turkey sandwiches for us. I hope you like turkey?"

"That sounds great."

Once they were settled, David handed her one of the sandwiches and set the big bag of chips between them. They munched happily and waited for the fish to bite. Hannah wondered what it was that David enjoyed so much about fishing. It was a little slow and somewhat boring to her, but it was nice to just be out and on the water, relaxing in the sun.

"I'd like to say that it's usually more exciting than this," David began. "But it's not. This is a pretty typical day. I just like being out on the water either hanging with a friend or just relaxing and getting my mind off work."

"It is relaxing out here. I can see why you enjoy it."

David laughed. "You're being polite. You think it's boring. I can tell."

"I wouldn't exactly say boring. Relaxing is a good word. I really do get it. Sometimes it's just nice to be alone and think or not think at all and let your mind drift. Do you ever fall asleep out here? I almost did, until you caught that fish," she admitted.

"Sometimes. A tug on the line always wakes me up though."

Hannah finished her sandwich and a healthy amount of chips and stretched, feeling full and almost ready for another nap.

"I have some iced coffee in the cooler too, if you need a little pick me up." It was almost as if he'd read her mind. She didn't really want to fall asleep in front of David.

"Do you want some? I'm going to have a little." She found the thermos of coffee and opened it.

"Sure. I'll take a splash."

She poured them both a half cup and added a little cream and sugar to hers. David drank his totally black.

"So, how did you get discovered? Did you always know you wanted to sing?" David asked as he leaned back and sipped his coffee.

"No. I never really wanted to perform. But I always loved music and have been writing songs for as long as I can remember. I took piano lessons first, when I was about seven and the teacher said I had a natural ear for music and perfect pitch. I could hear something on the radio and then sit down and play it almost perfectly."

"That's impressive." He grinned. "I'm pretty much tone deaf. But I sound fantastic in the shower. At least I think so."

She laughed. "Everyone else in my family is tone deaf too. I'm not sure where I got it from."

"So, did you go to Nashville right after graduating college?"

"No, I actually went to Hollywood first. My roommate was a theater major and wanted to get into TV or film and I wasn't ready to go to Nashville by myself so I went with her. I started playing open mic nights there because it was the only way to get attention to my songs, and a few months later, a record producer from Nashville was at one of my sets and he liked what he heard."

"Did he offer you a record deal?"

"He invited me to come to Nashville to create a demo tape that he could show to his bosses. I explained to him that my real interest was writing not performing, but he said my voice was a big part of his interest and he thought his bosses would agree. And they did. They offered me a deal and we put together a full collection of songs and I moved to Nashville and started playing whenever I could get a booking around town. Once my album started getting radio play, things went a little crazy."

"I think I remember that." David started singing the opening verse to her first hit single and she couldn't help laughing. He wasn't kidding when he said he couldn't hold a tune. He was totally off key but his enthusiasm was endearing. When they'd sung together in the car with the radio playing, she hadn't noticed how bad he was.

"I can't believe you know that song and know all the words."

"It's a good song. I can see why it was so popular. Do you write all of your songs?"

"Most of them, yes. Though now and then someone brings me a song and if I like it, I'll do it. There are a lot of talented writers out there. What about you? Tell me more about your business."

"Well, it's not nearly as exciting as what you do, but I enjoy it. There's about thirty or so people in the company now. We have a big warehouse on the Riston line and trucks and drivers that cover the whole region. We mostly serve smaller restaurants and pizza shops. I really like the buying part the most, getting a really good deal on cheese for instance and buying up a bunch of it, betting on the market not going lower."

"Like cheese futures."

"Exactly. The prices fluctuate and I've had customers quit me over a five cent difference in cheese. That doesn't happen as much now."

"And you love it." It was a statement, not a question. David's passion for his business was clear when he spoke about it.

"I do. It's been fun building the company. I'm lucky to enjoy what I do. I'm sure you feel the same way?"

"I do, usually." She grew quiet for a minute, thinking

of the stalker but David assumed she just meant she was tired.

"It must be hard to travel so much, being on the road for weeks or months at a time?"

She smiled. "Some people really love it. But I'm more of a homebody. I like to be home creating the music more than out performing it. I've actually been selling more of my songs recently and having other people perform them."

"Is that strange? To see someone else singing your words?"

"Not really. It's actually pretty wonderful to see them bring it to life and to put their own spin on it." She jumped as she suddenly felt a tug on her line and the pole dipped. She grabbed it tightly and reeled the line in. She was half-expecting another sandal or something other than a fish and was thrilled to see what looked like a big trout fly into the air and then land on the boat. She felt bad as it struggled though and was somewhat relieved when David said her fish was too small too, by only a half inch, and he tossed it back over the side. As much as she enjoyed eating fish, she didn't like seeing them in pain.

They continued to fish for another hour and just when they were about to call it quits and head in, David's pole started jumping and he reeled in what looked like a huge trout to Hannah.

"Is that one a keeper?" She asked once he got it free from the line.

"It is. I'm going to put it out of its misery now, so it won't suffer while we transport it back."

Hannah turned, so she didn't have to see how David was going to do that to the fish. She liked that he said it would be quick so the fish wouldn't suffer. She couldn't help feeling a little guilty though.

"You can turn around now. And don't feel guilty. It's a natural thing to eat fish," he assured her.

"I know. It's just different to see it up close." She grinned. "I'm used to having it arrive on my plate, fully cooked."

"Well, if you don't have plans tonight, I can make that happen. I'm pretty good at grilling fish and there's plenty here."

"I don't have plans tonight," she said.

"Good. Why don't you stop over around six then?"

Hannah agreed and they made their way back to the neighborhood dock. As David was about to pull the boat up, Hannah had a better idea.

"You're welcome to tie it up on my dock. There's room for several boats there and at the moment, I don't have any."

He looked at her uncertainly, "Are you sure? I don't want to impose."

"You're not. Really. It's the least I can do since I stole your house." She grinned and he laughed.

"All right. I'll tie up there for now. But feel free to tell me to take it back anytime."

He pulled the boat up to the dock, jumped out and tied it securely to the pier.

He held out his hand to help Hannah out of the boat and she felt a tingle when their hands touched. She wondered if he felt it too. He didn't show any reaction, so she just smiled and thanked him again and asked what she could bring for dinner.

"I don't really need anything, just come over."

"I have to bring something. How about a bottle of red wine?"

"I won't say no to that."

D avid put the fish in his refrigerator, jumped in the shower and then headed to the supermarket. He'd invited Hannah for dinner and he didn't have much else in the house besides fish. And it had been a very long time since he'd cooked for anyone, especially a girl. He didn't want to screw it up. As he walked into the market, he decided to consult an expert. Maggie answered on the first ring.

"Hey! What are you up to?"

"I'm at the market and I need your advice. Are you busy?" It was a little past four, kind of an in between time for the restaurant.

"Not yet. I'm just cutting fruit and getting ready for tonight."

"Okay, so I went fishing with Hannah today and she's coming over tonight to eat what we caught. I'm planning to grill the fish, what else should I do?"

"Hannah's coming for dinner? That's great. Hmmm,

why don't you grab a bag of those little new potatoes, slice them in half, toss with some olive oil, salt and pepper, wrap in tin foil and let them cook on the grill along with the fish. Do the same with some asparagus, just add a little lemon and parmesan."

"I think I can manage that. What about dessert?"

"Go to the bakery and find something chocolatey. Every girl likes chocolate."

"Got it. Thanks, Mags."

"Anytime. Tell Hannah I said hi. And don't worry. You've got this."

David smiled as he hung up the phone. He could always count on his sister. Maggie didn't ask any uncomfortable questions, she just gave him the information he needed and wished him well. He loved that about her.

He quickly found everything he needed and got everything prepped and ready to go so that when Hannah arrived, he could throw it all on the grill. He was surprised to find that he was a little nervous too. He couldn't remember the last time he'd felt like this around a girl. He knew that it was partly because he couldn't get a good read on Hannah. She was pleasant enough and she seemed to have a good time out on the boat, but he couldn't tell if she was interested in him, that way. He hoped that he'd find out soon.

———

"CHARLIE, I NEED YOUR EXPERTISE. WHAT KIND OF WINE would you recommend with grilled trout?"

"Hmm, well the obvious choice would be a crisp Sauvignon Blanc, but I know you're more of a red wine drinker. A light pinot noir would go nice too or a Beaujolais, just go easy on the lemon."

"I was wondering if Pinot Noir might work. Thanks, Charlie."

"Did you catch this fish?" Her brother asked.

"No, mine was too small. David caught one that was big enough."

"And you're cooking it?"

"No, he is. I'm heading to his house soon and wanted to bring some wine."

"Interesting. Is there a love connection here?" He asked.

"With David? I don't think it's like that. We're just friends. I'm glad we're getting along, finally."

"Hmmm. Yeah, things were a little prickly with the two of you at the charity event. I'm glad that it's better now. David's a good guy."

"Thanks, Charlie. I'll see you at Mom's tomorrow for brunch?"

"Wouldn't miss it." Their mother often had them over on Sunday mornings to catch up.

Hannah went to the local wine shop, and chose a bottle of her favorite pinot noir, Belle Glos. When she got home, she took a long shower and dressed in a fresh pair of dark jeans and a soft cashmere v-neck sweater in a pretty peach shade. She curled her hair so that it fell in long, loose curls and added a touch of makeup, just a bit of mascara, blush and lip gloss.

At a few minutes before six, she grabbed her purse, and the bottle of wine and made her way to David's house. He came to the door right after she knocked and showed her in. She handed him the bottle of wine and he set it on the kitchen counter. As she looked around she saw that his house was about the same size as hers, but had a decidedly masculine feel to it, with lots of dark wood and greens and blues. He noticed her looking around and smiled.

"Do you want to see the rest of the place? The layout is actually pretty similar to yours. I think it was the same builder." He showed her around and it was very similar. The only thing missing was the dock and view of the lake.

When they came back to the kitchen, David found a wine opener and poured them each a glass of the wine that Hannah had brought. He had several tin foil packages on the counter and brought them out to the grill which was already smoking.

"Is there anything I can do to help?" She offered.

"Just keep me company while this cooks." They sipped their wine and chatted on his back deck while everything cooked on the grill. After a while, David checked to see if it was done and after a few more minutes, he brought everything in and let it sit on the counter in the foil packets for a few more minutes to rest. Hannah knew this meant the food would continue cooking but also the resting period would distribute the juices back through the food as it cooled slightly.

"I'm excited to try it. It doesn't get much fresher than this."

"That's very true." David filled two plates with food and they ate at his dining room table. It was a sleek glass table on top of black wrought iron. It was still light out and there was a pretty view of his garden which was a mix of flowers and vegetables. "What are you growing? Your garden is gorgeous. And this fish is delicious." Everything was good. The vegetables had a smoky flavor from the grill and the fish was light and nicely seasoned. As Charlie had suggested, it went well with the wine.

"I have a little of everything. Besides the flowers, I have zucchini, eggplant, green beans, rhubarb, cucumbers, tomatoes and blueberries. Do you like to garden?"

Hannah smiled. "What is it called when everything dies? That's me, the opposite of a green thumb. A black thumb maybe? I forget to water and they die. It's very sad."

David chuckled. "That sounds like Maggie too. Oh, be sure to save some room for dessert."

Hannah perked up at the mention of dessert. "Oh, what do you have?"

"Some kind of chocolate cake. The box said lava, though I'm not sure what that means. The girl behind the counter said it was her favorite."

"Molten lava cake is one of my favorite desserts. If we heat it in the microwave for a few seconds, it makes the middle all gooey and melty so when you cut into it, it oozes out."

"Like lava. That sounds…interesting."

348   PAMELA M. KELLEY

"Just wait...if you haven't had it before, I bet you'll love it too."

"I'm easy. I like all desserts."

When they finished, Hannah carried their plates into the kitchen while David got the cake, cut two slices and put them into the microwave for thirty seconds.

"Do you want anything else to drink? I could make us some coffee," he offered.

Hannah shook her head. "No, thanks. I still have half a glass of wine and I know from experience that it goes well with chocolate cake."

"Oh, I might need to top mine off then." He added a splash to his empty glass and a little more to hers too. They took their desserts and wine into the living room and sat side by side on his leather sofa. It was buttery soft and Hannah sank into it. When they were both settled, she took a bite of the cake. It was as good as she remembered.

"What do you think?" She asked after she'd taken a few bites.

"I didn't like it at all," David said and she laughed when she saw that his plate was completely empty. He set it on the coffee table next to his wine glass and leaned back and stretched his arm across the back of the sofa, behind her.

She finished her cake and set the plate down next to his. When she leaned back against the soft leather, she turned toward David and he was smiling.

"Thanks for spending today with me. It was a really great day."

"It was. I had so much fun. Thank you for teaching me how to fish."

"There's something I've thought about doing all day." David looked into her eyes and smiled slowly and she felt the air shift between them.

"What's that?" Her voice came out breathy, which surprised her.

David leaned in and she felt his arm on her shoulder, drawing her closer to him. His lips touched hers and it felt amazing. She kissed him back and they stayed like that for a while, slowly kissing until finally, David pulled back and brushed a long strand of hair off her face.

"We need to do that again soon," he said.

"Fishing?"

He laughed. "Sure, that too. But I meant this." He leaned over and gave her a quick kiss.

"Oh, that! I'd much rather do that than go fishing," she said quickly and he laughed.

"Well, as much as I enjoy fishing, I'd have to agree with you there."

Reluctantly, Hannah stood. It was getting dark out now and she didn't want to be out too late, since they were going to her mother's in the morning.

"I should probably get going," she said.

David jumped up. "I'll walk you back to your house."

"You don't have to," she protested.

"I know, but I want to. It's dark out and there's a streetlight out. I don't want to worry about you getting home safely."

"All right then."

He walked her the short distance to her house and Hannah was grateful for it. It was darker out than she'd realized. David gave her another quick kiss before she went inside and waited until she was in and the door locked behind her before he turned to walk home.

CHAPTER 12

The next week went by in a whirl for Hannah. Things were going almost too well with David. They saw each other almost every day. He took her to his favorite restaurant, a small Italian place called Mamma Mia's that was in the next town over, Riston. And he took her to River's End ranch on Thursday night to play trivia. One of his best clients, Wade Weston, ran the ranch and some of his family and friends played trivia most weeks. It was a lot of fun and Hannah got a kick out of an older couple, Jaclyn and Simon that David said always played with them.

Jaclyn acted as though she already knew Hannah when David introduced her. She was sweet though a little eccentric and muttered something about how the fairies were up to their shenanigans again. Everyone just nodded when Jaclyn said things like that and no one seemed to think anything of it. Especially when she knew the answer to the final trivia question which meant their team came in first place and won a gift certificate to use the following week.

She gave Hannah a warm hug when they left and whispered softly, "I'm so pleased. The fairies told me that you'll be back again and I'm looking forward to it." It made little sense to Hannah, but she'd just smiled and told her that she hoped she'd play with them again soon.

"Oh, I have no doubt that you will. The fairies know, my dear!"

Hannah smiled as she remembered the evening. She'd enjoyed meeting Wade and his wife Maddie, and the rest of their group. This was exactly what she'd hoped for in moving to Quinn Valley, a tight knit community of family and friends.

Maggie and Charlie seemed thrilled for both of them. They'd met them out Monday night, which was Maggie's night off. They'd gone bowling and had pizza afterwards. Hannah hadn't bowled in years and was surprised by how good Charlie and David were. She was glad that Maggie was as bad as she was. It was still fun though and they laughed for several hours as they threw one gutter ball after another.

"My brother seems smitten," Maggie said as they turned their bowling shoes in at the end of the night.

"You think so? He's a really great guy."

"I agree, he is and yeah, I haven't seen him like this in a very long time. I think you two could be really good for each other."

"I hope so. I'm beginning to think we might be," Hannah admitted.

"So, how is it going with Hannah? Seems like you guys are getting along pretty well," Charlie said while Hannah and Maggie were at the shoe counter.

"It's going great. I didn't expect this at all. Hannah has been a pretty wonderful surprise."

"I'm glad you're just a few doors away. I feel safer knowing you are nearby," Charlie said. The comment surprised David.

"Quinn Valley is a pretty safe place."

"Oh, right. Yes, of course it is. I just meant that it's nice in case she needs you for anything or if you need her, you guys are so close."

"Right. I have to admit it's certainly convenient. And my boat is at her dock now. She was nice to offer that and of course I jumped on the opportunity. I don't mind not having the house now that I have use of the dock," He grinned.

"Well, I think that benefits her too. She was thinking of getting a small boat, but now maybe she'll just use yours."

"I'm fine with that."

David was amazed by how well things seemed to be going with Hannah. She was so easy to be with and even easier to kiss. Kissing Hannah was one of his new favorite hobbies. He loved the softness of her lips and the feel of her long, silky hair and whatever the soap or lotion was that she used, the smell of it drove him crazy. It was sweet and slightly floral and uniquely her.

He was looking forward to the charity event for the kid's center being over with though. Even though she didn't say anything, he could tell that Hannah was feeling somewhat stressed about it. Every time it was mentioned, he noticed a shift in her, a nervousness or apprehension. He wished that he could just tell her to forget about it, but the ticket sales had gone crazy. The money raised from the event would fund the kid's center for a very long time.

Once it was over though, he looked forward to a more relaxed Hannah, one who could focus on her songwriting and spending time with him.

CHAPTER 13

The Wednesday before the event, Hannah woke to sun streaming through her window and the feeling that it was going to be a good day. Her nervousness about performing was starting to fade. She thought it might have something to do with the time she'd been spending with David and she knew that they were going to be raising a lot of money for the kid's center.

She was starting to feel her creative juices flowing too and was excited to start planning her songwriting workshops and class for the kid's center. As she went to sleep the night before, it was to a new melody and she even had an idea of some lyrics to go with it. As soon as she got up, she made her coffee and then settled at her piano with her notebook and pen and tried to capture the music that she'd 'heard' the night before.

It came right back and she played the chords and was pleased with how it sounded. When it was right, she felt something deep within her and every time she'd had the feeling, the song had gone on to be a huge hit. She stayed at the piano for hours, playing bits and pieces of the song and jotting down lyrics, discarding and trying new words until the fit was right. When she was finally done, her stomach was growling, reminding her that it was time for lunch and her coffee was mostly untouched and ice cold. But she was pleased with the work that she'd done. The song was just about finished. It needed a final fine tuning and she thought she might debut it at the show on Saturday to see how the crowd liked it.

She stood and stretched out her muscles. She had a tendency to sit for too long when she was in the flow of a project. She heated up a can of soup and settled at her kitchen island with her laptop. She hadn't checked her email in a few days and figured if there was anything earth-shattering, her assistant, Mary would have called or texted her. She picked up her phone and while there were no voice messages, she was surprised to see three urgent text messages from Mary asking her to call ASAP.

Before she did, Hannah opened her email and her jaw dropped when she saw several hundred messages, way more than usual. Before wading through them, she googled herself to see what came up. Sure enough, she was in the news. The Lewiston arena performance was in the headlines along with a rumor from an 'inside source' that Hannah had changed her mind and was putting together a new national tour. There was lots of speculation from multiple sources on what that would look like and she was amazed how so many were posting the information as if it was a fact, based on that one 'inside source'.

She picked up her phone and called Mary. She answered on the first ring.

"Have you looked online?" Mary asked.

"Yes, just now. It's crazy. Where do they come up with this stuff?"

"I have no idea, but it's ridiculous. I swear they just make it up to sell magazines. How many times has Jennifer Aniston supposedly been pregnant?"

Hannah laughed. "Right, I know. What should we do about it though? I don't want people thinking I'm going back on tour and then disappointing them again."

"I'll take care of it. I'll put an announcement on the website that there is no upcoming tour and if that ever changes, it will be announced first on the website. And I'll contact that magazine too and ask them to post a correction."

"Okay, that sounds good. Thanks, Mary." Hannah sighed as she ended the call and brought her attention back to her emails. Most of them were junk, ads for various online stores. But a familiar email address made her pause. She really had thought that her stalker was just someone fooling around, not anything to be taken too seriously. And she hadn't heard anything further until now. With a sense of dread she clicked on the email with the subject line, "You didn't listen."

It was a short email, but it gave her goosebumps.

"You said you were going to stop touring. And now you are selling out yet another arena. You lied. But, you are stupid too. Because now I know where you live, Hannah. I know about your nice house on the lake and your dock with the boat. If you don't stop touring, I'll find a way to make you stop. I am watching your every move, Hannah. It would be a mistake to ignore me."

Hannah sighed and pressed her hands to her temples. She felt a stress headache coming on. She'd had a bad feeling ever since she agreed to do the show. There was no way she could back out now though. They'd had to move to a bigger venue because of the demand to see Hannah Keane. There was too much at stake now, too much money raised for the kid's center.

She tried to keep busy the rest of the day. There were errands she needed to run, laundry to be washed and groceries to be put away. There was a dress rehearsal in the evening, a dry run for the performance on Saturday and a chance to make sure her security team was familiar with the venue. She was dreading it though and was eager to get the performance over with. David had said he'd be by after work to pick her up and head to the arena. She made herself a quick peanut butter and jelly sandwich for dinner and opened her email, hoping that there wouldn't be anything further from her stalker.

But there was. The subject line this time was In Case you didn't think I was serious. When she clicked on it, the message was short, and to the point.

"Cancel the show, and I'll leave you alone. If you don't, well, you can't say you weren't warned."

Hannah's headache came rushing back. And also the decision to put an end to this. She hadn't been smart about keeping her whereabouts secret in Quinn Valley. She wouldn't make that mistake again.

David immediately sensed that something was bothering Hannah when he picked her up to go to the dress rehearsal. They usually chatted and laughed when they drove anywhere and on longer drives often sang along with the radio. He'd been looking forward to seeing her all day. But Hannah wasn't singing. She was barely even speaking and when one of her songs came on the radio, she immediately changed the station even while David was humming along with the tune.

"You don't like that song?" He asked.

"Sometimes you get sick of hearing your own stuff." She spoke softly, then stared out the window.

"Is everything okay with you? You seem a little annoyed or something. It's not me, is it?" Her vibe felt so different that he couldn't help wondering if she was having second thoughts about their relationship. Which would devastate him.

She turned and smiled slightly and rested a hand on

his arm for a brief moment, to reassure him. "It's not you. I'm just not feeling myself today—stress headache."

"Do you get those often?"

"No, thankfully." She absentmindedly rubbed her temple and closed her eyes. "I took an Advil right before you came by, so it should ease up soon."

———

WHEN THEY REACHED THE ARENA, STACY WAS STILL THERE and came over to greet them and her eyes were apologetic as she reached Hannah.

"I think maybe I owe you an apology."

"For what?" Hannah and David spoke at the same time and then everyone laughed, which seemed to lighten the mood a little.

"Well, I'm not sure, but I'm afraid that I might be the 'inside source' that is being quoted online everywhere. I got a call a few days ago from someone looking to confirm that you were going to be performing here. They asked if you were starting a new tour and I said that I didn't know but that the demand was certainly there." Stacy sounded so worried that she might have been misquoted and caused trouble for Hannah. But Hannah reassured her that wasn't the case.

"Please don't worry about it. People write stuff about me all the time that isn't true. My manager is going to make a statement on the website that nothing has changed and if it does, they'll be the first to know."

Hannah saw that her security team had arrived and

she introduced them to Stacy, who showed them around so they could make their plan for the show. David left her alone to get ready and she appreciated the space he was giving her and his concern. She'd been thinking all day, ever since getting the emails and talking to Mary. And she'd made a decision. It wasn't one that David was going to like and she suspected her family wouldn't like it much either but she didn't feel like she had any choice at this point. Her stalker was escalating and since she wasn't going to cancel the show, she had to do the next best thing, which would be for her to sell David her house and leave Quinn Valley.

She'd go into hiding until this stalker understood that she really had given up touring. And she hadn't given it up because of the stalker but since that was what the stalker seemed to care about, she could easily comply. And then maybe her life could get back to normal and eventually maybe she could return to Quinn Valley. But she didn't see that happening any time soon. And it broke her heart because there was nothing that she'd like more than to stay and to continue this relationship with David. But she couldn't put the people that she cared for in harm's way.

And besides, she knows that David has a reputation for not getting serious. She knows that she's this close to falling fast and if she gets out now, she can protect her heart too. She can't imagine that David will mind all that much, he'll just go on to date someone new, like he usually does. So, it will be for the best, for both of them. She tells herself this but instead of feeling better about her decision she feels worse. She doesn't want to leave Quinn Valley, but she doesn't feel like she really has a choice at this point.

———————

DAVID WATCHED THE REHEARSAL FROM A DISTANCE AND with concern. He couldn't put his finger on it but something was definitely off with Hannah. She'd forgotten her costume and he knew she'd had it ready to go. He'd seen it in a bag on the kitchen table and assumed that she'd grabbed it when she followed him out. She seemed distracted and the biggest shock was when she forgot the words to her newest song. That had totally flustered her and she'd apologized profusely and blamed it on her headache. They started over and she sang it perfectly but he couldn't help but worry that the jitters might get to her on the day of the show too. He wondered if she'd ever forgotten the words during a performance before.

When the rehearsal was over and they were in the car on the way home, Hannah was quieter than usual after apologizing again for missing the words.

"It's just a rehearsal. I'm not worried. Have you ever forgotten the words in a performance before?"

"No, never. I don't know what came over me. I really think it was the stress headache. It absolutely won't happen during the show. I can assure you of that."

"I'm not worried about it. You're doing us a huge favor after all. And if you do, it's not the end of the world."

"It won't happen," she said again.

"Are you hungry? Do you want to stop somewhere and grab a bite to eat?" David just wanted to spend more time with her and to see his happy Hannah return. She was so distant that it was starting to worry him.

"No, I ate before you picked me up. I'm exhausted. I just want to go home and go to bed early."

"Okay. Are we still on for dinner tomorrow night with Charlie and Maggie? We were going to meet them after work at Quinn's. Maggie has the night off."

Hannah was quiet for a long moment. Too long. "I think so. But if I'm still feeling like this tomorrow, with the headache, I might want to just stay in and rest up."

"Okay. I'll check in with you tomorrow afternoon."

He pulled into her driveway and walked her to her door and pulled her in for a quick hug and gentle kiss. "Sleep well, Hannah."

"Thanks for understanding, David. I'll talk to you tomorrow."

CHAPTER 15

David took a coffee break the next day a little after ten and swung by Quinn's Pub. As expected, his mother had just arrived and was opening a basket of freshly baked muffins. He was in the mood for one of his mother's muffins and for the company of his family.

"Hello honey, this is a nice surprise. You've been so busy with a certain someone lately that we haven't seen much of you." His mother pulled him for a hug and a kiss on the cheek. "I happened to have made your favorite today, blueberry crumb."

David grabbed one of the muffins, which were still warm. He put it on a small plate and added a hunk of butter that was so big that his mother frowned.

"David Quinn, there's already a lot of butter in those muffins!"

He laughed. "There's no such thing as too much butter."

"I agree," his brother Ryder said as he added even more butter to his muffin.

His wife, Bethany laughed and reached for the butter herself. They were all sitting at the bar drinking coffee while Maggie filled out her bar order to call into Charlie. Bethany had a small chalkboard and was writing down the lunch specials.

"I have a bit of an announcement to make," his mother began and looked around the room to make sure she had everyone's attention. Everyone was busy eating except for her. His mother made the muffins, but very rarely had one herself. She looked pretty excited about whatever it was she was going to tell them.

"What is it mom?" Maggie asked as she broke off the top of her muffin and took a bite.

"Well, I'd like you all to join me in church this Sunday, it's going to be a special day. Harry and I are getting married." She held up her hand and Maggie and Bethany both gasped. She was wearing an enormous diamond engagement ring.

"Are you sure about this, Mom? You haven't been dating Harry all that long," David said. Ryder nodded in agreement.

"It's not that we don't like Harry. We do, but David's right. It feels a little quick."

Marcia Quinn laughed. "Harry and I have know each other for years, before any of you were born. This is anything but quick. Besides, when you know, you know and there's no sense in waiting around."

"Where will you live?" Maggie asked.

David couldn't picture another man living in the house that he'd grown up in, and that his father had built for them. But if that's what his mother wanted, he wasn't going to object.

"I've already listed the house with Missy Roring. The first showing is today."

"You're going to move into Harry's house then?" Ryder asked.

"No, he's listing his too. We want to start fresh and buy something together that we both like."

"I think that's a good idea," Bethany said.

"So, we're going to have a quick service, then head to the hotel for a small reception."

Maggie smiled. "How small?"

"Only about three hundred or so. Just our closest friends and family."

Maggie almost choked on her muffin and if David's wasn't gone, he probably would have done the same.

"How did you manage to pull that together so fast?" He asked his mother.

"Well, it turns out there was another wedding scheduled and the bride called it off at the last minute. All the food had already been ordered and the menu sounded pretty good, so it seemed like a sign. Once that was firmed up, I made a few calls and a few more people made calls and seems like most everyone is pretty excited to come on Sunday. It should be fun!"

Ryder shook his head in wonder. "Only you could have pulled that off, Mom. But of course we'll all be there. Does Ivy know?" His sister would need to fly in.

"She was the first call I made. She'll be here on Saturday. It's all coming together quite nicely!"

"Are you doing anything for a honeymoon?" Maggie asked.

"Harry said he has a plan, so I guess I'll find out on Sunday. But he said to pack my bags for ten days, so we're off somewhere interesting."

"I'm happy for you, Mom," David said.

"Thanks, honey. Be sure to bring Hannah. She's invited too."

"I'll mention it to her. I'm sure she'll want to come." At least he hoped so. He wasn't so sure of anything anymore with Hannah. He'd seen something in her eyes the day before that had scared him. It was like she was stepping back and shutting him out. He'd wanted to mention it to his mother and get her take on it. He'd counted on her telling him it was nothing to worry about, but he didn't want to ruin the festive mood now that everyone was so excited about the upcoming wedding. He'd have to figure out the Hannah situation on his own. Hopefully she was just having a bad day.

At around four, David called Hannah to confirm their plans with Maggie and Charlie. He hoped that she was going to be back to her normal cheery self, but he had a sinking feeling as the phone rang and then went to voicemail. He left a quick message for her to call him back and said he had some good news. A few minutes later, his phone rang and it was Hannah.

"Hey David, I'm sorry I missed your call, I was just getting out of the shower." That was encouraging. He hoped it meant that she was getting ready to go out.

"No problem. How are you feeling today? Are you up for coming out still?"

Hannah was silent for an awkward long moment and then sighed.

"I'm sorry, David but I really don't think that I'm up to being social tonight."

"I could reschedule with them and just come by and

we could have a quiet night if you'd rather?" He didn't care what they did, he just wanted to spend time with her.

"No, I don't want you to cancel on them. I just, I'm really not up for any company tonight. I just took a shower hoping it might help with my headache but it's still there and I didn't sleep well last night. I think I just need a quiet evening in and a good night's sleep."

"Okay. Well, I have some good news to share. My mother is getting married on Sunday and she said to be sure to let you know that you're invited."

"She is? That's wonderful news. Please tell her I said congratulations."

"You can tell her yourself if you come to the wedding with me. What do you say?" David felt like he was pushing, but he wasn't sure what else to do. It felt like Hannah was slipping away from him.

"I'll go with you on Sunday."

He relaxed a little. "Okay, great. Rest up and I'll talk to you tomorrow."

"Thanks. Tell Maggie and Charlie I'm really sorry and I'll see them soon."

"I will."

David hung up the phone and tried to turn his attention back to work. At least Hannah had agreed to come to the wedding, that was something. He pulled up his emails and tackled the highest priority ones first until there were just a few remaining and one looked a bit odd. The subject line didn't seem like his other emails which were mostly related to customer food orders. This one simply said, Open now or regret later.

He clicked on the email and read the short message several times, trying to make sense of it. It was from a promoter in Nashville and mentioned the show on Saturday.

"Just in case something happens with Hannah Keane and she continues her streak of unreliability and cancels on you, one our top performers, Ruby Shaw, is available on short notice. Fans of Hannah would enjoy Ruby's performance."

David didn't quite know what to make of the email. The name Ruby Shaw was vaguely familiar to him. She was a lesser known country artist. David couldn't think of a single song of hers but her name was memorable. He didn't want to mention it to Hannah, especially the bit about being unreliable. After her forgetting her own lyrics he didn't want to put anything into her head that would make her worry about doing it again. Something about the message didn't sit right with him.

When he arrived at Quinn's, Charlie was sitting at the bar and Maggie was taking off her apron. They decided to go to the Irish pub that was a short walk from Quinn's.

Once they were settled at a table and had ordered a round of beers and a pizza to share, David told them about the strange email that he'd received. And also about Hannah's stress headache and missing the words to her song.

Maggie and Charlie exchanged glances before Charlie spoke. "I've never known Hannah to miss even a single world. She must have been really rattled."

"Do you think?" Maggie asked him and he nodded.

"There's something we should probably fill you in on. It's really Hannah's business to share, but it sounds like maybe things have escalated, given your email. So, I'm making the decision to tell you." Charlie told him about Hannah's stalker and the emails she'd received.

"I suspect you might be right. She was like a different person at dress rehearsal last night. Do you think my email might be connected to whoever is hassling her?"

Charlie nodded. "It's possible. Likely even. Your email might give the police something to go on. The stalker may be somehow related to this Ruby person. Her name sounds really familiar but I can't think of her music."

"I thought the same thing. Do you know Hannah's assistant? If I forward the email to you to get it to her, maybe she can forward to the police. I assume they're already investigating this?"

"They met with Mary, her assistant. But they haven't had much to go on. This might help."

———

WHEN CHARLIE GOT HOME, INSTEAD OF BEING TIRED AND full and ready for bed, he was wired and wide awake. He'd only had one beer and then switched to coffee. He couldn't get his mind off the email he'd received. He sat at his kitchen table and opened his laptop and began

googling, looking for everything he could find on Ruby
Shaw.

It took him a little over an hour before he connected
the first dot. Ruby had been one of Hannah's backup
singers during her first big tour. So, they knew each other.
He saw that she'd been a backup singer for two other
well-known female country singers too. In each instance it
had been for one tour, which was unusual because his
searching also told him that Hannah's other two backup
singer were with her for every tour. Why had Ruby left?
And why did she leave the other two artists as well?

He didn't have enough to go on, but his gut told him
that Hannah's stalker was either Ruby herself or her
manager, the promoter that had emailed him. A quick
search also interestingly showed him that the promoter,
Jeff Stevens, also managed one of the other artists. He
wasn't sure if that was relevant or not but he jotted everything down. And then he emailed Ken Pearson, a private
investigator he'd used several years ago when there was
an issue at his company. An employee had been skimming from the warehouse. He'd known that but couldn't
figure out who. Ken had discreetly investigated and
discovered that one of his employees was in serious financial debt and a little more digging discovered an email
trail.

He sent Ken all the information and asked if he'd dig
in and see what he could find out. And he stressed that it
was urgent timing-wise. He wanted this situation with
Hannah resolved as soon as possible so they could go
back to how things were. He also sent all the information

he'd uncovered along to Charlie to have Mary forward to the police.

And at two in the morning, totally exhausted but feeling like he was at least doing something, David fell into bed.

CHAPTER 17

Hannah was dreading the performance on Saturday. When David came to pick her up, her headache was like an ice pick pounding into her temple. She knew it was just stress related and she took a double dose of Advil which lessened it to a minor ache by the time they reached the arena. David seemed in an unusually good mood which made Hannah feel even worse. She'd decided that after the show on the way home, she was going to tell him about the stalker and let him know if he was still interested that she'd sell him her house. She didn't imagine he'd still want her to go with him to his mother's wedding, but she would if he did, as a final goodbye. Her eyes welled up at the thought of leaving Quinn Valley and leaving David especially. She blinked furiously to keep the tears from spilling over and twisted to look out the window so he wouldn't see her struggling to keep her composure.

"So, I got a look at the menu for tomorrow. It looks

pretty amazing. Turns out someone cancelled their wedding at the last minute and my mother swooped in and took over the date and the catering. It should be fun." His enthusiasm was contagious and Hannah couldn't help smiling.

"That sounds meant to be," she said.

"And I told my mother that you're coming. She's thrilled. They're going to be at the show tonight too."

"Oh, that's great."

"I think half of Quinn Valley will be there, actually. Everyone at my office was talking about it. Not to make you nervous or anything, though you're used to big crowds, I imagine."

"I'm not sure if I ever really got used to it. I just somehow managed to get through it. Getting up on stage is the hard part. Once I start playing music and singing, it's fun for me too. I don't really even see the crowds on stage, with the lights and all."

"Well, I'm sure tonight will go great. And your security team seemed really solid so there's nothing to worry about." Something in his tone caught her attention. He'd never mentioned her security people before.

"I'm not worried. They do a great job."

"Oh, I'm sure they will. I just meant, everything is taken care of. All you have to do is get up there and sing."

Hannah smiled. "Just get up and sing. I can do that."

AND SHE DID. THE EVENING WAS A TREMENDOUS SUCCESS.

The crowd loved Hannah and she even sang a brand new song that no one had heard yet and they went crazy for it. David had no doubt that it was going to be her next big hit. Between the ticket sales and the silent auction during the reception, they raised an unprecedented amount of money for the kids' center. His mother and Harry came up to them after the show and his mother was so cute, she was gushing over Hannah's performance.

"My dear you were so amazing. I know you're a professional and all but I had no idea how truly talented you are. It's a wonderful thing that you did for this good cause."

Hannah smiled. "I was happy to do it." And she did look happy. Now that the show was over, Hannah seemed more relaxed and calm. She was quiet on the way home though and David worried that she was pulling away from him again. When they reached her house, she invited him in which he took to be a good sign. Until they stepped inside.

"I need to talk to you, and I didn't want to do it while we were driving." She didn't look happy, and David braced himself for whatever was coming.

"Do you want something to drink? I have water, beer, wine, soda."

David sat on one of the island stools and shook his head. "I'm good. I don't need anything to drink. Just tell me what's on your mind."

"Okay." Hannah sat next to him and took one of his hands and gave it a squeeze. She took a deep breath and then she told him everything, all about the stalker, moving to Quinn Valley and the latest, more threatening emails she'd received. "It's my fault for not being more discreet about being here."

But he shook his head. "No. I don't accept that. If anything, it's my fault for pushing you to do the show. I should have accepted your initial reluctance, especially now that I know it was with good reason."

Hannah smiled. "It's not your fault. I still could have said no. But it's gone too far now. I think it's best that I go somewhere else. I'm not sure where, but I don't want to put anyone here in any danger. I'm happy to sell my house to you, if you still want it."

David squeezed her hand and held on tight. He wasn't about to let her go now.

"I don't think you need to do that. I'm pretty sure your stalker emailed me too." He told her about the message and aggressive suggestion to hire Ruby Shaw instead.

Hannah's jaw dropped. "Ruby was my backup singer."

"I saw that online. I noticed that she only lasted for one tour with you and then for one tour with two other artists. Seems to be a pattern."

"Ruby was a bit….difficult. She's talented, there's no question about that, but she wasn't a good backup singer. She wanted to stand out, a little too much and it just didn't work. She wasn't happy when I had to let her go at the end of the tour. The other two girls refused to stay on if I kept her and I didn't want to, anyway. I suspect something similar happened with the other two artists she toured with. Do you think she is the stalker? Why would she do that?"

"I'm not 100% sure that it's her. I actually have a buddy of mine who is a private investigator doing a little digging. He can go places online that I have no idea how to access. But I figure it's either her or her promoter."

Hannah shook her head. "I don't think it's him. He's a good guy with a great reputation. It might make sense if it's Ruby. She was very impatient and wanted immediate success. Maybe she thought with me not touring, she'd have a better shot at getting gigs. But she's not at the level of headlining a national tour."

"That seems a little delusional," David agreed.

"For someone to send emails like that, it shows they aren't thinking straight," Hannah said.

"The good news though, if it is her and I'm pretty sure that it is, I don't think that you're in any real danger. It seems like she just wants to scare you off. And she's done a pretty good job of it so far."

Hannah sighed. "She has. I hope it's her, so I can be done with this. It makes me so angry though to think that she would do something like this. It really makes you feel vulnerable and afraid. I don't like to think of myself as a weak person."

David stood and wrapped Hannah in a hug. "I'd say you're anything but weak. Most people wouldn't have done the show. That was brave of you."

"I really don't want to leave Quinn Valley," she admitted.

"And I don't want you to leave either. Hopefully this will be resolved soon and you can put it behind you."

"I hope so." Hannah yawned and David looked at the time. It was late, after eleven and he imagined that Hannah must be exhausted. It had been a stressful day and night. He knew that he was ready for bed himself.

"It's late. I'll let you get to bed. I'll be by in the morning to head to church and then the reception. You are still coming, right?" He held his breath waiting for her answer. He didn't want to go without Hannah. It wouldn't be the same.

She smiled slowly and he felt his heart melt. "Yes, of course. I'll be ready."

CHAPTER 18

Hannah was ready and waiting when David arrived the next morning to pick her up. She was wearing her favorite dress, a long, floaty cocktail dress in varying shades of pink with layers of ruffles and a flattering halter style top. She'd curled her hair and pulled it back in a pretty comb and let the curls tumble down her back. And she'd found the perfect shoes. They were pale pink cowboy boots and looked really pretty with the dress.

David smiled when he saw her. "You look incredible."

"Thank you. You're looking pretty sharp yourself." And he was. David was wearing a charcoal gray suit and a deep purple tie that brought out his blue eyes. They drove to the church and Hannah was glad that they'd arrived earlier than usual because it was packed to capacity. Maggie and Charlie were already there in the front row with Ryder and Bethany and Avery and Carter walked in right behind them. A few minutes after they joined the others, David's youngest sister, Ivy, came rushing in with her new husband.

The service started right on time and tears came to Hannah's eyes when she saw David's mother walking down the aisle. She wore a pretty mint green suit and Harry was waiting for her, wearing a gray tux and matching green cummerbund and bowtie. He looked distinguished and radiant when his eyes met Marcia's. The two of them were beaming at each other as the pastor had them recite their vows and then pledge their love to each other before pronouncing them husband and wife.

When the service finished, everyone made their way to the Quinn Hotel. Roxane Quinn was there to greet them. Her husband Ciran was close by. Roxane was the event coordinator and handled all the details for the wedding and was there to make sure everything went smoothly. She was also there as a guest, since she was a Quinn. And Marcia had requested a selection of Ciran's mouthwatering tacos as appetizers. David had brought Hannah to Ciran's taco truck for lunch once and she'd been blown away by how good the simple tacos were.

Roxane pulled Marcia into a hug as soon as she saw her. "Auntie, we are so happy for you! And I've made sure that everything will be perfect."

"Thank you, honey. I have no doubt that it would be. Thank you for taking such good care of us."

Hannah watched with amusement as Marcia made the rounds of the crowded room. Everyone in town seemed to know her and they were all at her wedding.

The food was fabulous and there was plenty of it. Hannah and David were seated at a big round table with the other siblings and spouses. They'd just started eating slices of the wedding cake when David's phone beeped and she saw a text message flash across it. She couldn't see what it said though. David glanced at it and a look of excitement crossed his face.

"Will you excuse me? I need to make a quick call. I'll be back in a minute."

"Of course." She wondered what was so important that he was rushing off in the middle of his mother's wedding to make a phone call. Ten minutes later, she found out.

David walked up to the table, pulled her into his arms and lifted her up in the air. No one paid much attention to them because by this time just about everyone was out on the dance floor.

"It's over, Hannah. It's really over now."

A sense of relief and joy swept through her. "Tell me."

He set her back down, took her hands and looked into her eyes and what she saw there shook her. She saw love and trust and her future.

"My buddy the private eye, just let me know that he connected all the dots. I don't know exactly how he did it, but he confirmed that it was Ruby and that she was doing the same thing to the other two artists, trying to scare them into not performing with the delusional hope that she could become a huge star. It's all over for her now. He's turned everything over to the Nashville police and they're going to take it from here. I don't think Ruby is going to be playing anywhere for a very long time."

Hannah released the breath that she didn't even realize she'd been holding. A single tear spilled over and she wiped it away and shook her head. She was not going to cry. "Thank you. I really can't thank you enough, David."

He smiled. "I was happy to do it. That's what you do when you love someone. You want to try to take their pain away."

"You love me?" Had she heard that right?

"Yes, Hannah Keane, I am head over heels totally in love with you. I hope that's not a problem?" He grinned.

"No problem at all. I might love you too."

"You might? You're not sure?" He teased her.

She laughed. "Oh, I'm sure. Want to dance?"

"With you? Always."

———

AN HOUR LATER, AFTER DANCING SONG AFTER SONG, Hannah excused herself to go to the ladies room. On her way back, as she reached the table where David and the others were sitting, she overheard David saying something too Charlie. "I don't feel right asking her to do that. The show was enough." She smiled as she'd caught the band looking her way and talking amongst themselves. And she'd had an idea earlier but didn't want to suggest it if it might not be welcome. It sounded like it might be. Instead of sitting next to David at the table, she pivoted and headed toward the band. They were just finishing up a song and wrapped up quickly when they saw her approach. She ran her idea by them and they were more than happy to comply.

———

DAVID WAS STARTLED WHEN HE HEARD HANNAH'S VOICE over the microphone. He turned and saw her standing there addressing the crowd.

"So, I have another new song that I recently finished. No one has heard it yet, but I thought it might be nice for this occasion because it's a love song. It's a slow ballad so if anyone feels like dancing, come on out to the dance floor." David's mother and Harry were the first couple out there and as Hannah began to sing, David noticed his mother's eyes looked suspiciously wet and Harry tenderly wiped a few tears away as they swayed to Hannah's song, which was absolutely perfect.

———

"When the world fades away and there's no one left but the two of us,

　know that I love you.

　I always have and I always will 'til the end of time.

　The two of us together…"

IT WAS A GREAT SONG FOR A WEDDING AND EVERYONE seemed to agree. The dance floor was packed and if Hannah wasn't singing, David would be out there too. Hannah's eyes met his several times and if he didn't know better, he'd swear she was singing it just for him. When the song ended, the applause was loud and long. David's mother went over to Hannah and gave her a big hug and Harry did too. Hannah was still smiling when she reached David.

"I guess they liked it," she said softly.

"And that would be the understatement of the year. That was very generous of you. I know my mother loved it, Harry too. It was a beautiful song."

"Thank you. I wrote it last night after you left. I thought I was so tired, but then I couldn't get to sleep. The music was trying to get out. The whole song came in a rush. I couldn't get the words down fast enough. I love when that happens."

"I can't begin to understand it, but I think I love it too."

Hannah laughed. "And I love you for saying that."

CHAPTER 19

TWO WEEKS LATER.

Y ou're a good sport for agreeing to go fishing with me again," David said as they walked to the boat. It was a sunny Saturday, unseasonably warm and a little past eleven.

"It's a good day for it and I'd like to maybe catch a fish this time—as long as you promise to take it off the hook. I still don't want to watch that part."

"I can do that for you." David took the heavy picnic basket that Hannah had packed for their lunch. She held a thermos of hot coffee in her other hand.

They climbed into the boat and David steered it to his favorite spot, and they spent about an hour there with no luck before moving on to the area where he'd caught his fish last time.

"I probably should have come straight here, but you never know."

Once they had their lines in the water, Hannah opened the basket and took out some cheeses, a rich and buttery St. Andre, a sharp cheddar and an aged goat cheese with fragrant truffles. She also had some sliced hard salami, assorted crackers, bread and cotton candy grapes—the oversized green ones that had an unusually sweet flavor.

She topped off their cups with a bit more hot coffee and they spent the next hour snacking, listening to their favorite country music station and waiting for the fish to bite.

It was a lazy, relaxing day and Hannah wasn't in a hurry to see it end. After a few hours though, David suggested that maybe it was time to call it a day. Just as Hannah was about to reel her line in, her pole dipped and she felt a tug. There was something on the end of her line! She held on tight and determinedly reeled it in and gasped when a good-sized trout flew into the air and then flopped next to her on the boat.

"Good job, Hannah!"

"What do you think, is it big enough?"

"Oh, that's plenty big enough. We're going to eat well tonight." Hannah let David take over getting the fish off the line and packed into the fish box to bring back with them. She was thrilled that finally, she'd caught something. David rinsed his hands and dried them on a towel, then came towards Hannah with a funny smile on his face. He took her hand, then reached deep in to his coat pocket and pulled out a small box and got down on one knee.

Hannah felt light-headed. She didn't see this coming at all, certainly not while they were out fishing.

"Hannah, I thought of something my mother said recently, when we asked if she might be getting married too soon. Ryder and I thought it was too quick. But she reminded us that she and Harry actually went way back and that when you know you've met the right person, there's no reason to wait. My mother's a wise woman. And I don't want to wait. I love you Hannah. More than I thought possible. Will you marry me?"

"Of course I will!" Hannah felt her eyes fill with happy tears as David slid the ring onto her finger. It was lovely, but she didn't care what it looked like. It could have been a plastic toy ring and she would have been just as excited, because it was from David. And there was no one else she could imagine spending the rest of her life with.

"I'm so glad that I moved back to Quinn Valley. We're going to have a wonderful life together."

David pulled her close to him and kissed her passionately. "Yes, we are. And you don't have to come fishing again with me if you don't want to. I know it's probably not that exciting for you. I don't know why I like it so much."

Hannah leaned over and kissed him again. "I don't have to do anything. I wanted to come fishing with you, because you love it so much and I love you. We got to spend an afternoon together, in the sunshine, eating good food, listening to music and drifting around the lake. What's not to like? And now we have tonight's dinner too."

David laughed. "Have I mentioned that I love you?"

"Feel free to mention it anytime. I don't think I'll ever get sick of hearing it."

CHAPTER 20

EPILOGUE

CHRISTMAS EVE, FIVE YEARS LATER

Davad waited until everyone arrived before he and Hannah shared their happy news. They were hosting the Christmas Eve feast at Hannah's house, or rather their house. Funny how he still thought of it as Hannah's house even though he'd moved in when they got married and they'd sold his house.

All the siblings were there, except for Ivy and her husband. They were touring together overseas and couldn't make it work with their schedules, especially as they were coming back for good in mid-January. Ivy was a mega country music superstar now and always seemed to be on the road. David was happy for her but was also glad that Hannah never got the bug to go back on the road.

She did the occasional mini-tour locally, in Lewiston and Seattle, but that didn't take much time and she preferred to be at home working on her songwriting and the workshops and classes she was teaching.

Ryder and Bethany had three small children now and they were running in a circle around the Christmas tree. The littlest, Avery, named after her aunt, was just over a year old but she started walking at ten months and was a speedy little thing.

Avery and Carter had two children now and they were with the others by the Christmas tree. Maggie and Charlie didn't have any children and didn't have any plans to have any. They had a houseful of animals, shelter cats and dogs that they'd rescued and they loved spoiling their nieces and nephews rotten and babysitting occasionally on long weekends to give their siblings a break.

David and Hannah had just about given up on having children. They'd gone through multiple rounds of fertility treatments and it had really taken a toll on Hannah, on both of them really. They got their hopes up each time, only to have them dashed when the results came back negative, again. They were on a six month break and both had decided that maybe it wasn't worth it to try again. Maggie and Charlie were happy as could be without children. Maybe it wasn't meant for them either. So, they relaxed about it and stopped even thinking about it for a few months.

And then the strangest thing happened. Hannah thought she was gaining weight, she seemed to be hungry all the time. They didn't think anything of it at first. After

all, the family was in the food business and David was
constantly bringing home samples of new food to try
from different vendors. But one morning as Hannah was
getting dressed, he couldn't help but notice her much
fuller figure. Her stomach was still mostly flat, but she was
spilling out of her bra.

"Honey, I'm not sure exactly how to ask this, but have
you gained a little weight?"

Hannah laughed. "I guess maybe I have, a little. I
didn't realize it was that noticeable."

"It's not, when you have your clothes on. Is it possible? I mean, when was your last monthly thing?"

"You mean my period? Last month I think. I'm not
always regular." She was quiet for a minute then pulled
out her cell phone and looked at the calendar on it. And
then her jaw dropped.

"Maybe it's been longer than I realized. But we
haven't been on any treatments. I don't think it's possible.
It's highly unlikely, anyway."

"Anything's possible, honey. Do we have any tests
left?"

"Are you kidding? I bought them in bulk at Costco. I
have plenty."

"Do you want to check, maybe? Just in case. It's probably negative, so we won't get our hopes up."

"Okay." Hannah went off to the bathroom and came
back ten minutes later with a dazed look. She held up the
test stick. "It's probably a false positive. That happens
right?"

David knew, without a doubt that it wasn't a false positive.

"I think we're really pregnant."

A visit to the doctor the next day confirmed the test results. They waited on telling anyone about the pregnancy until Hannah reached the three month mark because the doctor said she might be more vulnerable since it had been so hard for her to get pregnant. The doctor wasn't done giving them good news though, at their twelve week appointment, she did an ultrasound and they were excited to learn the sex of the baby.

"It's a boy!" She announced.

"We're having a boy!" David gave Hannah an excited kiss. The doctor had a mischievous look on her face.

"You're having a girl too. Twins."

"So, what's the big news?" Maggie asked. She looked excited and David knew she was hoping they might have baby news. She knew how badly they both wanted it.

"So, we've been sitting on this news for a while, but we just went for our twelve week appointment yesterday. We're pregnant and the ultrasound showed that it's a boy." There were cheers and congratulations all around and then Hannah stood and everyone quieted down.

She grinned. "And it's a girl. David and I are having twins!"

"I am so happy for you both! That's the best news ever. Twins!" Maggie said.

Hannah's mother and David's mother both looked like they'd won the baby lottery. They rushed over to congratulate both of them and give hugs and kisses.

ONCE ALL THE COMMOTION DIED DOWN, EVERYONE turned their attention to the food. Hannah set out platters of steamed shrimp, chips and dips, crackers and cheese, stuffed mushrooms and a big bowl of Prosecco punch that was very popular. She'd frozen fresh strawberries and grapes and they bobbled in the bowl instead of ice cubes.

David helped cook the main meal which was beef tenderloin with béarnaise sauce, roasted potatoes and asparagus. An assortment of cookies and pies waited on a side table for dessert and many glasses of wine were poured, though none for Hannah. She happily sipped a cold glass of sparkling apple cider and didn't miss the alcohol a bit. It was funny how her taste had changed since she was pregnant. She didn't even like the smell of wine anymore and she used to love it. And she'd been having some odd food cravings lately. Pickles and grapenut custard were her favorites this week. It changed often.

She glanced around the room and smiled. Everyone seemed to be enjoying themselves and outside, it was starting to flurry a little. It felt like Christmas. There was a sense of joy and wonder that always came at this time of year.

Tomorrow they'd be at David's mother's house. It was the one holiday of the year that she still insisted on doing all the cooking. And she really was an amazing cook. Hannah was looking forward to relaxing and trying everything.

She was also looking forward to after everyone left tonight and she and David would have the house to themselves. They always exchanged gifts on Christmas Eve and she'd stuffed his stocking with his gift earlier in the day. She was excited for him to open it and she hoped that he'd like what she'd chosen. She had a feeling that he might.

Maggie and Charlie were whispering and laughing and Hannah heard her brother say, "Go ahead and tell them."

"So, I have an announcement to make too. Hannah isn't the only one that is expecting." A shocked silence fell over the room and Maggie burst into laughter.

"No, it's not that! It's Jamie and they think she'll have eight or nine pups soon. There was some kind of mixup with the shelter that we adopted her from. They thought she was already spayed. Apparently, she wasn't. So, if anyone wants a puppy, we'll have plenty to go around."

"We might want a couple," Harry said. Marcia immediately swatted his arm.

"A couple?!"

"Well, you always want to have two so they can keep each other company."

"Hmmm. We'll talk about that later. It's been a long time since I've had a puppy."

"I think it's a great idea, Mom. You and Harry can spoil them rotten," Maggie said.

"That might be kind of fun. We'll see."

Hannah smiled as three sets of desperate eyes stared at Ryder and Bethany. "Please, please can we each get a puppy?" Eloise, the oldest asked.

Bethany looked pale at the thought. "I don't know about that. One, maybe. Two possibly. Three seems a bit much." She looked at Maggie and made a face. "Thanks a lot, Mags."

Maggie laughed. "Sorry." She looked around the room, "Any other takers?"

"I might want one, or maybe even two. What do you think, David?" Hannah asked.

"A puppy or two might be fun. We've talked about getting a pet once we got through the fertility stuff."

"Okay, just let me know when you all decide." Maggie cut herself a big slice of apple pie and added a scoop of vanilla ice cream.

Hannah's mouth immediately watered. "I'll take some of that too."

THREE HOURS LATER, THE HOUSE WAS QUIET EXCEPT FOR the soft sound of Christmas carols playing in the background. All the dishes were done and put away and David had just added another log to the fire.

"Are you ready to do our stockings?" Hannah asked.

"I'm ready." David pulled both stockings down from the mantle and brought them over to the soft leather sofa where Hannah was curled up under a cozy fleece throw. She had a cup of hot tea by her side.

"You go first." Hannah watched as David reached into his stocking and pulled out the first of his gifts. A new tie, navy with embroidered rainbow trout all over it.

"This is awesome, thank you." He leaned over and gave her a quick kiss.

"Keep going," she urged him.

He reached back in and pulled out two giant chocolate bars from the UK. They were dark chocolate Toblerone with bits of chewy nougat inside. It was his favorite. She liked them too. And then he reached to the bottom and pulled out a jeweler's box and opened it.

"This is great. I needed a new watch. Thank you."

"It's waterproof and is a fishing watch…all kinds of data for you, fishing conditions, GPS. It practically tells you where the fish are." She laughed. She'd seen it online and ordered it months ago for him. It seemed perfect.

"This is truly awesome. I didn't even know they made fishing watches."

"I didn't ether. But when I stumbled onto it, it seemed meant to be."

"Okay, your turn now." David watched as Hannah reached into her stocking and pulled out two pairs of fuzzy socks. She was always cold and always losing her socks. He'd gotten her two soft pairs, one pink and one blue.

"I love them, thank you."

"Keep going," he urged her.

She reached in and pulled out a giant bag of red Twizzlers. Her favorite candy. She liked when they got hard and stale, which made David laugh. She knew it was an odd quirk, but she really preferred them that way.

"Thank you!" She didn't have to be told to keep going and reached deep into the stocking and pulled out a slim jeweler's box. She had no idea what he'd gotten her. Hannah didn't wear a lot of jewelry. She opened the box and there was a stunning diamond tennis bracelet sparkling in the firelight.

"David, it's too much. You shouldn't have. I love it though." She lifted the bracelet up and draped it over her wrist and then smiled at the clasp. It was two stones that linked together, one pink and one blue. To represent their babies.

"I couldn't resist it. It made me think of you and our family." He helped her fasten the bracelet and she held it up and looked at it from all angles. It was stunningly gorgeous.

"I don't want to ever take it off. But I suppose I should. I'm wearing it tomorrow though. I can't wait to show your mother."

David grinned. "She's already seen it. She may have been with me when I picked it out. I didn't want to screw anything up."

Hannah leaned over and kissed her husband. "You did very well." She snuggled into his arms and rested her head on his chest. He ran his fingers through her hair and gently massaged her scalp. She loved when he did that. It was so relaxing.

"Merry Christmas, David. I still love you lots."

"Merry Christmas, Hannah. Love you lots too. Always and forever.

———————

THANK YOU SO MUCH FOR READING THESE STORIES! HAVE you read my books in the River's End Ranch series? They have a similar feel.

If you prefer women's fiction, you might enjoy my Nantucket series, beginning with The Nantucket Inn.

And at the end of May, I have a bigger book, a stand-alone story called The Restaurant, about three sisters that inherit a popular Nantucket restaurant and have to spend a year working together there.

Please join my Facebook reader group, where we chat about what we are reading and I share cover reveals and ask your advice now and then.

Made in United States
North Haven, CT
02 April 2022

17798673R00243